I AM IN BLOOD

BLOOD

OLD MURDERS NEVER DIE

JOE MURPHY

BRANDON

D1396177

First published 2015 by Brandon,
an imprint of The O'Brien Press Ltd
12 Terenure Road East, Rathgar, Dublin 6, Ireland.
Tel: +353 1 4923333; Fax: +353 1 4922777
E-mail: books@obrien.ie; Website: www.obrien.ie

ISBN: 978-1-84717-695-0

1 2 3 4 5 6 7 8 9 10
15 16 17 18 19

Editing, typesetting, layout and design: The O'Brien Press Ltd
Printed Nørhaven, Denmark

The paper in this book is produced using pulp from managed forests.

The O'Brien Press receives assistance from

DEDICATION

To my wife and our two boys.
This, and everything else, is for you.

ACKNOWLEDGEMENTS

This book wouldn't have been possible without the hard work, expertise and patience of a number of people and I think it's only fitting that I acknowledge that right from the off. First, to my agent, Svetlana, thanks for planting the seed for this book. Without you, this story wouldn't exist. Secondly, my editor, Rachel Pierce, deserves a huge amount of gratitude for her delicate touch in putting a shape on what was something rough-hewn and bloody. And last but not least to my friends and family, for things too numerous to mention and for reminding me who I am and where I come from. Those two things are precious and you can lose them without even realising how poor you've become. Cheers.

1892 was on its knees. *A dying year at the end of a decrepit century, muffled in winter fogs, howling out its last in December gales.*

He arrived in Dublin during the withering hours of December the eighth. The Feast of the Immaculate Conception. Across the Irish Sea he came. The crossing was more than choppy, the waves turned into slate fangs by a wind that itself had teeth. The snarl of the sea, the slap and suck of its salt maw, was the only thing that spoke to him on that crossing. The elemental reek of it seeped around him and lined his throat with its stink. The cabin he sat in yawed to the pitch of the water and wind. The lamp overhead, swinging from its beam, cast him in light, then shadow, then light again. For the duration of the crossing the season bawled its lungs out. Then, as the lights of Dublin Port glimmered, fragile, in the weeping dark, the wind died and fell silent. The ship slid into harbour as though on a slick of black oil.

He stepped off the gangplank and on to a quayside greased with lamplight. He stood for a moment amidst a throng of ragged people and listened to the alien bray of Dublin accents. He breathed in the stench of the docks. The organic odours of wood and rot and salt and tar. Of blood and sweat. He stood; black coat, black hat, black bag. He stood; an avatar of the season.

A dying century. A dying year. A killing presence.

CHAPTER 1:

DUBLIN, DECEMBER 1892

Mary Shortt. Slight and wizened. A woman of blackening teeth and failing lungs. A woman born of Dublin's back alleys and the redbrick labyrinth of its tenements. A woman who stood now on the corner of Sheriff Street and lifted the hem of her skirt as men passed her by. Coaches rumbled over the cobbles. Curtains twitched. The slow sootfall of Dublin's countless chimneys made the black night blacker. Deadening the air. Catching in the throat and griming the lungs with carbon talc. Her calves pale in the darkness. Her thighs. Her skin candle-coloured in the gloom.

Her legs were her best asset. Her dugs, withering year by year, she kept buttoned up behind her bodice. Then again, none of her customers seemed to mind. As they panted on top of her. As they breathed into her ear. No brothel room for her. No damp bed. No yellowing sheets. No oil lamp softening the scene. Lending a false intimacy to what was, after all, a business transaction. An exchange of services. All Mary Shortt needed was an empty alley or a quiet dead-end.

And every single soul who frequented or plied their trade in the reeking spread-eagle of Dublin's fleshpits would swear to see not a thing. Anything could be happening. Rutting against a wall. Fellatio in a doorway. And all and everyone turned the head and dropped the eyes. Even the Metropolitan Police. Everyone. To do else would be to acknowledge what was happening. To force a moral judgement. To take a stance. God forbid that in Ireland anyone might actually do something about the plight of the poor. About the degradation. About what people were forced to do. Day after day. Night after night.

The quick fumble and the moment of pain.

The folded note and the clink of coin.

It wasn't much of a living but, for someone like Mary Shortt, there wasn't much of a choice.

She stood on her corner and smiled thinly at anyone she thought might throw her a few pennies. Smiled as the cold crept down and the night grew deeper.

God, she thought. What she wouldn't give for a bit of warmth.

Her little patch was emptied of people now. No coaches rattled past. No voices in the soup of smoke and gathering fog. In the distance the sough and suck of the River Liffey gumming at the hulls of steamers and merchantmen. Everything made dislocate by the winter damp. Everything muted and far off.

She was thinking of going home. She was within an instant of saying to hell with things for this evening and scabbing a bottle of gin for to heat her guts in the long cold of the December dark.

But in that instant, a figure appeared.

She watched him come. Up from the docks with quick steps. A tall black hat. A long coat with a cape collar. A fat bag dangling from one hand. Black on black. A deeper shadow in a world of them. She watched him approach and something stirred in her. Something trilled with unease.

On the footpath his shoes clicked in brittle little hacks of noise. All else silence and about his face hot billows of breath.

He stopped in front of her.

'Howya,' said Mary.

The man inhaled slowly and then exhaled slowly. He smiled then and said nothing. That note of unease trilled in Mary once more.

'Are you alright, mister?' she asked.

'Perfectly and precisely.'

Plummy accent. Tone all clipped and vowels narrowed to a

sneer. A toff. Over from England, or Mary was no judge of a customer. She had had her fair share of this type. Across slumming it from their manicured estates. A little bit of Irish rough to dandle and brag about at the club, over cigars and brandy.

She'd done worse.

'Well,' she said. 'We'll make this quick. It's bleedin' freezing out here and I ain't got no flophouse to throw down in, so take it or leave it as you finds it.'

The man smiled again. A flat smile that tightened his lips but conveyed no humour or empathy. It was like the smile of somebody who's had a fine meal placed before them. A smile of satisfaction soon to come.

'I like it quick,' he said. 'Quick and clean and sharp.'

'Good. So do I.'

Mary led the man across the road and down into an alley clotted with the leavings of the surrounding tenements. She bent over a wooden box once used to hold apples and lifted her skirts. Her hams skinny and slat-muscled. Waxy in the nip of the night air.

'Well,' she said. 'Let's get this over with.'

Before the pain came she felt the blade in the flesh of her gullet, the soft mesh of her arteries. So sharp its edge was numbing as ice. The brutal intrusion of it though, its alien substance, was a violation against which she instinctively recoiled.

She tried to scream but blood filled her throat and when she gasped, she inhaled the warm flood of her own dying.

Her lungs pulled in all that streaming red wet, then spasmed and jettisoned the stuff all over the alley wall.

His hand cupping her chin. Cold hand. Hard. That hand lifted and she struggled, but the second cut came. Deeper than the first. She again tried to scream. To rail against what was being done. Alive and fully aware that in a moment she would not be, she strove to fight it. But her lungs were churning the blood to froth and she was drenched in her own fluids. Soaked and dying as the man steadied her at arms' length, holding her like a marionette.

He watched her drain.

Then her legs gave out and he allowed her to slump onto the alley floor. Down she slumped, down into the mess of her own mortality.

The last thoughts of Mary Shortt were, 'Oh God. Dear God. Please. No.'

The blood coursing in his veins and the throb of his blood-beat in the stilling of the whore's. Her blood on the cobbles. Tracing a pattern like spilled ink on dimpled parchment. A pattern traced by man over and over again. Leaking down the ragged channels of time. To the last syllable of humanity's final utterance. Order manifest in the primal tracery of a life emptied out and ended. All that blood coiling out and mingling through the years, a confluence of all the elements that made up humanity. Merging and flowing in perpetual flux.

She was still conscious when the man really went to work.

I AM IN BLOOD

★ ★ ★

Dublin Castle was a weeping slab of grey in the December dark. Station Sergeant George Frohmell of the Dublin Metropolitan Police sat at a desk and watched water puddle in the corner of one windowsill. The window's frame had been out of joint for months now and was becoming more and more mildewed and rotten. Like most things in this benighted corner of the Empire, he reflected.

The sun never sets on it, my eye.

Ever since the Act of Union in 1800, Dublin had slumped further and further into a morass of poverty and dilapidation. The Georgian redbricks around Mountjoy Square and Gardiner Street had been chopped up into squalid flophouses and flats. Three families to a room. Between the Gloucester Diamond and Sheriff Street, a maze of panting hovels sprawled and filled with whores and their customers. The Monto, they called it, those who rutted and ploughed in its filthy recesses.

The once-great townhouses of the Earls and Lords of the Irish Parliament all gone to rack and ruin. All made a flea-market of by vulture landlords, men who picked over the corpse of the body politic and rented out its carcass to pimps and opium merchants. Dublin had fallen and continued to fall. Once the Second City of the Empire, it was now a degraded and pestilential pit of a place.

George was named after the English King who presided

over Ireland's humbling. George's family, good Protestants all, descended from Hessian mercenaries brought over to help put down the Great Rebellion of 1798. George's great-great-grandfather, Wilhelm Frohmell, had escaped the pikes that had slaughtered most of his comrades and when Lake's cannon had eventually put a stop to the Croppies' gallop, he had settled down in Kingstown, by the sea, and made a modest fortune in tailoring.

Like everything else in poor oul' Ireland, each proceeding generation of the Frohmells fell on slightly harder times. Now, in the final decade of the nineteenth century, the last scion of the Frohmell dynasty, unmarried, unmonied and, at the moment, unwashed, sat in his policeman's uniform and watched the weather come in.

This was a joke altogether.

The room he sat in was cramped and stank like a latrine. The duty desk stood in the middle of the flagstoned floor. Its surface was empty apart from a mug of cold tea and a single pewter candlestick. Beside it sat a reeking spittoon into which Inspector Dunne was in the habit of fountaining streams of saliva dyed brown by chewing tobacco. The desk at which George sat was an altogether more cluttered affair. It was known affectionately as The Work Desk. George was of the opinion that he was the only one in the whole DMP who used it for anything other than storage space.

Overhead, the gaslight hissed. Only the best, most modern,

contraptions for the seat of British administration in Ireland. Only the best, of course, for its tireless guardians.

George threw a withering glance at the dead fireplace with its black scrawls of ancient kindling and shuffled through the papers on his desk.

Dublin was an awkward place to police.

Factions within factions and not a single person in the whole shabby place would give you a straight answer. Especially when you wore the Queen's uniform. The old aristocracy, with their threadbare sense of entitlement, looking at you as though you were the footman they could no longer afford. The merchant classes who preened and patronised and lied through their teeth. The ordinary people of Dublin who wouldn't piss on that uniform if it was on fire and the man inside it screaming. Wheels within wheels and a law that meant something different depending on who you were talking to.

Some of the soldier boys over from England had run into trouble because of the slippery nature of the place. If you weren't from there, Dublin was as slick as eels.

George would have bet good money, money he didn't have, that the lads in Scotland Yard wouldn't have half this trouble. The Pinkerton's over in the States definitely didn't. At least, as far as he could make out.

George was thirty years of age, and he didn't let on to anyone, but he read voraciously. Penny Dreadfuls and novels and tales of derring-do all became dog-eared and broken-spined in his hands. The stories of the Pinkerton's were his favourite. They were alien things of the Wild West, hectic with six-guns and horseflesh and desperate last stands.

Not once were they ever described sitting in the sallow sneer of light leaking down from a gas lamp, feeling the cold soak into their bones, deeper and deeper with every passing minute. George exhaled slowly and saw the very stuff of his existence condense in the air before him. Outside, the fog grew thicker and the evening darker.

He rubbed one hand across tired eyes and pinched the bridge of his nose. Then he went back to his drift of reports and roster sheets.

The knock, when it came, was so soft that he almost didn't hear it. He fastened the silver buttons of his uniform jacket and the knock came again, more insistent this time.

'Come,' George called.

He could hear the rasp of his jaw against the stiff fabric of his collar. How long had it been, he wondered, since he last shaved? The drink did that sometimes. You put off the little things. Over and over, you put them off until they ceased to matter. You lost where you were in the world.

The door opened and a short, slight constable of the DMP, well below the regulation five-nine, stood in the threshold and saluted. He fiddled with the silver chain of his whistle and shifted his weight from one foot to the other.

'Sergeant Frohmell,' he began. Then he stopped and coughed as though the cold and smoke and fog had scoured his throat raw.

George watched him for a moment. The man was pale. Fish-belly pale. And shivering from more than the December weather. Although not particularly young, he looked inexperienced, his uniform seemed brand new, lacking any sort of patching or even wear at the high collar. A new man. A new man with bad news.

'Sergeant Frohmell,' he repeated.

'I am he.'

'I was sent to get you, Sir,' said the trembling little man. 'The boys are after finding a body.'

George frowned darkly under the dull glass bell of the gas light. 'Found? Who found? Where?'

The man coughed again. 'Two of the lads on beat in the Monto. A whore named Mary Shortt. They blew their whistles like mad, Sir, and I came running. I seen her too, Sir.'

George was questing around for his greatcoat and his revolver. Officially, the DMP went unarmed. Every single member of the DMP who had been killed while policing the foetid tangle of Dublin's streets and petty conspiracies was unarmed. Their eyes open at nothing. Their mouths gaping. Their blood lapped at by mongrels. Their shit caking their uniform trousers. All for want of a gun. If George was to be shucked by a robber or shot by a Fenian, he was going to make damned sure he could defend himself.

He glanced at the constable and absent-mindedly said, 'Buck up there, me lad. You'll see more than one body before the DMP are finished with you.'

'I seen bodies before, Sir,' replied the constable. 'I was a soldier, Sir. Fusiliers. But I never seen a body like this.'

Something in the man's voice made George stop and look up. George was holding his revolver in one hand, rolling the cylinder in the fingers of the other, carefully checking each chamber. But now he paused and regarded the slight figure before him with a growing sense of trepidation.

'She was cut,' the constable said. 'Cut open like something in a butcher's window.'

George's eyes narrowed. 'What's your name, man?'

'Burrowes, Sir. John Burrowes.'

'Well, John Burrowes, for a soldier such as you to shake so, I'd hazard a guess that there's something else, isn't there? Tell me.'

Burrowes looked uncomfortable and licked his lips. He coughed again before saying, 'She was cut open, Sir.'

He paused and held George's stare for a moment before briefly dipping his eyes downward and saying, 'She was cut open, Sir. *Down there.*'

'Jesus Christ,' breathed George.

And again, 'Jesus Christ.'

Like the start of a prayer he couldn't remember.

CHAPTER 2

DUBLIN, DECEMBER 2015

Nathaniel Jacob watched the coffin. His father's coffin. A box of blond wood and shining brass. Inside, he could see, actually *see*, the scrawny bundle of kindling that his father had become. His skin like greaseproof paper. His veins showing through like scrawls of blue ink.

It sat in the back of the hearse like an anvil weighing down the universe. Unmoving and immovable. Worlds heavy.

Nathan watched and with every passing moment felt himself thinning. Thinning and vanishing.

Nathan held the book he was reading in one hand, his finger marking the page. *Cannibals* it was called. It traced the careers of some of the world's most monstrous serial killers. A grotesque patchwork of interviews and time-lines. Psych reports and crime scene photos. True crime. It was Nathan's thing. Some people read about Harry Potter and magic. Nathan read about Gary Ridgway and headless torsos.

Around him, mourners and family friends and his father's business associates all milled in that awkward shuffling way common to funeral crowds the world over. Stage whisper-ing, like their voices could wake the dead.

Go ahead, thought Nathan. Give it your best shot.

It was the collar of his father's shirt that got to him the most. It orbited that skinny neck at a grotesque distance. The old man had collapsed into himself, shrunken absurdly inside his clothes.

Old man.

That was a joke for a start.

His father had been fifty when they found the cancer. Leukaemia. Cancer of the blood. That weird mummy lying in the coffin was fifty-two years of age. His father, fifty-two going on a thousand.

His father.

That was another joke.

The funeral car was waiting for him. For him and Saman-tha and James. It sat gleaming in the December morning like a carapaced insect. The black of it cold and alien.

Samantha was no help in this situation whatsoever. She

was looking at him like he'd something obscene tattooed on his forehead.

'For God's sake, Nato!' she snapped. 'Put that book away. They're disgusting. Horrible things. There's a time and a place.'

He looked at the book in his hand. She had a point. He dog-eared the page and stowed it away in his inside coat pocket.

'Sorry, Samantha,' he said.

It had been years since he could bring himself to call her *Mammy* or *Mam* or even *Ma*.

She wasn't any of those things. No more than the thing at the bottom of that box was his father.

He knew he was adopted. He even knew who his real-life, honest-to-God mother was. His real-life, honest-to-God father, though, that was another story. But that wasn't the point. The man he had called *Da* all his life was a better parent to him than a million blood relatives could ever have been. He was a *Father*. A *Father* in a sense of the word that so many of Nathan's friends wouldn't recognise. Not an absent, perpetually disinterested shadow behind a newspaper. Not a smirking jay, all bluster and swagger on the sidelines of the school rugby pitch. But just a man who loved the boy he had called, *Nato*.

Maybe he *was* his real-life, honest-to-God father after all.

Beyond blood and genetics. Beyond the cold calculus of traits and chromosomes. Beyond all that, he was a man of

warmth and kind words and knowing smiles. A man of mischief and tenderness in equal measure.

If that didn't make him a real-life, honest-to-God father, then Nathan didn't want to know what did.

Samantha, his mother-by-proxy, sobbed and listed into Nathan's brother-by-proxy, James. James, his brother, younger by two years. James, his brother, the million-to-one-shot baby. The product of twenty grand's worth of IVF. Like Nathan was a mistake they weren't going to make again. No more adoption for the Jacobs. No Siree. James, the miracle boy who sprang from a barren womb and runty sperm. The boy who never should have been. The boy with blood and genes and chromosomes all neatly arranged so that he looked the image of his dead father but crowned with his mother's yellow hair.

Watching them, so close, so tactile, made something in Nathan twitch.

The funeral director held the door of the car open and Nathan and Samantha and James all slid onto the beige leather of the back seats. Samantha's mascara was running and she was trying to stop it staining her cheeks like a bruise. She went to put her arm around Nathan, but something in the way he held himself made her pause. Her hand rested for a moment on his knee, instead.

'We're going to be alright,' she said.

That distance between them. That distance had been

opening up lately like the gap between continents. Things were falling into it. Off the edge and into the depths, never to be seen again. Nathan didn't really know why.

Or maybe he did.

When he looked at Samantha and James, he was reminded of his father's absence. Samantha and her son, her real-life, honest-to-God son, had always been close. But the man Nathan called Da held the whole thing together. He welded a family together out of scraps. Even before he died, as he slowly atrophied in the hospital bed, Nathan could feel those welds start to crack. He thought his father could feel it, too. Could see the way Nathan started to visit more and more often on his own. And Nathan could see the pain that that caused in him. No morphine for that. Nothing at all.

James was looking at him.

'Mam's right,' he said. 'We'll get through this. Da would want us to stick together.'

'How do you know that?' said Nathan.

James said nothing and instead pretended to adjust the slant of his seat-belt.

Nathan closed his eyes. Memory was all he had now. Memory of his father laughing and carefree and boyish. Memory of that connection that was always between them. Vital and tough as ligament.

A couple of years ago now, this weird duck arrived on the pond up by the Sandyford Industrial Estate. The pond was what was left of the reservoir that used to be used by Jameson's distillery. There was nothing left of the distillery now except this flat plane of water with its little island and its weirs. A little river flowed in one end and out the other and on a smooth, reflected sky ducks and swans glided and dipped and squabbled for the bread thrown to them by passersby. All about was fringed by trees and rushes, ringed with green.

The duck that arrived on the pond was all different shades of orange and red and blue. The pond was just down the road a bit from where Nathan and some of his friends lived so he was always down there, messing around in the woods or skimming stones on the water. He was always down there, so Nathan was one of the first ones to notice this duck and its strange colours. Compared to the other birds on the pond, this one looked like it was glowing. Like it was on fire. It bobbed its crested head and shook its cherry beak and everything else was background to its brightness.

Nathan and his friends weren't the only ones to notice the newcomer and suddenly there were people with video cameras and tripods, fellas with big black cameras and detachable lenses as big as your leg, camped all around the pond. There were people with reference charts and notebooks. Tom Devereaux swore one day there was an RTÉ television crew down there. Nathan told him how he couldn't see Brian Dobson talking about the Still Pond.

Tom looked at him and went, 'Who's Brian Dobson?'

I AM IN BLOOD

The following Wednesday, the *South Dublin People* had a four-page colour supplement on this weird duck. It turned out that this bird was some kind of rare Mandarin duck from central China. How it got there nobody seemed to know, but the fact it was there was seen as some kind of million-to-one chance. Ornithologists and curious locals started tramping the water's edge to mulch and people were throwing so much bread in the water that the ducks couldn't eat it all. Little sodden flotillas of the stuff began fetching up against the banks like some sort of bizarre algae growth.

Then one day Nathan was down at the pond on his own and heard this one woman talking to her little daughter. She's going, 'Aifric, look at the beautiful duck. It came all the way here from China. Like that girl in your class.'

Then she lifted up her daughter for a better view.

They were looking at a moorhen.

Everyone seemed to have gone nuts.

Life continued like this for a week or ten days and then Nathan's Da brought it all to an abrupt halt.

Vivid as a picture, Nathan remembered everything.

He and his Da were down by the pond and the few people who were around earlier seemed to have gone home. The initial excitement over the duck had died down and now most people who wanted to see it had seen it. The Council, however, had arranged a visit from BirdWatch Ireland and no less than Don Conroy himself for the following week. There was talk of a Sandyford Mandarin Festival. All this for a duck.

This particular day, Nathan and his Da had the place more or less to themselves. The sun was a yellow bullet-hole in the sky and the August heat had painted Nathan's limbs brown and dashed golden highlights in his hair. They stood at the water's edge and they skimmed stones across the pond's surface. Every glistening skip of a pebble shattered the blue of the reflected sky and sent ripples like shockwaves from one reedy horizon to the other.

Nathan loved this. On his own with his Da. Removed from Samantha and James. Removed from the baby-vomit beige of their too-big house. Removed from their sneering looks. Nathan and his Da. Hanging out. Just like a billion other Nathans and their Das the world over. A closeness of temperament and feeling. Ties that bound stronger than blood.

They stood at the water's edge and Nathan's Da stooped and lifted up this gunmetal shard of slate. It was about as big as his palm and jagged around the edges. He leaned back and let fly. From where Nathan was standing he could see all the sleek, big muscles clench and release across his Da's shoulders. Under his T-shirt it looked like there were animals moving.

This was when he was fit. Middle-aged and not yet beginning to slacken.

This was before the cancer robbed him of himself.

I AM IN BLOOD

The slate whipped out from his hand and hit the water with a sound like a fist smacking flesh. It hit the water and then rocketed off again, leaping out of its own nest of ripples. He'd thrown it so hard that it struck the water twice more without slowing down in the slightest. They started to cheer. Nathan and his Da. Like little boys. They started to cheer because that piece of jagged slate looked like it'd go on forever.

It was at that moment, as the cheers started to build in their throats, as smiles began to hook at their mouths, it was at that moment that the Impossible Chinese Duck came paddling out of a patch of rushes.

The stone flat-smacked the water one last time and ricocheted upward. Its trajectory still rising savagely, the stone spun once in the air and Nathan and his Da stood slack-jawed, knowing exactly what was about to happen. They stood helpless as the piece of slate hammered into the duck's head.

There was no explosion of gore. There was no eruption of brains to colour the scene with unreality like in an action movie. There was just a horrible sound like a hurl connecting with a *sliotar* and then a wet plop as the stone dropped into the water.

Nathan and his Da stood there for a second, blinking and looking at the duck out there on the pond.

Then Nathan's Da said, 'Maybe it's alright.'

Then he said, 'Oh shit.' Flat as the sound of slate against bone.

Out on the pond the duck's head was starting to loll. First it rocked from left to right, as though the vertebrae of its neck were turning to jelly. Then a quiver ran through it and its jelly neck tensed and curled stiffly, carrying its elegant, crested head back between its wings. It stayed like that for a moment, with its neck in spasm and its beak shivering at the sky, and then, without a sound, the duck rolled onto its side and was pushed along by the current over the weir.

Nathan and his Da watched it in shocked silence. Its feathers were glowing like embers as they tumbled in the white froth and its dead eyes stared at nothing as the little river carried it away.

Nathan looked at his Da and then at the ripples on the pond and then at his Da again. Nathan knew, even back then, that if anyone found out about this, they were in big trouble.

Nathan was terrified and he felt that he was within inches of just running the hell away. His mouth was going dry and he could actually feel his heart against his ribs. He could feel the thud-tha-thud of his own mounting panic.

Nathan was terrified.

But his Da wasn't.

Nathan looked at his Da and then at the ripples on the pond and then at his Da again and something was happening to his face.

His Da's eyes followed the dead bird downstream and then

he turned to face Nathan. He couldn't possibly have meant to hit the thing, but what happened seemed to have lit a fire in his brain. His eyes were shining like there was a candle behind each one and his lips were split in an impish smile. He was like a child in a schoolyard after doing something bold. In that one expression, nearly forty years of life and long hours were effaced. Removed from Samantha's withering presence. Removed from the accumulation of money and stuff he didn't need. Removed from everything, the flare of who he really was burned through.

Nathan stood there, thinking all this, and then his Da said, 'For God's sake, don't tell Samantha or James about this.'

The he laughed. A laugh of mischief and good humour. A laugh of freedom and release.

He ruffled Nathan's hair and said, 'Don Conroy's going to be really pissed.'

With eyes closed, Nathan smiled as the funeral car glided forward, following the hearse with its freight of blond wood and dead meat.

And James's voice went, 'Nato? Nato, are you okay?'

Okay? *Okay?* Right then, Nathan thought there would never be an *Okay* again. He sat in the silence of his own misery and watched the sky roll up the windscreen and disappear out of sight.

At the graveyard, after all the handshakes and all the *sorry for your troubles*, the blond box with all that shining brass was lowered into a hole in the ground. It didn't even have the good grace to rain. A bloodless December sun, half-hearted and apologetic, slicked the surrounding tombstones with melting frost. In the watery brightness, in the Advent cold, Nathan could feel the bite of the straps he had used to lower the coffin. He could feel the weight of all that wood and all that brass. How much of it was the weight of his father, he didn't want to know.

Nathan was seventeen and it was felt by everybody that he was man enough to do this. Man enough to shoulder what was left of his father. Man enough to consign him to clay.

For Nathan, the most awful thing about the whole ritual was that ridiculous astro-turf mat they used to cover the mound of excavated soil. The deplorable inadequacy of it. It draped over that mound like the too-green fleece of a plastic animal. It did the precise opposite of what it was intended to do. It drew your attention to all that muck and spoil and nudged the mind to picturing it avalanching into the cavity of the grave.

Looking at that green mat, Nathan could hear the stones and clods hammering around his father's head.

And now he was gone.

Seventeen years old and man enough to feel a man's grief.

Across from him, across that fathomless hole in the ground, James leaned into Samantha.

Nathan watched as Samantha wrapped her arm around

her son's shoulders and bent her head to kiss the boy's golden fringe. She was crying, and her mascara was bleeding down her cheeks again. When she lifted her head, she left wet smudges in James's hair and on his forehead was feathered the red stain of her lipstick.

★ ★ ★

The house Nathan grew up in sat at the top of a short driveway with a putting-green lawn to one side. Five-bed and detached. Large even for the Kilmacud Road. It sat on its own little plot, massive and vulgar beside its neighbours. It sat like a monolith just before the turn up the hill on to South Avenue. It sat not quite in Mount Merrion, but definitely not in Stillorgan. Samantha stressed this quite a lot. Usually with volume mounting in direct proportion to the amount of Jacob's Creek pumped into her.

Vulgar and detached. To Nathan, that pretty much summed up everything.

Now the house was filled with relatives and friends of his parents. Everyone was wearing black and everyone was talking really low so that the house filled with a sort of sibilant thunder. James was in the back garden with a gaggle of his mates from school. They flocked around him, all dressed in the hippest funeral chic imaginable. The girls looked like they'd broken into Morticia Adams's wardrobe, with delicate black eyeliner to match. The boys stood in black skinny jeans or razor-seamed black trousers. Their hair all spiked up and quiffed over as if a Justin Bieber tribute band was what you wanted at your father's funeral. Nathan watched them. The pack of fakers.

Inside the house, distant cousins and people he had never met before shook his hand again and again, again and again, without ever meeting his eye. Samantha sat in the living room and sipped a never-ending glass of Cabernet Sauvignon. People queued to say how much her husband would be missed.

Nathan thought that none of them, not a single one, knew what it was to miss someone as much as he missed his father right now.

No one from school was there for him. Not even Esther, who, if you got right down to it, would have fit right in. She looked like she was attending a funeral twenty-four-seven. He would have liked to see her. Her smile. Her eyes that went from green to gold to hazel like the seasons, one after another, shimmered in her every glance.

Lately, he felt he might be in love with Esther.

Eventually, the distant relatives and the family friends and James's Third Year chums all filtered away. The caterers cleaned up all the paper plates, said how sorry they were for everyone's trouble, and then they left, too. They left behind them the chemical stink of paraffin burners and a half-eaten sandwich unnoticed under the couch.

It was funny how quickly the house emptied of people. It

was as though someone had pulled a plug and the black swirl of mourners eddied out before you even noticed they were going. Nathan stood alone in the kitchen. He listened to the enormous silence that seemed to suddenly stuff the world. It was like the air was clogged with little deadening fibres. His father's absence was a hole in reality. Nathan felt dislocated. Standing there in the empty room with its Mediterranean blue-and-white tiles, its rustic Kiltrea crockery, its great slab of a central counter, he felt like he was floating loose. Nothing bound him to this place anymore. The universe felt tissue-thin. Like he could tear it as easily as spider silk.

Samantha and James came in. Her arm was hooked around his shoulders again.

She looked at him, then looked away. Looked. Then looked away. Eventually she asked, 'Are you okay?'

Stupid, stupid question.

Nathan shook his head. 'No, Samantha, I'm not.'

He walked past them and left the kitchen.

Down the hall and up the stairs and he could hear Samantha and James murmuring to each other. In his head he could hear his own words. *No, Samantha, I'm not.* He'd become a cliché. A walking cliché.

In his room he sat on his bed and stared at the glossy toes of his shoes. His hair slumped forward in a frizzy tangle. He dragged his fingers through it and winced as they snagged in the knots. He hated his hair. It wasn't curly and it wasn't straight. It was an unravelled Brillo pad and, no matter what he did with it, whenever he looked in the mirror he despised what he saw. If it wasn't his hair, it was something else.

Nathan was bright enough to know this was all part and parcel of being a teenager. This didn't help in the slightest. Knowing stuff sometimes made other stuff worse. Sometimes his life felt like that green fleece overlaying the grave mound. He knew something horrible sat under the surface.

He also knew he shouldn't blame James for this. But he did all the same.

The million-to-one-shot baby. The apple of his mother's eye. The golden boy.

James's reflection of his parents cast Nathan in a darker light. His sameness underscored Nathan's difference. James's provenance could be traced in every curve of his features, every strand of his blond hair, every line of his carriage.

Nathan was a gangly thing, all angles and hard edges. A face that looked carved out of salt. A ragged crow in a nest of peacocks.

He had never belonged here. All of a sudden, he couldn't remember a time when he had belonged. All of a sudden, he couldn't remember a time when that distance didn't exist between James and him. And out of that distance a tiny voice mewled that if James had come first, if nature had delivered her punchline two years earlier, then Nathan wouldn't be here.

I AM IN BLOOD

Where would he be?

In care, probably.

In care, or six feet under like the mess of a woman who birthed him.

Kelly Brook stared at him blankly from the opposite wall. Kelly Brook wearing a bikini with just the right amount of cleavage showing. Samantha pretended she didn't notice, but she definitely did. She couldn't help but notice.

His father was different. His *Da*. His Da walked in the day after Nathan had nervously Blu-tacked Kelly onto the patch of wall that used to belong to Gandalf. Nathan was lying on the bed texting on his phone and his Da had stopped, performed a *Loony-Toons* double-take and smiled at his son.

He smiled and said, 'Gandalf looks well in a swimsuit.'

Then he told Nathan he had cancer. Leukaemia. A corruption of the blood.

That was Nathan's Da. He couldn't hide anything. Pretence wasn't in his make-up.

When the cancer took him, it took away something of Nathan, too. It gutted him.

Now, sitting on his bed, dressed all in black, Nathan felt his phone vibrate. When he took it out, the screen read: *Message Received: Esther Gilsenan*.

He smiled. In the middle of all this grief and all this heartbreak, he smiled. Still smiling, he thought, how could he?

With his Da dead and in a hole in the ground, how could he smile?

He opened the message. He read it. He frowned. He read it again.

Esther was the only person Nathan knew who could communicate so much of themselves through texting. Her message, a mass of chunky characters without a smiley-face or sad-face or lol to be seen, read: *Hey Nato, how are you? Stupid question, I know. I'm sorry I wasn't there for you today. I can only imagine how lonely you feel right now. I'm sure James is loving the attention. I'll see you tonight. Stay awake.*

Every comma and apostrophe exact. Fullstops and capitals all in their allotted places. Everything precise and ordered and so unlike every other text in his inbox that her messages stood out like pieces of glass in a bowl of baby food. There was something sharp about Esther. Something hard-edged and bitter and glittering. She was unique among the Interchangeable Sorchas that packed their school. Golden Retriever hair-dos and arch expressions. Every one of them wanting to be a mini Rosanna Davison.

Fakers. Every single one of them, fakers.

The screen of his phone had faded to black. He didn't know how long he had sat there frowning into space. Her message now was black on black.

Stay awake.

What did that mean?

I AM IN BLOOD

From downstairs a static quiet seemed to creep up through the floorboards. He could imagine Samantha and James down there. Their heads pressed together. She, with her glass of wine. He, with his hand in hers. His straw hair, his father's eyes. Both of them talking about him.

What will we do about Nato?

Outside it was already dark. December nights fall fast and deep. Through his window he couldn't see the sky. The light from his bedside lamp polluted the glass and slicked it over with a counterfeit image of his room. He looked back at himself, pale and dark all at once. He knew that out there other homes had Christmas lights turned on and real, honest-to-God trees spiced hallways and sitting rooms with the smell of pine sap and sawdust. Sagging swags of multicoloured bulbs swung suspended across the streets, arcing from telegraph pole to telegraph pole. Out there, the Season of Good Will to All Men was ripening under the brittle constellations. Out there, Christmas was coming.

Not in here, though. Not in this house. Not in this room. Ho, ho, ho.

He lay back on his bed, then sat up and fished in his jacket pocket. He took out his book again. *Cannibals*. Bold font. Front cover of dead eyes staring in the distance. Staring right through you like you weren't even there. He turned it over in his hands. He couldn't get over the description, the exhaustive detail. The banality of the lives and the savagery of the crimes. The world's most awful murders spread out before him. Men who had not only killed and killed again but men who had butchered their victims like veal calves. Men who had cut off heads and boiled them in stewing pots. Men who had made lampshades from the flayed faces of unlucky hitchhikers. Monsters. A freak-show gallery of the worst of human nature. Dahmer and Chikatilo and Garavito. *The Picture of Dorian Grey* made flesh over and over again.

The back of the book tried to dress this up as some kind of public service publication. It hailed the depth of the research and lauded the writer for trying to find the causes behind these men's actions. As if the writer was a mechanic and the human race was a car with a badly wired fuse. One wrong spark and you'd never know, you might eat little Seán from next-door. As if God could do a product recall.

Nathan wasn't fooled. He knew the book was just an excuse to describe the awful things done to people you didn't know, thousands of miles away. Misery porn. Like all those books written by kids who spent half their lives locked in an attic or under the stairs. Just before his Da died, Nathan had gone into Eason's on O'Connell Street to buy a book so that he might have something to read in the hospital. He had actually laughed out loud when he saw it. A whole, entire section called *Shattered Lives*. People loved to wallow in the quag of other people's misfortune. How else could you explain *EastEnders*?

I AM IN BLOOD

Nathan was comfortable with this. He knew why he read books like *Cannibals*. Why he read books like the other dozen on his shelf under the window. He knew it wasn't out of some public-spirited drive to understand why serial killers kill. He read them for the same reason that people wrote them. For the same reason that people went to see the *Saw* movies. Because blood and guts and carnage gave him a nasty little thrill. The lurid fascination of the voyeur.

Any other reason was delusion.

Samantha was horrified by these books. She said even the thoughts of them gave her nightmares and James thought he was a freak, anyway. His choice of reading material only confirmed matters.

How he missed his father. His Da.

He lay back on his bed and opened the book about half-way through. There was a section of glossy crime scene photos a few pages on. Sometimes you had to turn the book around and around like a steering wheel until you could make sense of them. They were always in black-and-white and the blood in them always looked like spilled ink. Most of them looked the way Francis Bacon's studio would look in black-and-white. All messy with stuff thrown all around. Except Francis Bacon didn't keep a torso in the bath.

The violence and chaos of creation had a lot in common with what a mass murderer did. Especially the really bad ones.

He lay there, reading the book, until he heard someone,

probably Samantha, come up the stairs. The someone stopped outside his door for a minute and Nathan could feel that little electric gap open up. That little buzzing moment when you know someone is thinking about doing something. But then the moment passed and Nathan heard footsteps shuffling down the landing.

Stay awake.

That's what Esther had said.

Stay awake.

What was she up to?

Nathan looked at his phone. Eleven o'clock.

Eleven o'clock and all was not fucking well.

CHAPTER 3

DUBLIN, DECEMBER 1892

The street, if it could be called such, was a narrow, stinking defile between two blocks of tenements. The gaslights and window lamps of Sackville Street and College Green were mere suggestions of illumination here in the Monto. Even in the daytime its alleyways were dark things, swamped in stench and oozing with shadow. This was a dark place for dark business. This was a place of deep doorways and covered windows, a place of hidden faces and secret lusts. In the still December night, it was a place of cold fog and abject horror.

George Frohmell, respected sergeant of Her Majesty's Own Dublin Metropolitan Police, tightened his lips as Constable Burrowes vomited into the gutter. George took a discreet step to his left, as much to give the man a modicum of privacy as to avoid the splatters, and glanced upward. Here the redbrick flanks of two tattered old townhouses reared to either side of him. Once the urban mansions of some country lord, they were now home to a crawling, yapping, litter of Dublin's poorest. Unwashed and brazen and selling their bodies to pay the rent.

About halfway up one wall, a tiny window looked out onto the alleyway and in it, touchingly, a feeble candle flickered in the dark. A nod to the Christmas season. A light to guide the wanderer home.

George hated the Monto and everything in it. He wasn't a religious man, but its very existence curdled the severe Protestant blood that gave him life.

'Sorry, Sir,' said Constable Burrowes.

'Wipe your chin, man,' said George and returned his gaze to the uneven floor of the alley.

Advent candles, my arse.

In front of him, two constables of the DMP were standing over something that looked like a rumpled pile of stained laundry. When George had first arrived he was forced to concentrate, in the dark and in the fog, forced to focus all his attention in order to ascertain that it wasn't. And when he discovered this, his whole body recoiled, reviling the fact that what he was concentrating on, the thing that he was staring at, rapt and intent, was, in fact, a dead body.

A very dead body, reflected George.

Once, in his first few months on the job, George had helped hook a drowned Welsh sailor from out of the Liffey. The man had been dead for a long while, his body submerged beneath the heavy anchor chains of a West Indies steamer. The poor unfortunate had blundered to his death and hadn't even been missed until his ship was about to set sail. They had found him in the water, a great hawser pythoned about his torso. If he had been a slim man when he entered the water, he certainly wasn't when he emerged from under it. The water had worked its own particular necromancy on him. He was bloated as a sea-cow and fungus pale. George had managed to sling a rope around one sausage arm and two helpful stevedores had sunk steel gaffs into the cumulous belly. The three men had heaved the corpse ever upward, it belching gas and leaking black fluids with every jerk of the ropes. They heaved, until, without warning, the rotting carcass split in two.

The sound it made was like tearing fabric.

That was as close to vomiting on the job as George had ever come.

The body now before him had brought back that old nausea.

She was a whore. There was no doubt about that. She sat with her mouth open and her head tilted back against the brickwork of one alley wall. Her throat was opened from ear to ear and the tacky spillage of her veins and arteries made a black bib across her chest. She sat as though paralysed with drink, her eyes glassy and staring at the invisible stars in the invisible sky, her dress and petticoats all bunched up and dishevelled. From beneath the tattered confectionery of her finery her two legs jutted stiffly. Splayed like a broken wishbone.

Beneath her and all across the alley, her blood made a viscous lake. She sat in a puddle of her own mortality and the fluids that had once sustained her existence now clabbered about her.

George had lifted those petticoats. He had seen where all that blood came from. He had seen the wounds. Her abdomen had been opened up in a wide, bloody yawn. Between her legs there was a razor-edged void. The wounds were clean. Sharp. A butcher's work, but with a surgeon's eye.

In his greatcoat pocket George kept a hipflask. Dublin in the wintertime was a bleak place. The grey of it got into your bones. The air was full of dank and foul humours. A drop of whiskey was always welcome. It warmed you from the inside out, warding off chills and infections and all the sour contagions that the season brought with it.

He had told Catherine that for two years.

Two years, until their engagement keeled over and died like a calf brained with a sledge.

He remembered her eyes. Every day he remembered. He remembered the shock in them. He remembered her cheekbone beginning to swell, a bruise showing already. He remembered the pain in his knuckles. Even through the whiskey haze, he had felt it.

Two years of warming little mouthfuls slugged in sheltered nooks around town. Two years of hiding the slur in his voice, the numbness in his lips. Hiding the rage that sometimes swarmed up in him, swarmed up in the dark watches of the night.

A hipflask of whiskey to ward off the chill.

It was in his hand before he even knew he was reaching for it. He watched the two constables as they looked through the dead whore's clothing. Delicately, they fingered petticoats like inexperienced lovers. Lifting each one like the turning of a page. One of the men kept a handkerchief pressed to his nose and mouth.

They were looking for the knife that did this. The weapon that opened the dead whore so horribly, so neatly.

He unscrewed the cap of the flask and took a quick, aggressive pull.

The dead whore.

He stowed the flask away and said, 'You said her name was Mary Shortt?'

Burrowes wasn't looking at him. Very pointedly, Burrowes wasn't looking at him. The hipflask always went unnoticed by everyone.

'Yes, Sir,' said Burrowes.

'How do we know?'

'One of the lads knows her, Sir. Knew her, I suppose, now, Sir.'

'One of *our* lads?'

'Sir.'

'What's his name?'

Burrowes cleared his throat. 'Just one of the lads, Sir.'

George arched an eyebrow. Burrowes was looking at the corpse and the two DMP men poring over it.

George glanced from the corpse to Burrowes and back again before saying, 'Well, ask him for a list of Mary's clients, if he can get it. Tell him he can keep his own name off it.'

'I will, Sir. Thank you, Sir.'

The constable with the handkerchief straightened up, arched his back and breathed out in a long billow of grey. He looked past George and nodded toward the mouth of the alleyway. There, a crowd of onlookers had gathered. They muttered and craned their necks and made scandalised little noises as the policemen went about their business. They gathered, their pantomime morality exercised by the constables' hands rooting through the petticoats of one of their own. Their disgusting curiosity piqued by the rumours that skittered through the surrounding tenements.

George didn't turn. He simply looked at the constable and asked, 'What about them?'

'There'll be newspaper men here, any minute, Sir. They'll

be trying to set up their damned cameras, Sir. We should get her inside. Give her a bit of dignity, maybe. There's no knife, here, Sir. Whoever did this is long gone and he took his blade with him.'

George nodded. 'Maybe. But we don't know that. I'm not having her moved until I have her looked at by someone who knows what they're doing. But we might as well do this as quickly as possible. Get a hold of a horse and cart and a sheet for to cover her with. Be ready to get her gone the second I tell you.'

The constable seemed mightily relieved and stepped gingerly, daintily across the slick of blood that surrounded the corpse. In any other situation, he would have looked comical.

As he passed, George caught him by the elbow and pulled him close. 'And you listen to me, Francis Delaney, not a word are you to breathe to anyone about this. Not a word. If I see any details of this scene appearing in any of the local rags tomorrow morning, I'll know where they came from.'

Delaney swallowed but his voice was level. 'Of course, Sir. I understand, Sir.'

George smiled at him, a smile with a ragged edge.

Still holding his arm George said, 'Good lad.' Then, 'And Francis?'

'Sir?'

'Get me Dr O'Sullivan. Number 53, Stephen's Green West.'

Delaney frowned but nodded once. 'Yes, Sir.'

'And Francis?'

'Sir?'

'You can leave the few bob you pilfered from her purse. I'll drop it into the poor box.'

An hour later and George Frohmell stood in the alleyway and fumed. He had commandeered a few threadbare sheets from the surrounding flophouses and had jury-rigged a make-shift screen to hide Mary Shortt's body from the eyes and lenses, bad luck to them, that had gathered now at both ends of the alley. He wanted this over with and Mary Shortt's body off the street. If this scene appeared in any of the local scandal rags, there'd be uproar amongst Dublin's great unwashed. And if that happened, the Castle would want answers.

Ah, Dublin Castle. It was more than just a centre for bureaucracy. It was the headquarters and garrison of an alien army. Ireland occupied a peculiar interstice in world affairs. It was a place there but not there all at once. A nation cowed under the gaze of a bullying neighbour. A proud Home Nation of the greatest empire the world had ever seen. A febrile birthing pool for unrest and dissent and Republican ideals. A stagnant backwater, a meander cut off from the flow of the world, silted up with old ideas. Ireland was a paradox. A people kept at heel by a foreign army whose members were one-third Irish themselves. It worried George, some-times. Sometimes, at three in the morning and his hipflask empty, he wondered at the capacity of his fellow country-men to hold two opposing views simultaneously, to be pulled by two opposing poles. He felt it was only a matter of time before a weak spot fractured and gave way. He felt it was only a matter of time before the DMP and the RIC and all the brass-buttoned Tom Lobsters in Dublin Castle would be forced to fix bayonets.

God save the Queen and God save Ireland.

Blood for blood without remorse.

Croppies lie down.

Boolavogue.

All things and everywhere simultaneously.

The entire place was a contradiction in terms.

And Dublin Castle stood at the heart of it. And at the heart of Dublin Castle stood George Frohmell and the DMP and hundreds of soldiers confused and frightened and hated by everyone.

So George stood now as newspaper men were jostled by DMP constables. The tripods for their cameras were kicked over again and again. But like the sea, they just kept on coming. Arguing with the policemen, scribbling notes, reset-ting their blasted cameras. Trying to snatch a glimpse at the emptied body of Mary Shortt.

The Castle hospital was a brick box without any of the ostentation that clad the rest of the Castle's buildings. It was a functional bunker of a place and tended to be occupied only in times of emergency when constables and soldiers were wounded by stones and bottles hurled by threadbare mobs or beaten by members of the working men's clubs that were lately springing up all over the place. George smelled trouble in them. Rats' nests of discontent, all.

But there was no hospital for Mary Shortt.

He watched as one of the DMP constables trying to hold back the mob at the end of the alley deftly brought his truncheon down and laid a member of Dublin's fine citizenry spark out. That's the stuff, thought George. Whatever about Mary Shortt, that poor fecker will need a stitch or two.

George hated hospitals and he hated the men who ended up in them. For however long they remained convalescing and sipping sweet tea and gurning at the nurses, they were a gap in his roster.

Two years before, George had been taught a most valuable lesson by the man who once wore the sergeant's chevrons before him. A gaggle of peasants from the countryside had come into the city looking for work and had stoked up the passions of some of the locals, who accused them of undercutting their wages. Heads were staved in and glass was broken and in the middle of it all Daniel Harford, one of the bravest men George had ever worked with, was brought low by a swinging chair leg.

George was kneeling beside him, sheltering him, nursing his split skull.

'What are you doing?' asked his sergeant. 'Get back to your duty.'

George looked at him wonderingly. 'It's Harford, Sarge. He's one of the best men we have.'

The sergeant sneered at him, openly and without any compassion, and said, 'Not anymore he's not. The best men we have are those that are able to do their duty.'

He pointed at the scrum of police and rioters and said, 'One of those lads is our best man now.'

George had resented those words at first. He had thought them bred of disdain and callousness. His sergeant had seemed in that moment a distant effigy in his dark uniform, a carving of something heartless and inhuman. In the months and years since, though, George had come to realise the truth in his old sergeant's words. What made you good, what gave you the right to call yourself a man, was the ability to carry out your duties.

A flash from one of the thronging cameras illuminated the alleyway like a lightning strike. The hanging sheets fluoresced like ghosts forever suspended in the dank of the Dublin night. Magnesium stink filled the place.

Carry out your duties, thought George. He curled his lip, puffed out his cheeks and prepared to do just that.

Dr Oliver Patrick O'Sullivan stood across from him. Between the two men was a slick of drying blood and a DMP photographer setting up his equipment. The legs of the tripod bit into the crust of the blood and pushed it up in viscous ripples. The vital fluids of someone become jelly. Pudding.

Dr O'Sullivan was a balding, lean gentleman of fifty-three years of age. He was old enough and wealthy enough to expect an unbroken sleep in the cold of a December night, without DMP men hammering on his door. He was rather flustered and sleep still gummed his eyes and gave his voice a false baritone.

He looked from the body to George, to the DMP photographer and back again.

'This is obscene, George.'

'I know. It is sickening. Such savagery is beyond rational thought.'

The doctor snorted. 'That's all well and good, but to have her photographed and laid out like this is beyond indecorous. I really don't see the need. It is obvious how she died. Baring her poor body to the camera in this way is verging on the immoral.'

George was nodding. Nodding in that distracted way that people do when they expect to agree with the sentiments of the person across from them. It took a long, silent moment for Dr O. P. O'Sullivan's words to register. When they did, George felt he must look like a fool.

'Are you suggesting, Doctor, that we box her up and throw her in a hole and have done with it?'

Dr O'Sullivan's mouth twisted and he regarded George

with an expression halfway between hurt and exasperation. He straightened up from where he was bent over the corpse and breathed out a fog of warmth and moisture.

'Don't be such a nettle, George. My heart goes out to the soul of this poor unfortunate. I don't want to even imagine the awfulness of her final moments. But be that as it may, I fail to see why we should pile indignity upon insult. She's had her throat slit and her lower abdomen cut open. Then she died. No doubt this was an act perpetrated by one of her customers.'

This last word slipped from his tongue like a bubble of bile.

George raised one eyebrow. 'Oh, for God's sake, spare me your piety. Does your wife still dance, does she? Still turn her ankle at the sight of a fat wallet?'

Dr O'Sullivan stilled. A static charge suddenly radiated off him like the crackle of St Elmo's Fire. The DMP man paused in the preparation of his camera. He had extended the accordion-like housing for the lens and was busy readying the blitzlicht for the flash. Now he stilled.

'Would you like me to leave for a minute, Sir?' he asked.

George ignored him.

He needed a drink.

'I apologise, Oliver,' he said. 'I should not have said that.'

'No, you should not,' snapped the doctor.

George stared down at the defiled remains of Mary Shortt. He watched as the DMP man with his camera ducked down under the heavy black cowl to sight through the lens.

'Mind yourself, doctor,' he said. 'Unless you want to be pictured with a murder victim.'

O'Sullivan stepped carefully out of the frame and the camera's flash etched the alley in actinic brilliance. For an instant, everything was hard-edged and intense. The shadows blacker. Mary Shortt's opened throat all the deeper. Her flesh all the whiter.

George stood batting acrid smoke from out of his eyes. Through the heavy folds of the stuff he could see O'Sullivan returning to scrutinise the corpse.

'We need to find out how this was done, Oliver,' said George. 'We can't let this rest. I can't let this rest.'

Dr O'Sullivan's face softened and he looked up. Almost in a whisper he said, 'Is this about Rosie? Are you worried about her?'

In spite of everything, George smiled. 'Nothing gets past you, Oliver, does it?'

'I try to keep abreast of things.'

The DMP man gave a polite cough and muttered, 'I just have to get something, Sir. I'll leave you to it for a moment.'

George watched him step around the screen of hanging sheets. His lovelife was become a joke. At least some of the men still maintained an air of discretion.

He shook his head and said, 'I haven't seen Rosie in two months but, yes, the more I think about what happened to the poor creature in front of us, the more worried I become.'

Two lonely months. Trying to wean himself off her. The whore and the policeman. The punchline of every barrack-room joke.

The doctor was looking at him, an oddly gentle expression on his face. Reading his mind like a medium reading cards.

'Why are you worried?' asked O'Sullivan.

'You know those books and pamphlets I like to read?'

'Dreadful things, George. Immoral scandal rags, every one of them.'

George shook his head but pressed on. 'Yes, yes. Penny dreadfuls. Lurid tales to fascinate the ignorant. But I read about this. I recognise it.'

'Recognise what?'

George gestured with his right hand. A curt spasm of a movement, as though his very muscles were reluctant to carry him any closer to the body on the cobblestone floor.

Dr O'Sullivan looked at him wonderingly. 'You *recognise* what's been done to this girl?'

George nodded and said, 'I need to know what weapon or implement made these wounds. I need to know if there was a professional hand involved, a butcher, maybe, or a ...'

The doctor was regarding him now with an expression of growing awareness. He licked his lips and asked, 'Or a what, George?'

'Or a surgeon.'

The doctor's face took on a grey cast and he blinked at George's words. He was a man for whom a curtain had been drawn back and the vista behind that presented itself was one of absolute horror.

'No,' he said, appalled. And again, 'No.'

He looked from the corpse of Mary Shortt to George and back, all the while saying, 'That's a despicable thing to even consider. A doctor would never do something like this. *First, do no harm.* A butcher, yes, but a doctor ...'

George let him babble for a moment before cutting across him. 'I need to be sure. Could a doctor have done this?'

'No,' came the answer. Flat and hard and cutting as broken slate.

George's eyes narrowed. Dr O'Sullivan with his upper-class piety, Dr O'Sullivan with his upper-class mores and sensibilities, Dr O'Sullivan with his upper-class intelligence, was being obtuse, evasive.

'I'll rephrase that,' said George. 'Might a man with surgical training be capable of making wounds such as those we see before us?'

In the distance a cab horse whinnied and in the cold fog of the night a lone mongrel sent up a yowling howl. In the alley, this defile of gore and death, all was silent. Dr O'Sullivan ran one hand over the grey tangles of his hair and shook his head.

'To what end, George? What would make you think a

person with medical training did this? Why would they take a knife to such a beautiful young girl?'

George thought the good doctor was being a tad generous in this eulogy. Her face upturned and blank in death, Mary Shortt was a gap-toothed thing of pinched features and cankered skin. Nevertheless no-one, no matter their trade or position in society, deserved to be slaughtered like an animal. No-one deserved to be opened up in a wide red gape with their life sluicing out across the filth of a Dublin alleyway.

He stepped forward, his voice pitched low. Should any of those damned vultures in the press hear what he had to say, there would be hell to pay.

'I've seen the wounds,' he said. 'Oliver, I've seen with my own two eyes what he did. I need to find out if he's done any more to her. I need to find out if he's taken anything.'

'Dear Christ,' breathed the doctor.

Over his muted outrage George continued. 'I told you, I recognise the wounds. I've read about them. If I'm right, if they are the same wounds, he might have done the same things to her as he maybe did to those others. He might have cut the same things out. Like a surgeon.'

'Oh God,' hissed Dr O'Sullivan. And hefted in those two words was a whole world of nausea and revulsion.

'Whitechapel,' whispered George, as though the name itself was a curse or a conjuration of something vile. 'You must have heard of them. The Whitechapel murders.'

'Oh no,' said O'Sullivan. 'No. No. No. That couldn't be. Not here.'

'The Whitechapel murders,' said George again. 'Each one had their throat slit. Their abdomens were cut open. In at least two cases, Annie Chapman and Catherine Eddowes, they were disembowelled and their intestines drawn up over their shoulders. They also had internal organs removed.'

The doctor's face was slack now. Haggard, like the decades still to come of his life had fallen on him all at once. He shook his head in mute horror, but George kept speaking. Quietly and relentlessly.

'He took things, Oliver. This killer took things. Kidneys. Wombs.'

O'Sullivan retched.

'The Whitechapel murders,' said George for the third time. Like a mantra.

Casting a spell or casting out a demon, he did not know.

CHAPTER 4:

DUBLIN, DECEMBER 2015

Nathan couldn't stay awake. The events of the past few days and weeks had tracked him down and ambushed him, lying on his bed, his head full of blood and gore. Exhaustion gently mugged him.

When he woke, his phone was vibrating so hard it had slipped off the pillow. It lay on his duvet, skittering like a wounded wasp and Nathan blinked at it. That moment when you wake up, those few seconds when you're drugged with the last dregs of sleep, that's what Nathan felt blinking at his phone. Stupidly he reached for it and stupidly he fumbled at the buttons and stupidly he answered it.

'Yeah. Hello?'

Yeah. Hello? Without even looking at the number.

'You were asleep, weren't you?' said Esther.

Her voice in his ear. That false intimacy ached through him.

'Yeah,' he replied. He kept his voice low. 'I dropped off halfway through Chapter Six. I didn't even know I was asleep until I woke up.'

'Chapter Six mustn't be much good.'

'Too much psychology.'

Psychology. Lies and snake-oil. Nathan knew this because Samantha had insisted that he visit a psychiatrist a couple of years ago and all he did was ask how Nathan felt about stuff. Over and over again. The psychiatrist with his corduroy slacks, the psychiatrist with his sandals and his earnest expression, wouldn't accept *Grand* as a feeling.

Once, Nathan asked why it was that the amount of diagnosable mental illnesses had increased by a factor of ten over the last thirty years. Nathan asked the psychiatrist did he not feel uncomfortable being part of a profession that basically invented stuff so they could make money off people. Like if you hired a builder to put down a patio, and you ended up paying for an extension that you never even knew you needed.

The psychiatrist looked at Nathan and then wrote something on his chart.

Samantha got a phonecall from him a few days later. This was at breakfast. She listened to the voice at the other end of the line. Then she frowned and then she hung up.

Nathan looked at her.

'Well?' asked his Da.

'He says Nathan doesn't have to go back. He says he's grand.'

Grand. Just like that.

'Told you,' said his Da and winked at Nathan. 'Right as rain, my boy.'

That was the last visit he'd paid to the psychiatrist.

But that was years ago.

Now, Nathan listened as Esther laughed down the phone.

'I despise psychology,' she was saying. 'I *loathe* it. Give me a gorefest. It's more honest, don't you think?'

Nathan was smiling, again. In spite of himself he was smiling.

'Why are you ringing?' he asked. 'Why did you want me to stay awake?'

'I'm out the front. We're going for a walk.'

Sneaking out was easy. The too-big house was full of too-deep carpets, beige and impossible to keep clean. You could walk noiseless as a ghost if you wanted to. Nathan went down the stairs and passed the door to the darkened living room. And stopped dead.

Samantha was on the couch. His heart cramped in his chest and he stopped breathing. She lay half-propped against a tumble of cream upholstered cushions. She lay, eyes closed, three empty bottles of Pinot Grigio upright on the rosewood table beside her. A last glass, half-finished, perched on the table's edge. She lay there, blue-white in the dark. Bloodless and still. Like a homicide victim waiting to be photographed.

And Nathan's thoughts ran to red. Asleep in the dark and Da asleep in the long dark. Endless and lightless and no coming back and I miss him. God, I miss him. Final ending and never-ending absence. Hole in my heart. Hole in the world. Swallowing it all down. Like a throat swallows wine.

He watched her for a long silent while and then went out.

He walked down the path by the side of the house. Nathan's phone said it was quarter to twelve at night and the stars had wheeled overhead, all but effaced by the light pollution from the city. The cold was a needle-clawed thing that bit into him as soon as he stepped into the back garden. He had thrown his jacket on over his black shirt, but the night air clamped onto his face and ears. Every inch of exposed skin was suddenly dimpled with gooseflesh. Frost webbed the world.

Esther stood at the end of the drive. She was the centre of a universe of freezing gossamer. The path beneath her feet glimmered in the streetlight.

She smiled at him and raised one hand and gave him a little cutesy-pie wave. All in black, her face white and her lips red. She looked like something drained of blood. She looked like someone who'd read *Interview With The Vampire* one too many times. Which she had.

I AM IN BLOOD

Under her fingerless black woollen gloves Nathan could make out the netting of black lace that peaked out at the wrist.

Black coat, black scarf, black hair, black eyes. Her face floated like a petal on dark waters.

The instant he saw her, Nathan felt a vinegar tingle in his abdomen.

Nato Luvs Esther 4eva. Esther 4 Nato. T.I.E.D.

A thousand scrawls on a thousand copybooks. A thousand thousand ways to spell out teenage love. A thousand thousand ways for your heart to be bared and a thousand thousand reasons to be told you're *just friends*. That she *really really likes you but not like that*. A thousand thousand ways to be told *you're so sweet*. A thousand thousand reminders that you'd still do anything for her. Anything.

Some smart-arse last year drew a picture on the inside of one of the doors in the school jacks. It covered a space of about a foot by a foot-and-a-half. Someone had put a lot of effort into it. It showed a boy wearing a dress, swooning in the arms of a female vampire who was busy chewing on his neck. In case there was any confusion as to the identity of the drawing's subjects, somebody had helpfully scrawled two huge arrows. One was labelled *Nato Jacob*, the other *Esther Gilsenan*. Another hand had added *HE WISHES!!!* in massive, yawping capitals.

Someone had used a pen to add some colour to this

masterpiece. The blood spewing from Nathan's neck was inked an arterial scarlet and sprayed out over most of the rest of the door. Nathan tried to wash it off once, but two lads from 6C caught him and shoved his head into the jacks for his pains. Now, he just ignored it as best he could. Ignored it as more and more people added to it. Like it was a whole-school project. Layer upon layer of misery. Detail upon detail. Black on black.

He hadn't told Esther about it. He was sure she must know, anyway. He was sure one of the Interchangeable Sorchas had spat it at her. He was equally sure that Esther didn't really care about it, one way or the other. The reason he hadn't told her was because, in that one image and in the humiliating permanency of it, was the illusion that they were an *us*. That they were linked, somehow.

Under the bleary stars, under the sweet-wrapper-orange of the streetlight, he knew he was in love with Esther Gilsenan. Not falling for her. But already all the way there. He had hit the bottom in a cloud of dust like the idiot coyote in *Road Runner*.

'Hi,' she said.

Nathan fought the grin, failed and tried to make it look like he was grimacing in the cold. 'This is insane,' he said.

Esther stepped toward him and slipped her arms around him and squeezed. Nathan could smell her hair in the bitter night. She was summer in the middle of winter.

Into his chest she started talking. Into his chest so that the words were muffled and seemed to come from a long way off.

'I'm so sorry about your Dad,' she said. 'I can't imagine how you feel.'

He looked down at the top of her head. He could feel the warmth coming through her coat, her chest pressed against his. To the stitching of her knitted hat he said, 'Where were you today? I missed you.'

For *missed* read *love*.

She stepped away from him and her lips quirked up in a not-quite smile.

'I hate funerals. I hate seeing people I care about being so upset. I hate seeing people lifting a coffin. I want to remember your Dad the way he was before he got sick. I don't want to see a box every time I think about him. I don't want to think about you crying.'

Nathan said nothing for a long while.

'Are you okay?' she asked.

'No. I'm not okay.'

For *I'm not okay* read *I love you*.

Esther nodded and said, 'Maybe I can help.'

The laugh that came out of Nathan's mouth was a nasty thing. There was a broken edge to it that he didn't like. It was a twiggy sound, a winter sound. Sharp and gnarled.

'I appreciate the sentiment, Esther, but I don't see how.'

She smiled at him. She smiled and said, 'We're going to see your Dad.'

Nathan blinked. He went to say something, stopped, and went to say something again. He felt like that kid in Second Year with the stutter so bad it was like something was lodged in his throat.

Esther leaned into him and said, 'I promise it'll make you feel better.'

Nathan breathed out in the sub-zero air and into the cloud of his own body heat he said, 'Okay.'

And again, 'Okay. But you're crazy, Esther.'

Nathan's Da was buried within a mile of his home. He was at rest under ground he had trod for most of his life. From the upstairs bathroom of Nathan's house, if you leaned out the window and strained your neck, you could see the giant cedar trees that grew in one corner of St Raphaela's graveyard.

It was a short walk. In the cold Nathan and Esther's footsteps crunched on the footpath. She listed close in to him and linked his arm. She kept saying, 'I'm so, so sorry, Nato.' She leaned her head against him and stroked his arm with her free hand.

Nathan's footsteps crunched. Under his feet, ice. In his stomach, heat.

Her perfume came to him on the dead air. Every bob of her head twined it into the cold and the light pollution and the silence. In the buzz-saw chill, all was quiet. All, except Esther's voice going, 'I'm so, so sorry, Nato. I'm so, so sorry.'

To either side of the street, very expensive houses were very dark behind very neat hedges. Here and there, though, the lights of Christmas trees bloomed against window blinds where their owners had forgotten to turn them off for the night. Nato felt Esther huddle closer to him.

She breathed out in a plume of sudden ice crystals.

He breathed them in and said, 'Fire hazards.'

Like the uncool dad in a sitcom.

He couldn't believe he'd said that. Said it into the stained-glass night. Said it into the soft lights and hard cold. Said it so that it broke the moment between them.

She lifted her head and said, 'What did you say?'

Nathan nodded toward the house they were passing and mumbled, 'They shouldn't leave the lights on. Fire hazards.'

She patted his arm. She didn't stroke. She patted his arm and said, 'Oh, Nato. You're so silly. Always stressing about shit.'

Then her face became mischievous and she whirled away from him. Her Doc Martens dug shallow furrows in the thickening frost. Nato stopped and watched her. She laughed, capering and spinning and her voice broke from her in a cloud of cold smoke.

'Imagine, though! Imagine if they did go up. All those fancy fucking houses. All burnt to the ground by Christmas trees. Burning up like pagan bonfires. We should be celebrating the season with fire, like the Celts did. All hot and red.' She stopped and dragged exultant gasps into her lungs. 'Like the way we were,' she panted. 'Like Druids.'

In someone's backyard a dog started to yammer mindlessly.

Nathan shoved his hands deeper into his pockets and walked towards her.

'You've got to stop reading that New Age, hippy crap, Esther.'

Esther was an original member of the school's one and only Creative Writing Club. It was set up by Andrew Callahan, an odd-looking almost-albino, who Nathan knew, really *knew*, had the hots for Esther so bad it screamed from him. Andrew Callahan with his drippy philosophising. His glib banter, stolen line from line from indie rom-coms. He actually had the words *Colour my Life with the Chaos of Trouble* stencilled onto his schoolbag.

The boy was a loser and the fact that he stared at Esther in the same way that Nathan did made his jaws clench.

When Nathan pointed out that Andrew Callahan obviously fancied her and maybe she shouldn't be spending so much time with him, Esther simply said, 'Since his parents died he's been lonely. Writing helps him express himself.'

She said this with a strange not-quite-a-smile smile, almost mocking.

'You should come to the writing group, you know,' she

said. 'It's a real eye-opener. I'm sure it would help you find your inner voice.'

Esther was always on about stuff like this. She was one of the brightest people in Nathan's school. Top of every list. In Nathan's opinion, those lists included the one titled *Brighter than Most of the Teachers*. There was a vitality and energy to her that no other girl in the place could ever hope to have. She fired like a synapse all the time. And all the time Nathan felt himself pulse in rhythm with her. All the time, in spite of her Goth tendencies and bullshit ideologies.

The first time he had spoken to her was way back in First Year CSPE. Civic, Social and Political Education. Mr Mulroy, the bell-end that he was, decided to take the piss out of Esther by pointing out that wearing an army surplus jacket with the word *Anarchy* in permanent marker across the back wasn't exactly congruent with the *Greenpeace* wristband she had on.

He actually used the word *congruent*.

Esther, all composed and confident and cool, had smiled at Mr Mulroy. She smiled her cherry-bomb, fizzy-cola smile and said, 'I believe I'm trying to make a statement about the duality of man, Sir.'

The Interchangeable Sorchas had sniggered at that, but from then on Mr Mulroy left her alone.

On the way out of Mr Mulroy's class, Nathan had pushed his way over to her. Awkward and obvious. She saw him coming, paused in the packing of her bag, and smiled her not-quite-a-smile smile at him.

Without even introducing himself he allowed the words '*Full Metal Jacket*' to tumble from his tongue like clods from a spade.

Her smile had widened at that and she said, 'I knew I liked the look of you.'

Now, under December streetlights, she took two dancing little steps, gripped his elbow in both hands and whispered, 'Hippy crap's why you love me.'

She knew. She had to know.

St Raphaela's graveyard. A huge, flat field of granite and marble, fading bouquets and rotting limestone. And in one corner, under the cedar trees, a fresh mound of earth and a simple wooden cross with a brass nameplate tacked to it. St Raphaela's graveyard. Twice in the one day.

In front of Nathan, the grave mound was furred over in frost, the loose soil hard as concrete. Here, the streetlights were far distant and the moon lit the grave. Its light splashed across the front of the little wooden cross, splashed across the ditch and wall running along behind the cedar trees. Splashed across Nathan and Esther and the pile of muck that lay at their feet. In the light everything was given brittle edges and the shadows behind things were intensified. It looked like the entire world was one huge page from a giant pop-up book. In the moonlight the whole place looked two-dimensional and backed by nothing but empty space. Like a set in a B-movie.

Looking down at the grave, Nathan didn't feel like he thought he would feel. The pain stayed the same. It didn't intensify. It didn't slacken off. It just remained. A physical ache just under his ribcage. Tangible and raw. Like a broken bone or internal bleeding.

Looking down at the grave he heard his own voice ask, 'Why are we here, Esther?'

Esther was staring at him. In the dark her eyes looked like wellheads. From them, Nathan could feel pity and sorrow and compassion leaking out and drowning the whole entire world.

'I want to help you,' she said. 'I care about you a lot.'

For *care about you a lot* read *like you as a friend*.

Fuck sake.

He sighed. And in that sigh was freighted all the exhaustion and all the despair he was feeling.

'How? How are you going to help me?'

Esther smiled and in the dark that smile opened up her face and looked like a segment of bone.

'Wychery,' she said.

Nathan blinked at her. You could actually *hear* the *y* in how she pronounced it. Not *witchery* but *wychery*.

New Age hippy crap.

'For God's sake, Esther. This is my Da's *grave* for the love of Christ. You know I'd do anything for you – '

She cut him off. 'I'm doing this for you, you fucking dope. This has nothing to do with me.'

Then from out of her long, oh so black coat, she took a small, squat book. She had shown it to him before. She had bought it in some alternative therapy shop in Temple Bar. One of those ones with pewter fairies and trolls in the window. One that sold chess sets where each piece was a character out of *Game of Thrones*. It was bound in red leather and contained procedures for séances and rubrics for spells. It was called *The Necronomicon*, but Nathan knew this was just a cool sounding name for what was probably a load of crap. Nathan had read up on it because he was vaguely creeped out by how authentic the thing seemed. What he found out was H.P. Lovecraft had invented it in the 1920s for one of his short stories. It wasn't based on anything real. Definitely.

In the moonlight, though, with its red leather, it looked to Nathan like Esther was holding a blood clot.

Curious, appalled and annoyed in equal measure, he asked, 'What are you going to do with that thing?'

'I'm going to read and you're going to think of something. Then, if *weeee* do it properly, you might be able to say something to your Dad and, if we're really lucky, he might be able to say something to you.'

Nathan just stared at her. That pain, the one that felt like a broken bone or internal bleeding deep in his chest, that pain was forgotten. A small swell of resentment began to form inside of him. The arrogance of her nettled him, but it was this very sort of thing that drew him to her in the first place. The darkness in her. Once, when they were in Second Year, she had managed to get her hands on a Ouija board. The others hated it as the lump of crystal moved from letter to letter, spelling out the names of Demons and dead relatives. The girls squealed and withdrew their hands. The boys scoffed to hide their discomfort and swaggered away to play football. At the end there was left only Nathan and Esther, hands joined, revelling in the power this stuff granted them. The act of transgression and the fact they were willing to hold on when all the others walked away. The ragged edge of things was in that moment theirs and theirs alone.

And here they were, in St Raphaela's graveyard. Teetering on that ragged edge once more. And for all of Nathan's distaste at Esther's presumption, they for the moment were each other's sole companion on that edge of things. He was repulsed and sucked in all at once, and he could feel his want for Esther grow in tandem with his dislike for what she was doing.

Ann Rice or Storm Constantine would have a field day with the crap in his head.

Esther opened her little grimoire and said, 'Think of the last time you and your Dad were alone and happy. Before he was sick. Think really hard.'

'I don't know about this. I mean …'

'I know. Don't worry, Nato. This is white magick. Good magick.'

You could hear the *k*.

Maybe it was something in her voice. Maybe it was something in her face. Maybe it was the fact that he was in love with her. Maybe it was all of these things, but from somewhere in his hindbrain a memory drew close, coming forward and brightening.

Standing beside his Da's grave, in the cold and in the dark, all this came to the surface of Nathan's brain. Clear as the sky above him. No light pollution there.

Esther was looking at him.

She said, 'Ready?'

Nathan swallowed and said, 'There's not going to be any fucking zombies, right?'

Esther frowned at him. In the moonlight he could see her brows scuttle together.

'No,' she said. 'There won't be any zombies.'

'Because I've seen *The Walking Dead*. I don't want my Da to pop up as some sort of a zombie.'

'There won't be any fucking zombies, Nato. Are you thinking of something happy?'

'Yeah. Yeah, I think so.'

'Okay.'

She took a long, slow breath, 'Here goes nothing.'

Then she started to read. A strange language. Consonants

shackled to consonants so that they sounded like the babble of a different reality entirely. Esther's breath gusted into the freezing dark and her breasts lifted and dropped beneath the fall of her coat. She had her eyes closed and Nathan watched her chest rise and subside, rise and subside. His hands twitched and her voice juddered on, clattering out those rattling chains of alien syllables.

The sound of her voice and the swell of her breasts outlined in the orange of the sodiumshine stirred something in his guts and the mound of clay, and the dead meat it housed, slipped from the forefront of Nathan's mind. Instead, his whole being thrummed to the working of Esther Gilsenan's diaphragm.

In the pitch cold of the December night, Nathan's palms were sweating.

And then he heard his father's voice.

It swam up to him, sudden and terrifying.

Esther obviously couldn't hear it. She continued her reading. Eyes closed, lips working around the impossible pronunciations.

It's okay. I'm here. I'll always be here. And you will be, too. It's warm here. So very, very warm. We're all here. All of us. All the way back. So very, very far back.

And then the voice changed in a way that flashed goose-flesh across Nathan's scalp and between his shoulder blades. Where before it was mellow. Welcoming. Now it was almost mocking. A sneer. Cold and hard.

We're all here. All of us. And we come back. Again and again, we come back. All the way back. All the way …

This was insane. The voice that clattered about inside Nathan's skull was a gibbering thing. Something of his own invention. Something that sprang from stress and grief. His father and his need for him to come back. To tell him that everything was going to be okay. It had to be. It had to. Looking at Esther with her little leather book, her lovely face plastered with an expression of faux-intensity. Looking at Esther over the mound of frost-fixed earth, he knew he couldn't take this anymore.

'Stop,' he said.

Esther looked up at him, her finger marking her place. Marking the line where all her hippy-trippy-earth-mother-hyphenated-fur-is-murder nonsense was leading to. Marking the line that Nathan would not cross. He was out here in the cold and in the dark because of her. Not because of his Da, a lump of cold meat in the frozen ground, not because of his loneliness and loss. He was here because he wanted to fuck the goth chick in front of him. Any other reason was delusion. He was letting her dictate this little charade because she wanted to. Because she believed in it as much as she believed the little pentagram she wore around her neck would protect her from harm. Genuinely believed.

Nathan didn't believe, but because her smile tightened the

muscles of his abdomen he let her bring him out here. Let her play necromancer with the memory of his Da.

That voice. That awful voice. There was no way that was his Da.

She was looking at him with this little petulant expression on her face.

Before she could start talking, before her voice and her touch and the smell of her hair robbed him of his backbone, he said, 'I don't want to do this. I want to go home.'

She was looking at him, but now her expression was one of pity. It was the expression that some of the teachers used when they spoke to the Special Needs kids. All soft and full of sympathy for the poor, useless simpleton who was baffled by everything.

'Okay,' she said and her finger came out of her little grimoire. 'Okay. I understand. We'll go home.'

Home. That was another black joke.

CHAPTER 5:

DUBLIN, DECEMBER 1892

Sergeant George Frohmell sat at the breakfast table. He folded and put down the newspaper. He sighed and looked around himself. Dr O'Sullivan's dining room was surprisingly understated, especially when you considered the good doctor's background. The man was private surgeon to half the businessmen in Dublin. His father before him had ministered to the last dregs of the aristocrats who sought to cling to a ragged existence in nineteenth-century Ireland. The Earls of Leinster had been notable clients. The male side of that illustrious family suffering as much from ill-luck as bad judgement should the number of venereal complaints be taken at face value. In spite of this, Dr Oliver O'Sullivan appeared to demonstrate quite a measure of restraint in his décor. The tables, carved and polished and laid with good silverware, were hardly ostentatious and the room was of adequate but not overwhelming proportions. Like most buildings here on Stephen's Green, however, the ceiling moulding was decidedly baroque, the plasterwork delicate and the gilt unblemished. Between the elaborate borders, the ceiling itself opened up in a wide, white yawn. No dangling gas lamp for the doctor as yet, let alone any of that American electricity. Lightning tamed and bottled and bloody dangerous, in George's opinion. In fact, there was nothing faddish about the entire place at all. Like the doctor himself, the place was a throwback to a vanished era.

'What do your bloody peeler's eyes see now?' asked Dr O'Sullivan.

George lifted one eyebrow and regarded the doctor with an expression halfway between exasperation and derision.

'This isn't my fault, Oliver,' he said.

Dr O'Sullivan turned away from the bay window looking out onto The Green. Outside, the rain that had fallen all night continued to thread mercury through the air. A cab trundled past across the mud, its horse steaming and its driver bundled about in streaming oilskin. Dr O'Sullivan snorted and commenced pacing the room once more.

'It's never your fault,' he snapped. 'All those years ago it wasn't your fault when you tried to arrest me.'

In spite of everything, George smiled. 'I wasn't arresting you. I was asking you to leave premises of well-deserved ill repute. I had no intention of arresting you.'

'The woman I ended up marrying was in those 'premises', as you so delicately put it. A wet-behind-the-ears constable throwing his weight around is what you were. I liked you immediately. The verve you showed was exhilarating. However, I had no intention of going anywhere unless she was coming too.'

'Raising her up from the gutter, is that it?'

'Don't be snide, George. Besides, when that reprobate felled you with a bottle you were glad I was there.'

'How many stitches did you end up giving me?'

'Ten, I believe.'

'And I didn't even give you a warning.'

'You did not. But you did develop a disturbing tendency to land trouble at my door at the slightest provocation.'

'I like you, Oliver. And you like me. Friends do nixers for each other all the bleedin' time.'

'*Nixers*? Is that what unpaid labour is called nowadays?'

'Only by us lower-class types.'

'You're being trite again.'

'I still don't see how this is my fault.'

'Of course this is your fault. You couldn't just leave the blasted thing alone. You couldn't just haul her last customer up in front of the magistrates. You're like a bloody dog

worrying a bone. What do you propose to do with my find-
ings, confound you?'

George smiled. Dr O'Sullivan had spun on his heel and
paused with his hands clasped behind his back. His face was
flushed and his hair was a grey, tangled mat, unbrushed and
oily. Behind him a ribboned holly wreath described a jagged
circumference where it hung on the dining-room door. The
blood-bonny beads of its berries winked out from the waxy
leaves like the eyes of rats.

'Is the Detective Division not interested in this?' the doctor
asked. 'Surely we, I mean you, shouldn't be the ones prying
into these things. This whole event is appalling. Beyond awful.'

'Detectives?' sneered George, a horrible sort of grin on his
face. 'There's no way in hell that a G-man is going to bother
his bollix with a case that has no medals in it. Unless it has
to do with Fenians or political intrigue, G Division couldn't
give a tinker's curse. A dead prostitute? In the Monto? No,
Doctor, I'm afraid we're on our own.'

'Why are you smiling?' the doctor snapped. 'You look like
a bloody death's head. There's no humour in your smiles,
George. You wear a rictus on your face. I'm not entirely sure
that you enjoy anything at all.'

'I'm enjoying this,' replied George.

'For God's sake,' exploded Dr O'Sullivan. He ran a hand
through his hair, adjusted the fall of the jacket he had been
wearing for two days now and cocked his other fist on his hip.

'I have had next to no sleep because of you, you uniformed ape. I would appreciate at least a modicum of reciprocation, since I have been engaged all the while in your ghastly business. And not a penny I'll see for it either, as is usual when you ask my professional opinion on some sordid happening.'

George's smile widened and he said, 'You could have told me you found nothing. You could have drawn a discreet curtain over this whole affair.'

Dr O'Sullivan looked at him. He blinked slowly and the capillaries of his cheeks were suddenly etched in stark violet against the red of his complexion. His nostrils flared.

'Are you taking … are you mocking me?'

'Always.'

'You are an insufferable man, you realise that, Sergeant.'

'Always.'

Dr O'Sullivan stepped quickly toward him, his brogues clopping on the floorboards. He dragged a chair out from under the table and flopped down onto it. His eyes watched George's features and he chewed the inside of his lower lip. He looked for all the world like a petulant and over-grown schoolboy.

At length, in the face of George's half-mocking grin, he growled, 'Oh, don't be so glib.'

George leaned forward, resting his forearms on the table's top. 'I couldn't let this be for the same reasons you couldn't lie to me. It wouldn't be right.'

'And we are righteous men, Sergeant?'

George laughed wryly. 'Not always.'

Dr O'Sullivan lifted his hands and dragged his palms down along his cheeks. His stubble made an audible rasp and his skin was pulled so out of shape that it appeared, for the briefest instant, that his face was no more than a mask of sacking about to be pulled free from his skull. He sighed long and low.

'There is an honesty to you that's quite disarming, George. There's a sort of desperation in you that I find fascinating. An angst that the world does not conform to your idea of what it should be.'

George laughed again, loudly this time. A belly laugh of genuine surprise and good humour.

'And there's a candour to you, Oliver, that most people would find insulting.'

'We all have our crosses to bear.'

The doctor's next question caught George a little off-guard. 'How's Rosie?'

George blinked and he hesitated for the barest moment, a reaction that prompted Dr O'Sullivan to smile.

George cleared his throat and replied, 'I don't know. I left a message under her door but she hasn't been in touch.'

'You should really tell her about this, George. Can you get her out of the city while this blows itself out? You have relatives down Wicklow way, have you not?'

George shook his head and a curious expression scuttled

across his features. An expression of bitterness and self-disgust and derision all at once. With his lips warping into a sneer, he said, 'I'm to send my pet whore down to my aged aunt, is it? Could you imagine the reaction?'

The doctor looked at him in sympathy and with genuine compassion and softening his voice said, 'Do not be so hard on her, George. Do not be so hard on you both. The human heart is a strange thing. It is a benign tyrant. Nobody can hope to gainsay its desires.'

George struggled to prevent a frown clouding his features. 'Is it as bad as I feared, Doctor? Should I be afraid for her? Have my bloody peeler's eyes seen true?'

O'Sullivan grew quiet. A stillness came over him like the storm-weight of approaching thunderheads. Only his left hand twitched and his thumb and index finger nipped at his thigh, plucking imaginary threads from his trousers. George watched him in the confessional quiet. Outside, a cornerboy shouted an insult and was replied in kind. A cart slopped past. In the doctor's house, all was silent.

'You were right,' O'Sullivan began at length. 'Your bloody peeler's eyes and your dratted bloodhound nose were right, damn you. No oafish hand was employed in the poor girl's death. The implement that was used to inflict her injuries was razor-edged but longer than a razor. Her throat was cut from ear to ear in two quick motions. No hacking or sawing. Two cuts, clean as anything I could do myself.'

O'Sullivan swallowed. All the while he never took his eyes from the fabric of his trouser leg. He never once looked up at George and his voice had taken on a droning quality, devoid of emotion. It was as though he were lecturing a medical student. Everything stripped down to facts. Anatomy as mechanics.

'Go on,' George prompted.

The doctor breathed through his nose and then his voice began again, still in that numb monotone.

'The incision severed her jugular, which prompted massive and immediate haemorrhaging. Death would have been far from instantaneous but would have followed quite rapidly.'

He paused again, coughed, and this time when he continued there was a slight fracture in his tone.

'At the point of incapacitation, but probably before the point of death, her murderer began to work on her genitalia.'

O'Sullivan shifted a little but George remained fixed, unmoving.

'He removed her labia and clitoris, again with very precise incisions. The amount of blood that resulted from these wounds leads me to believe she was alive when they were inflicted. He then moved on to her abdomen. He very neatly opened her up and removed one of her kidneys without so much as nicking her bowel, uterus or bladder.'

George allowed the doctor a moment to get his breath

before asking, 'How long do you think the whole process took?'

O'Sullivan looked up then and his face was calico. White with harrowing.

'No more than ten minutes. Probably less.'

'That little?'

O'Sullivan dragged in a long breath through the yellowing sieve of his teeth and replied, 'The fellow has done this before, George. This was a practiced hand at work. Clean. Everything precise.'

'Surgical?'

'For God's sake, George.'

'I want to hear it, Oliver.'

'Yes, surgical. Are you happy now?'

George laughed sourly. 'Oh, absolutely delighted. We have a maniac on the loose. Why wouldn't I be happy?'

The doctor pinched the bridge of his nose and asked, 'Did your men find her … her organs, at least?'

'No. They were taken from the scene.'

'This is exactly what you said it was, isn't it?'

George sighed and regarded the doctor's stricken expression, his whey complexion.

'The Whitechapel murders?' George replied. 'If not the same monster, then some creature remarkably similar.'

'Here in Dublin?' lamented the doctor. 'Has God not punished our poor degraded capital enough?'

He laughed then and in that laugh was all the warmth of December sleet. 'This will play havoc with property prices. Whatever are we going to do?'

George leaned back, clasped his hands behind his head and then suddenly scrubbed at his own stubbled cheeks. He reached forward and lifted the newspaper from where he had tossed it earlier. He spun it round so that O'Sullivan could view the front page. There, centred below *The Freeman's Journal* banner and sandwiched between adverts for caustic soda and The White Star Line, was a charcoal drawing of a panto-mime villain. Top hat and cloak and devilish features. Stark and hard-edged and holding a dripping knife. Beneath the sketch, the caption read: *John Bull's Butcher sent to Murder Ireland's Own.*

'What do you make of that?' asked George, his expression curdling.

'Dear God,' hissed the doctor. He lifted the newspaper and regarded the drawing with frank disgust. 'They're saying the British sent this monster over here on purpose?'

'They are. This will cause unrest. *The Freeman's Journal* deserves a fair degree of credit for this. They know what they're doing, I'll give them that.'

Dr O'Sullivan shook his head, folded the newspaper and flung it onto the floor with obvious distaste. 'Everything about these events adds a little more to my trepidation,' he said. 'So, I'll ask you again, what are we going to do?'

George stood and walked around the table, patting his

friend's shoulder as he went. 'I don't know about you, doctor,' he said, 'but I'm going to have a drink.'

George left O'Sullivan's house feeling angry. The sky above him was a solid slab of spitting grey, seemingly close enough to touch. The world in its entirety seemed balled close about him and yet to be simultaneously spinning away. Every atom of existence was bound in a chaos of self-destruction, ready to hurl itself into oblivion rather than remain shackled to its fellows in such foetid intimacy. For George Frohmell, the hectic edge that his world had suddenly acquired provoked in him the old lashing rage. The belch of boots in the mud, the shouts of carriage drivers, the whicker of whipped horses, all mocked him with their mundaneness. The circadian rhythms of Dublin jigged about him and for a moment, with the rain spattering on him, he hated every single part of it.

He set off along the footpath, greatcoat collar pulled up and helmet clamped onto his head. People hurried past in the rain. Women in dark dresses, the more fashionable scowling under a mask of water, their bustles overbalancing them in their haste, workmen in tweed or corduroy, hackney men in streaming gabardine. All saturated in the morning downpour. All darkened to charcoal, smeared across the day. And above, the sky was the colour of limestone and it wept onto Dublin and its people, mixing with the smoke of a million chimneys, stinking and damp and overlaying all like some dull, sogged pelt.

I AM IN BLOOD

Soaked and sour-humoured, George slogged his way up Sackville Street and then on to Frederick Street, turned on to Dorset Street, swung left up Eccles Street and came to halt outside a redbrick building. A perimeter of cannibal spikes, once white but long since grimed over and mildewed, sprang from out its frontage. Standing in the December rain, George breathed deeply, dragging into his lungs the smells of fried offal, of stewed tea, of open chamber pots. The smells of home. Somewhere a child was crying.

He stalked up the granite steps leading to the door. The door, black and topped with its perpetually broken fanlight like a false dawn over a dead sea, was always left unlocked and so it was this morning. George pushed it and it swung easily open with a soft sigh of noise and immediately all the scents of the place were intensified. In the lightless hall beyond, young Seamus Darby was playing in the shadows with a wooden horse and a handful of lead soldiers. He looked up as George came in.

'Morning, Sergeant Frohmell,' he said. Then he coughed and smiled apologetically as though he had done something wrong.

Dublin was a gangrenous place. Wet and cold. Old and poisonous. It'd kill you eventually.

George shook the rainwater from his cape collar and replied, 'Morning, Seamie. How's the chest?'

The child's head lowered and his fringe fell in front of his eyes. He set the soldiers in a line, saying, 'Ah, sure it's alright. Ma has it, now, though.'

George frowned.

'Tell her to rest and drink plenty of warming stuff. Tea or even a drop of brandy. Tell her I'll drop her in a package when I get the chance.'

Seamus smiled then and said, 'Da, won't like it. Taking charity from peelers and black Protestants.'

George laughed and set off up the stairs. 'Your Da's never feckin' happy.'

George lived on the third floor and every step of the way the stairs croaked at him, the treads sagging in the middle, the risers soft with rot. The building wasn't quite a tenement but wasn't far off it. Most of its tenants worked and a few were tolerably well off, but George knew from around town that the landlord was eager to knock walls and wedge in more families. From what George had heard, his greasy palms were itching for the rebates the Government offered to house the poor. Per head. Like cattle.

George unlocked his door and swung it closed again behind him. The rustle at his feet made him look down. There, shoved under the door, was a folded piece of paper. One edge was ragged, as though it had been torn from a book. It certainly wasn't writing paper.

George picked it up but didn't read it immediately. His rooms, if you could apply such a term to a bedroom and kitchen, were cold. The no-colour light of a rainy December seeped through the net curtains of his single window, doing nothing to alleviate the gloom. The fire in his little stove had gone out. How long had he been gone? How long since he had slept in his own bed, rather than at his desk or in a spare barracks bunk? He had no idea. This startled him a little.

He hung his coat and helmet on their hook, crossed to the press slouching against one wall and took out a bottle of whiskey. Then he sat in his single armchair, looking from the whiskey in one hand to the paper in the other. Across the paper a wild, loopy hand had pencilled the word *Georgie*.

George knew exactly who had written the note. He could almost smell her perfume in its creases. Cheap, though it was. Sugary and astringent all at once.

He set the whiskey down on the table and sat in the armchair. He could feel the cold of it. His coat shed fat drops on to the floor. He sat for long minutes with the damp of the place wreathing him about and the cold sinking into his flesh. He looked at the bottle of whiskey. He reached for it, paused, and unfolded the letter instead.

The same loopy hand had written:

Dearest Sergeant Georgie,
I got your message but I did not have the chance to write until now. Word about what happened to Mary Shortt has the wits gone

in everyone with the fright. What should we do? Could you meet
me? I'll be at the usual place all week.

> *Yours,*
> *Rosie Lawlor*

Rosie Lawlor.

Rosie Lawlor.

Rosie Lawlor.

He read her letter three times.

His pet whore.

Her perfume in the letter's every crease. Her voice in every line and every syllable. Her face. Her mouth. *Yours.*

George balled up the letter and flung it across the room. His life was a bad joke. A bawdy pub satire. A snigger on street corners. Did you hear the one about the brasser and the station sergeant?

In the miserly light of his room George Frohmell put his face in his hands and fought the tears and the anger that grew inside him. He had barely slept now for three days. He was on duty again tonight. He needed to sleep. He needed to rest. Frayed nerves and exhaustion were at work in him. That was all it was. Frayed nerves and exhaustion and horror piled upon horror and the ridiculousness of his life until Dublin and the DMP and the whole of existence seemed crushed into a jagged cutting thing that tore at him. Frayed nerves. Exhaustion. That was all.

Maybe this monster had done this before. Maybe had a record or was new-released from Mountjoy or Kilmainham.

Rosie on the streets. Blood on the cobbles.

He could not sit here, achieving nothing and thinking in circles. He would go back to work. There had to be something he was missing. He would go back to work, but first there was something he must do.

Panting, he lifted his face and reached for the bottle of whiskey.

Seamus Darby was surprised when the stairs beside him groaned in the gloom. He was even more surprised to see Station Sergeant Frohmell descend the stairs, his coat still dripping and his helmet fixed so that it shadowed his eyes.

'Hello, Sergeant,' he said. 'Out again already?'

George reached the bottom of the stairs and came over to Seamus. He was carrying the bottle of whiskey and he placed it down beside the boy's row of lead redcoats. Seamus looked up at him quizzically.

'It's for your Ma,' said George. 'For her chest. Tell her to put a drop in her tea. It might warm her up a bit.'

Seamus picked up the bottle and shook it so that the amber liquid glugged and sloshed. 'Are you sure?' he asked. 'There's near enough a full bottle there.'

George patted the boy on the head and laughed. 'There's precisely a full bottle there, you little rascal. It's never been opened.'

CHAPTER 6:

SUSSEX, JANUARY 1839

The Work. The Pattern. God, you could grow to love it. Knife and gloves and red wet in the lamplight. God, you could love the feel of it. The shank stab and twist of it. The breaking gristle. The sigh of blood the exhalation of blood the bright spray of it. All the time in the world. All the time to do our bit. The opened artery and the scarlet arc of it. And not a soul to see. Windows to it. No eyes. Put them out? No. Better to see the light go out. The snuffed candle the trimmed wick of it. God, you could grow to love it again. Here. Not in the green sulphur stink of the Eastend. Not among the Jewboys and the recreants. Here. Here. Here. They deserved it as much as the others. The it of it. The cut of it. The way it resisted and then broke. That instant that cutting instant and then the slap of all the stuff coming out. No fear. No bobbies. Oh,

the slither slap of all that stuff in the cold. The smell of it the steam of it.
Drag it in. Pull it in. Our lungs filling with the odour of it …

See the child, the father of the man to come. He was born
on The Night of the Big Wind. *Oíche na Gaoithe Móire.* That
night a hurricane came boiling in off the Atlantic and made
a cataract of all Ireland. A quarter of Dublin's houses were
flattened. In country places, sparks were sucked howling up
flues and then alighted like hellish sprites on the thatch below.
Cottages were become infernos. And infernos became funeral
pyres. Dead beyond number and nature as massacre.

Not that he knew anything of this. A baby knows nothing
and he knew nothing except for what instinct and ancestry
had bred in him.

He was born in an English manor house and he wailed as
Ireland was lashed. Above him, the Home Counties sky was
full of stars and a meteor dashed a bitter needle through the
hanging constellations. Orion lanced.

The last of eight children, his family were known as del-
vers in the earth and hewers of wood. His father built mills
and chimneys and happily married off his eldest daughter
to a duke. The weight of new money sat upon the manor in
which he spilled, puling, into being. It distorted the universe
around it like an anvil drags a magnet. Royalty and gran-
deur gravitated toward it and orbited about it. Open fields,
tailored and bland. Sculptured hedgerows and potted shrub-

bery. And in the distance husbanded copses that held yet a few last deer, too tame to course.

Into this world he came, four hundred miles from Ireland and its convulsions in fire and water and wind. All the elements melded in a paroxysm of destruction. All the humours of humanity soured. And what of the humours that combined to make up this little bloodied babe, this hairless squab of a thing? Was something soured even then? Clinging to his mother's breast, the heat of him startling, the flesh of him blushing from blue to pink, was there something ulterior in his squashed features and soft hands?

His first memories were all of his mother. For five years she was his world and cosmos. Servants and nurses and butlers and maids bustled in the spaces between him and his seven siblings, but his mother stood large in his life. More so than the others, his mother was his confidante and his friend. She nursed him herself, taking him to her time and time again with a wan determination. She weaned him and fatted him and was his playmate through his bumbling years. The others, with their little resentful faces, looked on as she gave him pears to suck and sweet things to glut on.

Once, when he was four, his father caned him for kicking one of his sisters. His mother went to him and from the bosom of her dress took a tin of Turkish Delight. They sat together on his bed and she fed him lumps of the stuff while his beaten hands reddened and throbbed.

'Remember this,' she said. 'Remember who loves you.'

The pulse of his hands, the sugar-marl of the sweets, the warmth of her beside him.

'Mama loves me,' he said.

His mother loved him for five years before the sister she was to deliver him carried off both infant and dam. Nameless child and bloodless mother were both committed to clay and he, five years of age, did not know why. After that, he was alone in the world.

He was always a bright boy. Bright but otherwise without feature. Unremarkable in every physical characteristic so that when he stood still his very ordinariness rendered him invisible to the eye. He stood still often. In his father's cavernous home with its small army of attendants, his brothers and sisters spread throughout the rooms, he was constantly losing himself.

With every passing day he felt himself thinning. Thinning and vanishing. Like toffee stretched between fingers until the light came through and it snapped.

Even newly minted and shining in this old world, there was a love of order in him. A mindless love. He would arrange things just so, wandering from room to room unaccompanied by anyone or anything. And should vase or painting or coal scuttle be moved from his precise alignment, he would feel things crawl beneath his skin until he had it re-fixed.

He bit his eldest brother once. Bit him to the bone. The older boy was taking pleasure in tormenting him. He was moving things about in a manner calculated to scald the wits of his youngest sibling. They would be replaced and they would move again. The younger boy waited to catch the person doing this. When he saw his brother, spare and lank like a bipedal spider, he launched himself at him. If he had been older, his teeth would have clapped closed and severed the digit entirely. As it was, his brother was left with the third finger on his right hand dead as bog oak.

His father beat him for this. For having the temerity to harm the son and heir. And when his father beat him, he left welts across the backs of his legs like narrow, livid drumlins.

His brother came into his room that night, his arm in a sling and his hand bound about with gauze. They faced each other in the lamplight, the heir to their father's bullion and the runt of the litter.

They faced each other until the older brother said at last, 'I never meant for father to beat you so.'

The boy said not a thing.

His brother raised his wounded hand. 'Did you mean to hurt me so?'

'No,' said the boy.

'No?'

'I meant to kill you.'

The older boy laughed as though his youngest brother had spilled out something clownish and humorous. Something that hung between and bound them both together in happy foolery. To do otherwise was to acknowledge the flatness of the boy's tone. The dead cobblestones for eyes. The otherness of him in this place of vulgar wealth. There was not a line of ostentation about him. He was simply a creature of a different type.

And so his eldest brother laughed his false laugh, clapped him on the shoulder and left.

The boy watched him go, the welts from the thrashing he had received pulsing evenly with his heart's every beat.

… whereon odour of purple sausage insides. Woman parts all sliced and folded away. Rashers in a shop. Bacon smell of dripping meat. Opened hole of emptied womb. Kidney slither and warm in our hand. Oh, the heat of it. Through the red wet of the gloves. The heat of it. The throb of it. The pulse of heart stilling. Feel the it of it in us. Feel the crotch throb of knife work. Oh, you could grow to love it. Knife and bag and wet and running. Red and slick and squeeze the juices from the leather. It soaks in. It always soaks in and the smell and the taste of it after. Oh, the memory. Put out the lights. The crotch wet of it all. And again and again. Here and here and here. Nice hotel. Money and accent and cufflinks. Black suit and black hat. Black bag and all the bright tools within. Nobody thinks. Nobody knows. Nobody sees. Nobody. God, you could grow to love it. Again and again and again. Here. Squeeze the fluids from the fingers from the palms from the thumbs. Twist the leather. The drip of it the lovely stink of it.

God, you could grow to love it.

CHAPTER 7:

DUBLIN, DECEMBER 2015

A few days later, the Friday after his Da had died, Nathan and his million-to-one-shot brother went back to school. Samantha offered him a lift, her face a furred, beige cake of make-up. When she spoke, the stuff nearly flaked off.

Nathan said he was grand and so she and James hopped in the Qashqai and left him in the driveway.

Given the traffic, he'd get there before them anyway.

He hadn't heard from Esther since the night of the funeral. Maybe she was giving him some space. Maybe she was angry at him. He tried not to care. He tried to tell himself that he had bigger fish to fry, that the concerns of someone who believed vampires were real were probably not a priority right now. He tried to tell himself this, but whatever crazy little guy was operating his controls didn't want to listen. Instead, for the last few days he checked his phone every five minutes and sent text after unanswered text to Esther's number.

The December cold tightened the skin of his face and he walked with his head bandaged in the vapour of his own breath.

He would see her at school. He wasn't sure how he felt about that.

Nathan's school used to be run by the Brothers. It used to have boarders. Now it was simply a large, grey, nineteenth-century mock-gothic edifice with a barrio of pre-fabs huddling up against it. Even in South Dublin the education budget was not what it should be. The pre-fabs trapped the heat in the summer, their fibreboard flanks sore to the touch and drying to a sort of brittle delicacy. Through any gouges or cracks in the grey cladding, the stuff would splinter and break up. It always reminded Nathan of Weetabix.

In the winter, though, they became freezer boxes. Over the years the window frames had warped and let the season slither in. Sometimes, some of the younger female teachers would forget to bring a jacket with them from the staff-room and what proceeded was a giddy thirty-five minutes of snatched glances and sniggering from the lads as the teacher tried to keep her arms folded at all times.

Inside the main building, the corridors were floored with

slick linoleum and the walls were painted in industrial shades of paint so thick it hung in petrified ripples from angles and brickwork. Everywhere was lumpen and heavy-handed and the marks of the uniform black shoes were like smeared charcoal on the skirting boards. The place smelled like an old folks' home. The noise of the alien children laughing and shouting in its cold hallways made echo from every hard surface, as though the building was affronted by the life within it.

Nathan was five minutes late. In his head, he blamed Samantha for it.

Mr Feeney was launching into *Macbeth* when Nathan knocked and entered the classroom. Nathan looked at his English teacher, tried to apologise for being late and could not. Every drop of saliva had curdled in his mouth and his lips worked soundlessly. He tried to swallow. Blinked. Then tried again.

Mr Feeney stood like a waxwork, his right arm outstretched, the *Complete Works of Shakespeare* a brick in his left hand, his face thin and his eyes fastening on to Nathan's own. Mr Feeney stood with his head shaved down to the alabaster skin, the bone dome emphasising his lean face, his scrawny neck. Mr Feeney stood, a revenant of Nathan's Da.

Mr Feeney lowered his right arm and said, 'Welcome back, Nathan.'

Then he seemed to notice Nathan's horror and he raised

his right hand again and rubbed it briskly over the smooth curvature of his head.

'Charity,' he said. 'Shave or Dye.'

Nathan didn't know what to say so he just nodded and stepped over the bags cluttering the aisles between the desks. He sat down beside Bethany Keogh. Bethany, who'd had the desk to herself for the guts of a week, shifted a little to one side as though Nathan had something catching. She didn't say anything to him and she didn't look at him and Mr Feeney started going on about how life is a tale told by an idiot, full of sound and fury, signifying nothing.

It turned out a few of the teachers had shaved or dyed their hair for charity. Even Mr Geraghty, who most people thought was a prick, had bared his big culchie skull like a great ball of scar tissue. Mr Geraghty was probably grand outside of school. But inside he was one of those young teachers who tried to compensate for the fact that he hadn't a clue by roaring and shouting all the time. He tried to come across as a disciplinarian but instead came across as a supercilious, petty dickhead. His maths classes were mausoleum things, with only the sounds of breathing and the clicking of calculators to be heard, dry and skittering.

Nathan was shit at sums.

It was in Mr Geraghty's class that Esther chose to text him.

His phone was on silent but he felt the vibration in his pocket. It had to be Esther. He flung a quick look at Mr

Geraghty, who was doing something with the roll book, his head down, his fingers trailing absent-mindedly over his shorn scalp, and took out his phone and held it under the desk.

Esther's message read: *Hey there. I saw you at little break but didn't want to bother you. I'm sorry for the radio silence but I've been trying to sort some things out in my own head. Can we meet up some time?*

Nathan shouldn't have had his phone switched on in class and Esther shouldn't have been texting in whatever class she was in. Probably Art, because Ms Sinnott was a pushover and would let anyone away with murder. Either way, when Nathan tried to reply, the phone slipped from his hand and bounced out across the linoleum.

It spun once and then stopped, with Esther's name staring at him from over a blank field of nothing. Anything he was going to say to her was suddenly academic, background to Mr Geraghty's anger.

The entire class had stilled.

Mr Geraghty rose from behind his desk like some pagan and bloody-handed God and in the static silence of the class-room his voice carried an almost physical weight. It pounded Nathan, every syllable a blow.

'What the hell do you think you're doing, Jacob? You come swanning back in here, thinking you own the place, taking the piss in my classroom. Who the hell were you texting? What's so important that you have to undermine my maths class? Well?'

And there we have it. A man so ill at ease with himself that anything out of the ordinary that happened around the school must be to do with him. Must be aimed at him and honed and designed to undermine his authority. Geraghty was the sort of teacher who patrolled the corridors and thought every laugh and every snicker was directed at him and him alone. Lacking in self-belief, but so self-centred that no comment or half-heard laugh was let go, because all of it must, must without a shadow of a doubt, have something to do with him.

Like the whole world could see through him and so the whole world held him in contempt.

Geraghty, true to form and overcompensating, didn't even wait for Nathan to answer. His voice just kept on rolling like a tsunami, mounting and mounting.

'Why in God's name do you think I've my head shaved? For cancer charity, that's why. And your dad dead a week from it. How do you think he'd like his son taking the absolute piss out of someone doing his bit for charity? Hah? He'd be ashamed of you. Ashamed.'

Nathan sat for a moment and watched his phone's screen go black and then he started to cry.

Some of the people in his class looked away or shook their heads. Some of them started to snigger.

Mr Geraghty watched him for long moments and then said, 'When you're finished, pick up your phone and go and wash your face.'

Nathan didn't text Esther. He just walked home that evening, in the Christmas chill and the gaudy spill of the Christmas lights. He walked home all on his own. He had to bring so much stuff with him to study for Christmas exams that he had to shove some of his notes into a plastic bag. The weight of all that knowledge distended the bag and dragged it out of his fist. On nature programmes, when an antelope gives birth, the baby comes out in a weird translucent sac, all knobbled and stretched by the thing inside. To Nathan, his bag of notes looked like that. He switched it to his other hand and started walking towards the house where he lived. Toward home. To get there he had to walk down North Avenue, on to South Avenue and take a right at the bottom. He'd walked this way a thousand times before but never before had he considered how different suburbia looked in the chill of a winter's evening. The neighbourhood he was walking through was well-off, affluent. To Nathan it might as well have been the set of a zombie movie. If zombies walked dogs. They only come out at night.

The paths were a conveyor belt for pensioners. Every old person was towed by a hyperactive terrier. Some of the terriers wore tartan jackets. Honest to God, thought Nathan. Honest to God, tartan jackets. In the twilight the old men and women looked grey and their wrinkles were swilled with shadow. He didn't talk to them and they didn't talk to him. They didn't talk to each other. Each one of them shambled along in perfect isolation. The volume of air between this one and the next was inviolable. Nathan walked against their flow and their dogs' nails clipped against the concrete.

Nathan wondered who these people were and why they were walking alone at night. Every one of them could see everyone else but no-one said a word. He wondered, were they like this during the day? Did they sit in silence in their expensive houses listening to the clock eat away their lives while their dogs snuffled at the dry scents of the old? He wondered, did the clip of the dogs as they passed sound like the ticking of the clocks in those silent rooms?

He was surprised by the last one in the procession. She smiled at him. It was a smile of habit. She didn't mean it and Nathan thought she knew because it just died on her face. It was a worm on a hook. He walked past her before her expression could change back again and now he was on the Kilmacud Road.

He didn't belong here. He just didn't.

★ ★ ★

The next morning was Saturday. He got up before Samantha and James awoke and went down to the kitchen. In his right hand, dangling from its strap, his schoolbag was filled with maths notes. Maths notes and another nasty, disingenuous book about mass murderers. On the kitchen table there were two bowls of cereal already poured out, the sugar bowl, a bowl of fruit and a little note from Samantha, scribbled on the yellow furl of a post-it. It read: *We'll get through this. I love you both.*

Nathan ignored it, plucked an apple from the bowl, his jacket from the coat-stand and went out the back door.

He felt like shit. He had come home the evening before and gone straight to his room. Samantha or James, he didn't know which one, left his dinner outside his door. He left it there, untouched, until it went cold. When he left his room to use the toilet, someone had taken it away. Everything done silently and with no communication. Everything dislocated and distant. He had read his book until he felt he should sleep. With the lights out he cried into the dark until his pillow was wet. Even with his eyes clenched tight the tears leaked out and he felt that weird combination of emotions common to all young men who find themselves upset and moved to tears. That weird combination of confusion and helplessness and self-disgust.

Feeling this, he fell asleep.

And still feeling this, he woke up.

His very self was coming apart at the seams.

The walk to the library was short. He headed right, walked into Stillorgan and then swung left. The library was a new building sitting between two 1970s redbrick shop-fronts. It was a glass-walled place of Ikea minimalism and halogen glare. It was a place that Nathan came to a lot. A place of quiet and rustling industry. A place where books muffled the bustle of the outside like feathers matting a nest.

I AM IN BLOOD

The librarian behind the counter nodded to him when he walked past her. He came here all the time to study and she was as much a fixture of the place as the Ikea shelving. Her familiar face was wrinkled and friendly and sensitive. Her gaze took in his chaos of hair, the stoop of his shoulders. The red of his eyes. Nathan didn't notice her noticing him but as he sat down at a study desk, her bearing took on something of the maternal. There was something bantam about her as she watched him reach into his bag and pull out the countless sheaves of his maths notes.

Nathan started with complex numbers. Zeds and i's and pretend numbers that weren't actually numbers at all. Page after page of scrawled stuff that looked like Cyrillic to him. This was a language he didn't understand, a language of definites and hard edges and absolutes. A language with no dictionary and no thesaurus and no context that he could work from.

Why was he doing Honours? Why was he doing this to himself?

He stuck at it for an hour and a half. He stuck at it until he reached into his schoolbag and instead of notes he pulled out another one of his books. He experienced a small stab of guilt; but only a small stab. He knew this was why he had brought the book. He knew he couldn't last too long poring over Mr Geraghty's exam tips and sample answers.

So, in this place of light and warmth and clean edges he began to read about the mind of a serial killer. A place of dark and cold and ragged edges. A place of filth and degradation. A place much more interesting than the drab monotony of arithmetic.

He was lost in a world of punctured innards and shallow graves when the librarian leaned over his left shoulder.

He jumped and closed the book with a spastic jerk of his hands. Like he'd been caught flicking through a porn mag. Which, he supposed, in a weird way he was.

He blinked and the librarian smiled down at him and said in a not-quite whisper, 'It's alright. I like all that True Crime stuff too.'

Nathan didn't say anything. He just looked up at her, dumbly grateful, like a spaniel thrown a scrap.

She kept smiling and kept whispering. 'You come here a lot, don't you? You used to get a lot of books out. Studying a lot these days, though?'

Nathan nodded. 'Yeah, Leaving Cert. I live around the corner. I like it here. I like reading. I try to write a bit too but, you know, it's hard.'

Then her expression took on a more sympathetic aspect and she leaned closer.

'Nathan Jacob, isn't it? I'm sorry for asking, but it was you whose father died last week, wasn't it? It was in the local paper. I'm sorry for your trouble.'

Nathan swallowed and mumbled, 'That's okay. It's been hard enough.'

'I remember losing my father. I couldn't think straight for weeks.'

Nathan smiled wryly and gestured to the rumpled drift of notes cluttering the desktop. He shook his head and said, 'My head is wrecked. I can't concentrate on this stuff at all. That's why I'm reading this instead.'

He lifted the book and showed the librarian the cover.

'*Manhunters*,' she read. 'Sounds interesting.'

Then a small frown dimpled the space between her brows and she said, 'I might have something here for you that you'd like. Follow me.'

She bustled off between the aisles of books. Nathan frowned and went after her. She moved in a busy sort of waddle but her eyes scanned the shelves, bright as tinsel.

Nathan watched her toddle around the corner into the History section, stoop out of sight and then bob upright again. 'Come on,' she said. 'There's a book here about old murderers and executioners I think you might like. Now where is it?'

Nathan paused. Smiled at the woman as she scanned the shelves, muttering to herself. He leaned one elbow against a shelf of books and let his eyes drift over the spines. Then he frowned and his hand reached out. Like his muscles and sinews decided to operate on impulse and instinct, his hand moved. And from behind his eyes the thinking part of himself watched it. His hand went out and when it came back, it held a small, jaundiced book in its fingers. He held it as the librarian bumbled back toward him, her hands empty and her face apologetic.

'I can't find what I was looking for. But what's that you have?' she said.

He held it up for her and she looked at it as though it were an alien artefact.

'It's history,' she said. 'I didn't even know we had it. I've never seen it before. It's history but judging by the cover, which you should never do, you'll probably appreciate it.'

Nathan turned the book in his hands. The cover was a sort of mustard yellow with the title printed in stately black capitals. It had the slightly greasy feel of old books much handled. The pages were dust grey along the edges and the colour of tannin inside. How many people's sweat and oils had seeped into the paper to discolour them so, Nathan didn't want to know. Generations of licked thumbs, of moist palms, of damp fingers.

'The Monto Murders,' whispered the librarian, as though the name itself was a curse or a conjuration of something vile. 'You know, I've never heard of them. Strange that.'

Nathan frowned and then said, 'The Monto Murders.' The syllables rolled around his mouth like sweetbreads.

And again, 'The Monto Murders.'

He could almost taste them.

CHAPTER 8

DUBLIN, DECEMBER 1892

Night wrapped around Dublin like a dirty, wet shawl and Dublin wrapped around George Frohmell like the arms of a drowning man. The air was cold and as he walked up Dame Street his breath fogged out in front and behind. Urchins sat on the doorsteps of businesses and tenements and asked for money or spat or flung insults. The uniform he wore. The helmet on top of the greatcoat. The silver numbers on his collar and on his shoulders. All cast him in a different light. The DMP didn't belong. Like the city which they served, they were a shadow people, neither one thing nor the other. Still, George reflected sourly, it could be worse. He could be in the Royal Irish Constabulary, instead. He wouldn't exchange the scolding of a Dublin brat for their lot, not for all the tea in China. Putting down half-arsed rebellions every few weeks. Being shot at. Hated by everyone. Seen as traitors to their own people. All George had to do was solve crimes.

Crimes like the RIC couldn't even imagine.

Crimes where women were carved open like something in an anatomy lecture.

Crimes where their organs were taken.

He had spent all afternoon trawling through the records of any violent offender known to be within twenty miles of the Monto when Mary Shortt was murdered. He had pestered the orderly at Kevin Street Barracks to run up to Mountjoy and Kilmainham and get a list of all those released from these gaols over the past month or so.

He sat there, behind a dune of paperwork, reading and re-reading the deeds of crooks and swindlers and rapists and murderers. The testimonies of witnesses. The comments of judges. He discounted nobody. To George's mind, a man who robbed a lady at knife-point was no more than six-inches away from becoming a murderer.

He had sat there and drank mug after mug of hot tea, sucking paper cuts and striving to connect anyone about whom he read to the savagery he had seen done to Mary Shortt. He had sat there until his Inspector ordered him to leave. To go home. To get some sleep.

But when he left, he did not go home. He had to see Rosie. He had to warn her.

Rosie Lawlor lived in a tenement just off Dame Street and just below Christ Church Cathedral. She tended to ply her trade in the Monto, on the corner of Buckingham Street, but it was here, basking in the dubious glamour of the Cathedral and the Castle, that she made her home. It was early, yet. The clock had not struck nine but the December night had fallen like a hatchet. George hoped Rosie would still be at home at this hour. Still be at home and would be still dolling herself up. Not that she needed it. As far as George was concerned she could spend all night dolling herself up, for she wouldn't be leaving that tenement tonight even if he had to sit on her.

In reaching for the bottle of whiskey earlier that day, George had come to a sudden realisation. The smell of Rosie's perfume still on his hands, he had reached for the whiskey bottle and stopped. How could he protect anyone if his mind was half-addled through drink?

A little slug to keep the cold out. To stave off sleep.

All the old excuses bawling out at him from the dark of his own skull.

How could he protect the woman he loved?

And there it was. Opened and raw and pulsing in front of him. The one surety of his existence. The punchline to the joke that was his life. He was in love with Rosie Lawlor.

The whore and the station sergeant.

Dr O'Sullivan would laugh his arse off if he could see him.

A sea of grubby little forms scurried out in front of him and frog-belly faces all gurned up at him.

'Mister! Mister! Are you goin' up the Castle?'

'Mister! Mister! Give us a penny, would ya?'

George stopped and around him milled a tattered squabble of tenement children. All were bare-footed and all were filthy and all had streaming noses and weeping eyes. George could feel subtle hands, soft and pliable, darting into his greatcoat pockets. In the inner city, nobody ever carried anything valuable in their outside pockets if they could help it, but the little urchins were a perpetually optimistic bunch.

George slapped them away and raised his voice to a theatrical pitch.

'Are you attempting to rob a policeman in the course of his duties?'

The children squealed their innocence and a few made to dash off but before they could, George reached inside his coat and took out his hipflask. Suddenly interested, the gang watched him warily.

'It's silver,' he said. 'Pawn it.'

Then he tossed it into the middle of them and walked away.

Rosie's building was different from George's own. Where George's was redbrick, Rosie's was limestone. Where George's was utilitarian, Rosie's was elaborate. Where George's had some semblance of respectability, Rosie's was a squalid pit.

I AM IN BLOOD

In former times, in grander times, the building in which Rosie lived often housed dignitaries and country bishops who came to conduct their business in the hulking, gothic monument to Protestantism that was the Cathedral. The building's front was columned and fluted and carved with Roman numerals. Now, though, its columns were mouldy, its flutes and carvings silted up with soot. Its interior hacked up and partitioned. The limestone itself looked to be rotting.

The door was unlocked, so George pushed it open and stepped inside. He stepped into a welter of noise. The bray of arguments, the crying of children, the bark of dogs, the rattle of pots. The air hot with cooking, dense with steam and smoke. He stood in what had once been a reception hall and empty doorways lined the corridor that stretched away in front of him. To his right a stairs mounted the wall. The stench of the place was a physical thing. George's lips twisted and his eyes began immediately to water. This sort of place disgusted him. The inhumanity of it, the degradation, the humiliation. The fact of so many families reduced to the level of animals. The place was a breeding ground for disease and disaffection. George could cut the crime rate in half simply by burning places such as this to the ground.

And yet Rosie was here. This was Rosie's place. The stinking hole from which she rose.

George shook his head at the absurdity of it all and made for the stairway.

He met Rosie on the first landing.

'What the hell are you doing here?' she said.

'Season's greetings to you, too.'

'Jesus Christ, Georgie. In your uniform and everything? You'll have me bleedin' tarred and feathered.'

George looked at her. Her dark hair. Her dark eyes. Her lips rouged so that they looked bloody. Her skin buttermilk in the splutter of light from the tallow candle fixed to one wall.

'Well?' she said.

'I got your note,' he said eventually. He was suddenly possessed of that awkwardness common to all men in love and who have somehow bungled in the eyes of their beloved.

Rosie cocked her fists on her hips and said, 'I suppose you read it, too? Did I not tell you to follow me up to Monto? Why in Christ's name would I want a peeler appearing at my door?'

Dearest Sergeant Georgie my arse, thought George. But what he said was, 'I'm on duty and I don't care what I'm wearing or how it affects your delicate sensibilities. I've something important to talk to you about and I'd rather not do it on the public stairs.'

'Oh, is that how it is with you?'

'It is.'

'I have work to go to.'

George stayed silent at this. His disgust at the word 'work' radiated from him like static.

'Fair enough,' she relented. 'We'll go upstairs. But we haven't long, mind you.'

'It won't take long,' said George, taking a step toward her.

'And don't be getting any notions,' she said. Then she turned and with a little flirtatious glance over her shoulder, she led him to her room.

There was no door to Rosie's room. It had been torn down for firewood years ago. Instead, a filthy sheet made a sort of screen that had to be drawn aside to enter. The room inside was old and high-ceilinged. All around the border of this ceiling, olive branches, shells and cupids were moulded out of plaster. All were flaking and blackened and crumbling away. At the far end of the room an extraordinary marble fireplace yawned coldly. The chimney had been bricked up long ago and now the fireplace, with its carven lions, was merely a pointless curio, all stained and yellowed as though with tannin. Damp and soot hung in the air and breathing hurt the lungs. The room was divided into three by means of dishwater grey fabrics sewn together and fastened onto lines at head height. Two families and Rosie occupied these three separate little worlds, Rosie paying more for the privilege of solitary living.

At the moment the swags were pulled back to allow the smoke and steam of cooking to escape out into the hall. As Rosie and George entered, one of the women looked up from where she was bent over a pot and exclaimed, 'Jesus, Mary and Joseph, Rosie! Why are you bringing that in here?'

Then she spat.

George arched an eyebrow but Rosie snapped, 'Would you ever feck off, Mary. Who do you think you are? With your airs and graces and your tongue hangin' out of ya like a bitch in heat whenever a soldier walks past you. Match you better to keep your panting bleedin' tongue in your head and not be passing comment on my business.'

The woman, Mary, lanced George an evil look but said nothing more as Rosie led him to her portion of the room.

They sat side by side on her bed and George looked around him and said, 'I don't know how you can live here.'

'I'm waiting for a handsome man to propose and take me away from all this.'

George smiled bitterly.

She reached up and touched his jaw where the stiff collar of his uniform bit into his flesh. 'Your Inspector still has nothing to say about … about us?' she asked. And her voice was now tender, the bravado and bluster and dancehall theatrics gone. She leaned in to him and he into her. A man and a woman in love.

'Oh, he knows,' George said. 'He hasn't said anything because we're so understaffed he can't afford to lose another Station Sergeant. He knows, Rosie. Everyone knows.'

She smiled in the strange light of the place. 'Whatever are we to do? The whore and the station sergeant. We're like the start of a joke.'

George laughed at this. A genuine roar of laughter that nonetheless had a frantic edge to it, a lunatic fraying that frightened him to hear. The start and the end and the entire grubby middle, too.

From behind the screen of fabric, Mary's voice shouted, 'Would you be quiet in there! It's hard enough to make dinner without the pair of you rooting and roaring in your sinful lust!'

'Shut up, you oul' hag, or I'll clatter the puss off ya!' came Rosie's ladylike response.

George grinned at her and said, 'That's why I'm here. I read your note and I've thought long and hard about a few, more than a few, things. And I've decided something.'

'What have you decided?'

There was a breathlessness to Rosie's voice, an eagerness, that George completely missed.

'I've decided that you're not going to … to work … until all this has blown over and we've caught whoever killed Mary Shortt.'

Rosie's jaw squared and the sudden disappointment in her eyes was immediately replaced by outrage.

'You've decided? *You've* decided? How dare you, sir. By Jesus, I've put up with a lot in my time in this world but I've never been *decided* for before. Who do you think you are?'

George blinked. 'Would you keep your voice down?'

'I will not. I will do nothing that you tell me to do. You,

with your uniform and your funny bleedin' hat.'

She was on her feet now and her voice was mounting. George grabbed her before she could say any more and dragged her back down beside him. Startled, Rosie stilled and stared at him.

Pitching his voice low he said, 'This murderer is different to any other we've seen. He isn't finished. If I'm right, he's not finished by half.'

Rosie's expression softened and her eyes took in George's haunted look. She saw the worry that was in him and she said, 'Oh, Georgie. You read too many penny dreadfuls. Your imagination is always running away with you.'

'No it isn't. Not this time. There are certain details that I'm not at liberty to divulge that suggest this may be the work of a monster who takes deliberate pleasure in mutilation. Mary Shortt's death wasn't robbery or anything of the sort. There's an evil at work here, Rosie, and I'm frightened for you.'

Rosie blinked and she said, 'You make it sound like those killings over in London. You know, the ones where all those working girls were killed. Whatchamacallit ...'

'The Whitechapel murders.'

From beyond the screen came a small intake of breath and Rosie picked up a hairbrush and flung it as hard as she could in its direction.

'Would you ever leave off, Mary, and stop your earwigging.'

In a whisper George went on. 'You can't go out tonight. Or tomorrow. Or ever again until this fiend is caught. Your friends are right to be worried.'

'And what am I supposed to do for money? How am I supposed to live?'

'I can help with that.'

'I'm not a bleedin' charity case, mister. I'll not take hand-outs.'

'For God's sake, Rosie. This isn't charity. I want to take care of you. I'm sick of seeing you go with scum for the want of a few bob. I'm sick of it.'

Rosie sat back and scrutinised his earnest face.

'Is that what this whole fairytale of yours is all about? You don't want me out on the streets because you're jealous?'

George tried to keep the anger out of his voice and said, 'For the love of Christ, no. Well, yes, I am jealous. But that's not it. I want to see you safe. You and your friends, too.'

Rosie smiled. 'You're jealous?'

'Of course I'm jealous!' George snapped. 'You mean everything to me. I …'

It was then, in the far distance but getting louder and being taken up again and again, that the sound of whistles came into the room. Came into the room and settled shrilly between them and broke whatever spell had lain upon them.

'You what?' pressed Rosie. 'You were going to say something. What was it?'

George was on his feet, listening. Through the pandemonium of the tenement, through the background bustle of night-time Dublin, through the whicker of horses and the rumble of carts, through the shouts of urchins and the cries of those lost in the dark, the whistles wailed out, metallic and cold and piercing.

'Damn it,' said George. 'Damnitdamnitdamnit.'

When he left, he left Rosie sitting crestfallen on her bed without telling her what he was about to say. Without pitching both their worlds over the edge. Over the edge of the acknowledged but unstated. Without saying what they both knew but what they both needed to hear. Without forcing the moment to its crisis.

'Ah, sure, he'll be back,' said Mary from behind her screen.

'Ah, go to hell,' said Rosie.

George followed the whistles all the way up to Monto. Up Dame Street with the whistles growing. Up Westmoreland Street with the whistles growing. Across the granite trajectory of Carlisle Bridge and up Sackville Street. All the time with the sound of whistles converging around him. Winded and panting now, he turned right down Talbot Street and kept going. Kept going under the gas lamps. Kept going with the sound of whistles at last beginning to die away. Kept going with the sound of his own heart whumping in his ears.

On the edge of the Monto he found them. A narrow

alleyway crammed with dark uniforms and cigarette smoke. Crammed with whispered conversation and the stink of something bleeding. Lit by the bull's-eye lanterns of an impotent police force. The Furry Glen it was called, this gully of filth and degradation. Called laughingly by prostitutes and whoremongers and the sweaty men who paid them. A joke. A pun to mask the nasty nature of the place. Redbrick walls stretched off into the gloom and a floor of sunken old cobbles was bisected by an open sewer. An open sewer that carried all the many fluids of humanity down to the Liffey, where brown water churned it into nothing. An open sewer now filled with black blood.

Overhead, whores and their children leaned out of windows and leered down at ten DMP men and the body of a woman.

George pushed his way past a waxy-looking constable and said, 'Who's in charge here? Someone get those women up there back inside and start taking statements.'

No-one moved.

Every eye was fixed on the body sitting propped against the alley wall. She looked for all the world as if she were asleep. Asleep with a black circlet around her neck. A black circlet that only if touched would reveal itself to be tacky and warm.

'Who's in charge here?' George asked again.

The closest constable turned to him and muttered, 'You

are, Sergeant. C Division's under strength. You've the command here, Sir. Like you had for the last one.'

'Christ's sake,' George spat. 'What a mess.'

He turned to two constables who looked particularly shaken and said to them, 'You two. On your bikes. Get into this whorehouse here beside us and start taking statements. Record everything they say. Everything. Do you hear me?'

Both constables saluted and backed away, palpably relieved.

'Who found her?' he asked.

A constable with an extravagant handlebar moustache took a long drag on his cigarette and stated, 'I did. I thought she was drunk. I thought she was asleep. I went to shift her.'

He sniffed and drew his sleeve across his mouth. 'Christ,' he said. 'I kicked her. I bloody well kicked her.'

'And she was dead when you found her? Did you move her at all?'

The constable swallowed and cleared his throat. 'When I kicked her, her head. Jesus, Mary and Joseph. Her head sort of flopped to one side. Her neck opened up from ear to ear.'

'Right,' said George. 'I want one of you fine lads to start sketching this scene. I want two others stationed at both ends of this alley. If anyone from the press, especially *The Freeman's Journal*, tries to poke his nose in, you have my express permission to wallop him.'

'Right,' said George again, more to himself than anyone. Then he bent down and lifted the dead whore's skirts.

I AM IN BLOOD

When he stood up his face was the colour of lard and his hand went automatically inside his greatcoat. No hipflask. No warming draught to ward off the chill. No burning slug to soften the blow of what he had seen. What he had seen, unseamed and sopping.

Someone asked, 'Same as before, Sergeant?'

George nodded and looked up, saying, 'Someone must have seen something. Have we a name?'

The constable who had found her was lighting another cigarette. He took another long drag and lifted his lantern, casting its watery illumination back down the alley, shedding light deeper into the recesses of the Monto.

'No name, Sergeant. But whoever she was, I don't think she was killed on this spot.'

'What makes you think that?'

'There's a trail of blood, Sir. Look. She's after being dragged down here.'

George's eyes followed the spar of illumination drifting out from the constable's lantern. Blood soaked the cobbles and pooled in the hollows.

'She mightn't have been knifed here, but she wasn't dead when she was brought. She was bleeding a hell of a lot.'

'Why would he drag her here, Sergeant? What's he playing at?'

George turned to the constable and asked, 'What's your name, Constable?'

'Patrick Sinnott, Sergeant. DMP 9252.'

'You've a natural eye, Constable. You'll make Detective before you're finished. We're going to familiarise you with that fine body of men immediately.'

'Sir?'

'You head to G Division straight away and you rouse whatever Superintendent is in charge at the moment. You tell him that Station Sergeant Frohmell demands the assistance of G Division. Tell him this is the second instance of such butchery in a week.'

'*Demands*, Sir?'

'You heard me, Constable. Tell him *The Freeman's Journal* has a theory as to who's behind this.'

'Sir?'

'Fenians, Constable. The spectre of Republicanism will have those Castle lapdogs over here like a shot. Tell them I said something about trade unionism as well. That should do it.'

Constable Sinnott was smiling. In spite of everything, he was smiling.

'I understand, Sir,' he said. 'I'll be back as soon as I can.'

'Good lad,' said George. 'We've need of good lads.'

As the DMP men dispersed, George stood over the mutilated corpse of another dead whore and thought of Rosie. How could he keep her from this? How could he stop this happening to anyone else? How and why had the killer brought her here without being seen? How did he kill and vanish? How had such a monster fetched up in a place so ravished by poverty and crushed by oppression? How could his poor, miserable city cope? How could he?

How he could use a drink.

CHAPTER 9

SUSSEX, SEPTEMBER 1846

The Work. The Pattern. The bell jars in the closet. The instructions on the door. The note. DO NOT DISTURB. The dull glass and the formaldehyde and the smell. No one questions. No one questions. Rich clothes dark clothes big man in his big room. No one questions. No one asks. No one disturbs. Ignorant peasants with their animal accents. Honking of geese. The squeal of them. Opened like pigs. The squeal of them cut off. No one questions. Money speaks louder and accent of money and entitlement. Plum in the throat spoon in the mouth. Servility as habit. Time and again. In this place. This place that is not a place. All on the edge of the world. World's ending. Here. Here and here again. Money and rich clothes and quiet. For the work for everything. The locked cabinet and the printed note.

I AM IN BLOOD

The smooth of muscle the silk of muscle. Taste of liver. All sliced and cut and neat as neat. The jars with them floating and the smell of it the reek of it. Knifework and fingers delicate and the pulse the throb the gush of it. All the world ours. All the time and all the time and decisions and revisions. Gone …

When he was seven, his father hired a tutor for him. The runt disturbed the father on some fundamental level. The beatings he administered seemed to have no more effect on him than if he had taken his riding crop to the wall's numb plaster. The boy's siblings were all schooled at home. Experts in mathematics and literature and French and German were drafted in and all were paid good money to bleed some little of that expertise into the young brains sitting before them. The boy, however, did not like to sit with his family. He did not wish to hear anything that fell on any other ear. He wanted things new-found and knowledge new-kindled for him and him alone. With the others around him he felt like some sort of clod-minded farm animal, herd-fed and herd-bound. He wished to be isolate. Not just without company, instead his oneness became an action, a done thing.

And so the tutor, a young man of Oxford, came with his tweed coat and smiling face to school him in abstract matters in the open privacy of his father's library.

This tutor sat day after day with the strange little boy in front of him and marvelled at his aptitude. The boy excelled at all things academic, but especially so in mathematics and literature.

Only in poetry was he lacking.

There was something at the heart of it that he could not grasp.

His tutor marvelled at this, too. He watched as the boy struggled to comprehend the sensitivity of Wordsworth, the humanity of Shakespeare.

And so, like any good tutor, he thrashed him for his incomprehension. The application of physical chastisement being well-known as a spur for the intellect.

The boy took it unflinching.

His father, however, was not renowned for his *sangfroid* and was appalled that a mere teacher, an upstart commoner, should raise a hand to his son, runt though he be. Like all those newly monied in that soot-blackened world, his father thought himself far above those fellows not so industrious as he. He had tossed away all memory of where his family had sprung from and had joyously embraced the amnesia of the nouveau riche.

The tutor took his upbraiding with the same unflinching detachment that the boy had taken his.

And then he had calmly informed the father that he was adhering to established pedagogical principles and that, if the father wished to see his son educated, then he should either allow the education to be carried out or terminate his contract immediately. For he would not be spoken down to, simply for doing his job.

The father listened and considered the difficulty in finding a suitable tutor. The next day, after thinking long and hard, and not for the first time, about the strangeness of his youngest son, the father spoke to the ostler whom he employed to look after the horses. The man had a son the same age as the boy and the following Monday this young lad accompanied the boy to class.

Like all new men, the father clung on to old ideas. Old traditions. Living like a lord of yore was not enough. To pretend to be an aristocrat was one thing. To actually become an aristocrat, one must behave like one. Behave to excess if needs be. Hence the vulgar mansion, the manicured lawns, the inordinate furnishings.

Hence the ostler's son. Now the whipping boy for his peculiar little classmate.

The tutor introduced the two boys.

'Hello,' said the ostler's son.

'I don't like you,' said the boy.

The ostler's son blinked and the tutor said, 'How do you know you don't like him? You've only just met.'

The boy regarded him with his flat eyes in his oh-so-ordinary face and said, 'I don't like anyone.'

'That's not so,' said the tutor. 'You like me.'

The boy said nothing.

The ostler's son proved himself to be extraordinarily precocious. He had never been to school before and could write only with the agonised expression and cramped hand of someone to whom the whole process was alien. And when he wrote, the only words that scrawled themselves into being were his name and the names of household items. Within a week he was reading quite complex sentences and within a month he was tackling poetry.

The tutor spent more time in those first few weeks with the new boy than the old boy. The ostler's son's enthusiasm was blinding and his love for the written word radiated from him. He began to write stories and simple verses about horses and life at home in his family's dreary little cottage.

The boy looked on and said nothing.

Perhaps it was the tutor's fault, in the end. Perhaps the enthusiasm of the ostler's son caught him off-guard. Perhaps his own love of literature was his Achilles' heel. Perhaps his distaste for the concept of a whipping boy made him sympathise with the ostler's son more than he should have.

For seven months the tutor did not have to raise even his voice to correct any member of his little class of two. But then the boy, silent and sullen, did something that forced him to take action.

The boy, jealous of the ostler's son, decided to give up on poetry entirely. He would not make a fool of himself anymore. Each time he read the words of a poem it felt as though boulders rolled about in his skull. He had come to the conclusion that poetry, in all its forms, was simply lies created by adults to hide the truth in things. Similes and metaphors did nothing to reveal the nature of reality. They covered things up. They showed the world in a way that it wasn't. To the boy they didn't mean a thing.

I wandered lonely as a cloud.

Clouds could not be lonely. It was all nonsense. Only people could be lonely. Painfully lonely.

And so he watched his tutor and the ostler's son revel in each other's company. The master and the protégé. And he simmered in dumb fury until one day he simply closed his book and pushed it away from him.

'Page fifty-seven,' said the tutor. 'Come on. You can do it.'

The boy said nothing.

The tutor picked up his cane, stood and moved in front of the boy.

The boy stood and held out his hands, his face blank as porcelain.

'Open your book,' said the tutor.

'No.'

'Damn it to hell, boy, open your book!'

'No.'

The boy lifted his hands as though offering up a sacrifice.

The tutor turned to the ostler's son, who was sitting quietly, his finger tracing the lines of the unfamiliar print on the page before him.

'Stand up,' said the tutor.

'Master?' said the ostler's son.

'I said stand up!'

The ostler's son rose timidly to his feet, his little face crumpling in confusion.

The tutor turned back to the boy and cleared his throat.

The boy frowned at him, but a growing sense of understanding was scuttling through his brain like a rat after something putrid.

The tutor cleared his throat once more and pronounced slowly, 'Should you disobey me again, I will be forced to punish your classmate, innocent though he is of any wrongdoing.'

The ostler's son stood agog while across the boy's face a smile opened up like a gash.

The tutor spoke again, the bleat in his voice horrible to hear. 'Surely you do not wish for that? Surely you would not wish to see an innocent punished for your wilfulness? Come now, be a good boy. Don't hurt this poor lad simply because you do not want to do your work.'

The boy said nothing.

Right then and there the tutor decided that there was something broken in the boy. Something broken that he had neither the skill nor the courage to fix. How could he allow an innocent lad to be beaten for no cause? The dubious reasoning behind the use of a whipping boy was to appeal to the better nature of the other, the boy who could not be touched. And yet here he was, cane in hand, trying to appeal to the better nature of a creature that appeared to have none.

And into his thoughts the voice of the ostler's son came soft and pleading. He had turned to his classmate and clutched at his arm in childish desperation.

'Please,' he said. 'Please don't. Don't hurt me.'

The tutor's cane cracked down on the whipping boy's right palm and the poor little creature yelped and cried out in terror, in pain. In confusion.

Three more times his cane worked its violence.

And the boy looked on. He was rapt and motionless save for that greasy smile, widening moment by moment.

The tutor lashed out then. Lashed out at that smile. Lashed out in revulsion. Lashed out in indignation. Lashed out with all the horror of the civilised man suddenly confronted by the unreasoning glee of savagery.

Today would be his last day as tutor under this roof. He would walk away rather than be exposed to that baleful smile, day after day. Rather than be forced to brutalise the innocent while those empty, depthless eyes looked on.

The boy rocked back on his heels. Where the cane had landed, a bright red seam had suddenly split open along his cheekbone.

There was silence then.

And into that silence the whipping boy curled over his pulsing hand and sobbed the word, 'Why?' Over and over again.

The tutor would never forget the expression that came into being on the boy's face at this unanswerable question. In dark nights to come, in bed alone or gripped by fever and sickness, that expression would shudder suddenly into view and he would think of that strange little boy and the awful things he must surely have done with his life.

… like the centre of empire fog and dank and wet. Night is the dear friend. Red dark. Hot dark. Steaming. Old friend. Faithful black and empty. Yawn of them all emptied out. Fog on the water. Smoke on the wind. No revisions. No bobbies. No questions. The floating things. Blind. No eyes. No soul. The filthy woman parts. The piss stink bundle of kidney. Wash and jar and cork and savour. All night. In the dark. In the cabinet. All night. The love of it. The start of it. Wash. Clean. Shave. All our tools glitter. Knife and saw and bright and sharp. Razor edge and bitter point. Stow all away. Fasten. Close up the belly. Suture in the dark. In the red dark. In the secret dark. Black bag black coat black hat. Black gloves. The smell of it. Press the nose. The smell of it in the leather on us. Impregnate. No one sees and no one asks. No one cares. Oh the howl of it. The free gale of it in us. Heft the bag. The weight of it. Razor edge and bitter point and empty jar. The weight of it in us. Time and time and time again.

The start of it.

CHAPTER 10

DUBLIN, DECEMBER 2015

Nathan ate dinner in his room. The day before Christmas Eve and here he was, eating dinner on his own, in his bedroom, with his laptop open and one eye on the spastic reactionism of Facebook. *OMG. Like.* Some American billionaire telling people they have x amount of friends. Nathan shovelled forkfuls of lukewarm beef into his mouth thinking, What, when you get right down to it, actually qualifies as a 'friend'? He read the illiterate venom that constituted ninety-nine per cent of Facebook and he suddenly found himself thinking, This is shit. He shovelled forkfuls of roast beef into his mouth and his mind wondered how Zuckerberg gets away with this. He sat there thinking, all the graffiti on all the toilet doors in all the world, all the scrawls and insults, all the *Nato luvs Esther*'s. All the bullshit. This was social networking. All the glitz and all the razzmatazz was plastered on to dress up something with absolutely no substance or consequence. And still he kept eating and kept reading. Refresh. Refresh. Refresh.

He was meeting Esther later.

Anymore did she qualify as friend?

Anymore did he?

Esther, with painful predictability, was heading to the Christmas instalment of her writing workshop. Nathan wouldn't have minded if anybody else was running it, no, no, *facilitating* it, other than Andrew Callahan. Andrew Callahan who looked at Esther as though she was the most beautiful thing he'd ever set eyes on. To make matters worse, Nathan used to be friends with Andrew. Nathan even went to the group a couple of times, but the Kum Ba Yah positivity of the whole thing made his skin crawl. It's like you couldn't do anything anymore without a support group. Self-help circles had a monopoly on human warmth. The writing group was meeting tonight in Andrew's house, just off Trees Road. Esther had rung Nathan to invite him along. For the umpteenth time. She was always on to him about going back to it. On to him about putting his thoughts on paper. On to him about his *voice*. His *vision*.

Nathan wanted to see her. Wanted to see her beyond anything. The ache for his father was fading and in its place the ache for her just kept on growing. The atmosphere in Nathan's house was getting more and more uncomfortable. Samantha and James had become a little support circle of their own. Their intimacy excluded the rest of the world. Nathan had decided that after dinner he would take a walk down to the writing group. Walk down to see Esther. To put his thoughts on paper. To clear his vision.

He hadn't talked to her properly in ages.

And now at last he had something to talk to her about. At last, beyond voyeurism and beyond the black blood of crime scene photos, he had found something real. Something real behind all the transparent self-justification and fragile worthiness. He had to speak to Esther about it.

And then he thought, for a good while now he hadn't spoken to anyone much. And then he thought that without Esther, he didn't really have much of a life. Without Esther, he didn't have friends much. He tried to remember when this happened, when he stopped going to parties, when he stopped talking to even the lads who lived across the road. He didn't know when he started drifting apart but all he knew was that when he was with Esther, he was happy. Wasn't he?

And then he thought of Samantha and James' dislocation from him. So seamless that he didn't even notice until one day a cold gulf existed between them and he was eating his meals alone. Was that gulf always there? Did his father's death just make it visible and felt by everyone. Manifest.

He thought, going to this writing group just to see Esther smacks of desperation. Watching Andrew gurn and simper made his head ache. Watching the other girls titter and whisper and make up stories and scrawl *Esther 4 Andrew* in the margins of their crappy short stories made him actually angry.

Nato Luvs Esther 4eva. Esther 4 Nato. T.I.E.D.

This was how it should be. How it should read.

And then he thought, I have to make it up to her. A support group of two.

He had texted her and asked her to call round on her way home.

No problem. See you around half eight, came the reply.

He smiled at this. He knew he shouldn't be jealous of her spending time with anyone. She wasn't his. Not really. But he still was.

Nathan spent the rest of the day in his room with *The Monto Murders* open on his desk and the internet open on his laptop. The whole middle section of the book was taken up by glossy pages whereon were printed photographs of dead women. Women empty of womb and slit-throated in the glare of the magnesium flash. Black ropes of blood wound around out-flung thighs. Black aprons of blood drenching their Victorian petticoats.

People always describe dead people as looking like they are asleep. These people didn't look asleep. They looked like what they were. They looked like butchered meat. The dispassion of the camera lens. A cold record of things.

And beyond the pictures, something else. Something he had found in the yellowing pages. God, he couldn't wait to tell Esther. Couldn't wait to show her.

He went downstairs at quarter past eight o'clock. The too-soft carpet of the stairs soundless under his stockinged feet.

The hallway was dark. Samantha and James were sitting in the living room. Both of them balled about in the glow of table lamps. No decorations, still. No tree. His father took care of all that. Without him, the place was left as it was. To do otherwise was to acknowledge the world had moved on without him. In this Samantha, James and Nathan were all in unspoken concord. Nothing had changed since his father had departed the world. Not a single thing moved or replaced.

Nathan stood looking through the glass panelling of the living-room door. Looking at Samantha and James. *Strictly Come Dancing* was on TV. They watched it unspeaking. Their own company. A silent communion.

Nathan stood in the darkened hallway. Watching them through warped glass. Then he walked in to the kitchen. He was going to make a pot of tea and get some sandwiches together or something so that he and Esther might have something to eat. He had a lot to talk about.

Not least what had happened at his father's grave.

At half past eight Nathan put the teapot, mugs and sandwiches onto a tray and brought them upstairs. At twenty minutes to nine, Esther still had not arrived. He had no idea why this provoked such unease in him. He pictured her and Andrew Callahan heading out for a drink. He pictured her texting to cancel things. He was about to ring her when his phone cheeped.

I'm outside.

He hurried down the stairs and opened the front door. James must have heard him because he poked his head into the hallway and said, 'Why didn't you turn on the light? Who's at the door?'

Nathan ignored him and stood aside to let Esther step in.

'Hey James,' she said.

'Oh, hey Esther,' he replied. 'Come here to be depressed by this loser or to see his handsome little brother?'

'You're funny,' said Esther.

'Don't humour him,' said Nathan. 'He's an asshole.'

James shrugged and went back to *Strictly*.

Esther went up the stairs ahead of Nathan and he couldn't help but check out how tight her jeans were as she mounted step by step.

'James is sort of right,' she was saying, but Nathan wasn't paying much attention. 'Your father's death has hit you really, really hard. Like, seriously.'

'And?'

They were in Nathan's room now and he closed the door

behind them. They sat side by side on his bed.

'Well,' said Esther. 'That's the reason I was trying to help you with *The Necronomicon*. It's like you've been hit by a truck. I think you need closure or something. Anything.'

That arrogance in her again. That infuriating hotness.

Nathan thought for a moment before saying, 'You know the way I'm adopted, yeah?'

'Yeah.'

'Well, all the time I have this rootless feeling. I never ever had it with Da. He always made me forget about myself. Like I belonged with him. More than just that he and Samantha took me in. It's like I was part of him and he was part of me. I'm not sure if that makes any sense.'

'Of course it does,' said Esther and her hand touched his shoulder, his cheek.

He leaned in to it a little and she drew back. Her hand dropped to her lap.

He sighed and went on. 'I never knew my mother. But I know there's a real part of her in me. I carry her blood for real. I always wondered if I could follow my bloodline and where it would lead me.'

'She died, didn't she?' said Esther carefully.

'Yeah. She was real troubled. I think she was a drug addict. I think Da used to help her out. I think he was the only thing close to family she had. That's why she left me to him. She knew he would take care of me.'

'Your father was a good man, Nato. A nice guy.'

Nathan smiled absently. 'He was always doing stuff like that for people. I feel sorry for my mother sometimes. I wonder what flaw was in her to drive her into the situation she ended up in.'

He stopped for a second. Stopped and then said, 'I never really wanted to chase down where I came from before this. Before, you know, Da died. I never felt the need. Whenever I was feeling all sort of dislocated, he was always there to nail me back down again. Am I making any sense here?'

Esther was looking at him, her face open and sympathetic. 'You should write this stuff down. It sounds like it might help you. You know, to find your place in the world. To see where you fit.'

'To find my voice?'

'Don't take the piss. I'm serious. You should do some automatic writing or something. Yeats used to do it all the time.'

'I've done a bit of that, I'm trying to get better at it,' said Nathan.

'You can't get better at it,' said Esther. 'You just do it.'

Nathan laughed. 'I prefer the True Crime stuff, to be honest. That's what I want to show you.'

Esther frowned but said, 'Cool.'

Nathan brought over *The Monto Murders* and spread open the central pages.

'Wow,' said Esther. 'Gross. What am I looking at?'

'Women who were murdered right here in Dublin. Back in the 1890s.'

'No way.'

'Seriously. They were killed just like Jack the Ripper killed people. All cut up and mutilated.'

They looked at the photographs one by one. Each corpse taken from various angles. The harrowing honesty of them. The objectivity. The dead eyes empty and staring.

'These are amazing,' said Esther. 'I knew they had cameras back then but these are really clear. Creepily clear. Cool.'

Nathan nodded.

Esther ran her finger over one of them, tracing the line of a knife cut.

'You can almost feel the blood. Imagine being that close to death. So close you can smell it and taste it and touch it. Why do men do stuff like this to women?'

Nathan looked at her. There was something rapt about her.

'Women seem wicked when you're unwanted.'

'They're preserved,' she said. 'Like suspended animation. Like life after death. You know, here we are a hundred years later looking at them. Just because they were murdered. Wow. It's like they're undead or something.'

Nathan watched her for a moment before saying, 'It's like you think there's something sexy about it. About blood. About life after death.'

'And you don't?'

'I'm not sure,' he said. But what he was thinking was the way Esther's eyes gleamed and her lips parted – parted just so – was incredibly sexy.

'How come I've never heard of this before?' she asked.

Nathan shrugged. 'Nobody has. I Googled them and nothing comes up apart from this book. Not even images. It's like the whole thing was covered up or forgotten or something.'

Esther was riffling through the pages, letting the grey suede of their edges whisper past her thumb.

'Where did you find it?' she asked.

'The library … but …'

'But what?'

'It's like it found me, not the other way round.'

Esther looked at him for a long time.

'Cool,' she said.

'You don't think that's strange?'

'Of course I do. That's why I said, *cool*. I wish they had something like this at the writing workshop.'

'Really?'

'Yeah, I don't think I really fit in.'

At this Esther dropped her head and her frown came back and deepened.

'It'd be different if you were there.'

Nathan felt a soft sort of warmth buffet him from the inside. She wanted him. She actually needed and wanted him. Esther had *wanted* him to come to the poxy writing group. She needed someone to lean on as much as he did. Peas in a pod. A support group of two, after all.

Nathan's hand went out and took hold of Esther's.

Her touch. The warmth of her. The fragility. Like bird bones.

'You're being harsh on yourself, Esther. I've read your stuff. It's amazing. Yer man, Andrew, must see that. I'm sure he's delighted to have you as part of his group.'

He tried to keep the grit out of his voice. He wasn't sure how successful he was.

'You're too nice, Nato. He's a loser. The stuff you write would blow his little mind if you read it out to him.'

'Really?'

'Really. God, the stuff he and the others come out with is atrocious. Stephanie Meyer has a whole lot to answer for.'

Nathan smiled. 'You're right. Storm Constantine is far better.'

She tilted her head and looked up at him. 'Are you taking the piss?'

'Out of you? Of course not, my dear.'

For *my dear* read *my darling*.

She was smiling too now and she shimmied around on the bed so that she faced him and placed both her hands on his thigh.

'So let's see this writing you've been doing.'

He shook his head. 'It's rubbish. Nonsense. I think I could

do without finding my voice. I think I'm better just sticking to things that are true to life.'

Esther looked around and then leaned forward quickly. There was a rustle from just under the bed. When she straightened she held an A4 sheet triumphantly in her right fist.

'Well, what have we here?' she crowed.

Nathan suddenly felt genuinely uncomfortable.

Esther was already scanning the page and with each line her mouth drew down and her eyes grew ever more clouded.

'What the hell is this, Nato?' she asked eventually.

'That's what happens when I let my mind go.'

'Really?'

'Yep. Told you I was better at the true to life stuff.'

'It's not bad,' she said, still frowning. 'But it's weird, Nato. Dark. Really, really dark. It's like the thoughts of someone out of *Gormenghast*.'

'I don't really think that's my voice, Esther.'

He felt more and more uncomfortable with every passing second.

'Whose is it?' she asked.

The cemetery. The graveside. In the cold and in the dark. That voice from the hindbrain. That gibbering thing. Deranged.

'I don't know,' he said.

She shook her head in confusion, 'You don't even talk like this. Do you think like it? Who even uses the word *whereon* nowadays? There's stuff like that all the way through it. It's like someone from the past or something. It's mental.'

Nathan looked at the floor. What if you could not find a voice? What if a voice found you?

Esther was watching him now. The piece of paper gingerly placed to one side as though it might cut, or bite, or chew.

'Have you ever thought of writing a book?' he asked.

'No,' she said. 'Have you?'

'I haven't thought about it until now. Until I felt the world come loose about me. Until Da died. Not in a million years. Then I took your advice. You know writing to nail down who I am and where I am.'

He gestured to the page beside her. 'That's what came out. But I want to write about something real. Not just random thoughts. Something really real. Something that speaks to me about me. Something that says to me that this is me and that this is where I belong.'

Esther was smiling at him now. An all-the-way-wide-open sort of smile. 'What are you talking about?'

'I want to write about this,' said Nathan and he dragged his new favourite book up in front of her face.

'*The Monto Murders*,' said Esther. 'I get it. I really get it. God, the photos alone are worth writing about. But what have hundred-year-old murders got to do with who you are?'

'This is what I wanted to show you. Read the name of the policeman who investigated them.'

Esther took the book, turned it round and squinted at the blurb.

Eventually her head snapped up and her eyes met Nathan's own.

'You're joking,' she said.

'See? See why I wanted to show you this? See why I want to find out more? Why I want to tell this story?'

'It's about you.'

'My mother's name,' said Nathan. 'Frohmell.'

CHAPTER 11

DUBLIN, CHRISTMAS DAY 1892

December 25 1892. Christmas Day. The rain had stopped but the clouds above Dublin still had a dirty look to them. A spiteful look. The city hunkered down between the mountains and the plains, the plains and the sea. Hunkered down and straddled the Liffey like a whore squatting over the stream of her own piss. God rest ye merry gentlemen. Silent night. Good people all.

My eye, thought George Frohmell.

People were cretins. Simpletons. Every single one of them. Even the woman sitting across the table from him. Especially the woman sitting across the table from him.

She was eyeing him now, pugnacious and proud.

'For the love of God, Rosie, would you see sense,' he said. He hated the note of pleading that had entered his voice. There was a bleat to it that was maddening.

'Why are you trying to ruin Christmas for us?' she said.

'I'm trying to have a conversation. Damn it to hell. I'm trying to make you listen to reason. To have a bit of cop-on.'

'Don't be cursing, Georgie. Curses make the baby Jesus cry.'

George breathed out through his nose. The sound it made was like a punctured bellows.

'You snore, Georgie,' said Rosie. 'Do you realise that? You snore outrageously. Like a boar with a cold in his head and a belly full of slops.'

Inexplicably embarrassed, George touched the bridge of his nose and mumbled, 'I got my nose broken. Twice, I think. It goes with the job.'

Rosie folded her arms and said, 'So does bullying people, it seems.'

She would drive a man to drink. George's hands had begun to shake over the past two days and yesterday he had actually begun to search his rooms for any empty bottles left lying about that he might suck the dregs from. Christmas Eve and he was flat on his belly looking under the presses for a forgotten bottle or a drop in a glass. The realisation of how pathetic he must look fell on him like a cold downpour and then he had gotten up and sat quietly for a long while.

'I don't bully people,' he said. 'I don't think asking you to live here with me is bullying you.'

'Yes it is,' she said. 'It bleedin' well is. And you know it is. It'd be a scandal is what it'd be. We're not married. You've not even bothered to propose. Filthy black Protestant that you are. Instead you want to set me up like some sort of oriental concubine. Who the hell do you think you are? The King of Siam? Who do you think I am? A bit of alright to come home to when you're not spending all your bleedin' time in the barracks or up the Castle or sweeping out the bleedin' station house?'

'A *scandal*,' said George. 'A *scandal*. How can you go on about morality when …'

He trailed off. The look on her face warned him that to go further would be to stray on to very dangerous ground.

'Go on,' she said. 'Go and say what you were going to bleedin' say and have done with it.'

'I thought curses made the baby Jesus cry.'

'To hell with the baby Jesus. Little bastard had a better flippin' birthday than anyone I know. At least he was warm and got a decent lot of presents.'

George laughed and said, 'Look it. We'll argue over this another time. It's Christmas Day and I'm glad you're here, with me. I'm glad you spent last night here, with me.'

Rosie smiled. She could feel the weight of the future

bearing down on her. In George's eyes she could see the want, the potential. Years and years to come, opening out and rolling away in front her. The tipping point of things. The word. The question. The statement. The bald expression of what they both knew. She waited and George licked his lips and his mouth opened and her unborn children were bright in his eyes.

And then someone knocked on the door.

'Ah, for God's sake,' she snapped.

George was frowning and unconsciously looking around for his revolver.

The knock came again.

'Who is it?' he asked.

'Your long-suffering friend and fellow-traveller along the winding path of life,' came the response.

Rosie's eyebrow arched but George only smiled and said, 'Come in, Doctor. Don't be standing out there on the landing. You'll bring down the tone of the place. People will talk.'

The door opened and Doctor O. P. O'Sullivan swept into the room. He was carrying a large basket draped over with muslin and his cheeks were berry-red and glowing. He looked for all the world like a shaven St Nicholas.

'Merry Christmas!' he boomed and placed the basket on the table.

Seeing Rosie, he bowed low over her hand and kissed her knuckles.

'The inesteemable Rosie Lawlor. What a pleasant surprise to see such a figure of loveliness in such a hovel as this. I'm so glad to see you again.'

'You're pissed, Doctor,' she said.

'You are as perspicacious as you are lovely,' he replied.

'Sit down,' said George and dragged over a stool. 'Let me take your coat.'

Doctor O'Sullivan perched on the stool and looked from Rosie to George and sighed happily. 'Ah, true love. A dream within a dream.'

George looked at him and said, 'It's three o'clock on Christmas Day, Oliver. Why are you here?'

'Have you eaten yet?' asked O'Sullivan.

'Rosie has some ham boiling and we've a few spuds left over from yesterday,' said George. 'You're welcome to have some.'

'Indeed,' said O'Sullivan. 'I was wondering what that smell was.'

Over Rosie's outraged snort he continued, 'I've brought some presents. I thought you could use some company. I wasn't aware that you had made arrangements of your own.'

'What did you bring?' asked Rosie, now curious. All insults were suddenly forgotten as she lifted one corner of the basket's covering, her face eager, like a child's.

'Good King Wenceslas looked out …' sang O'Sullivan and he swept aside the muslin.

Under it was revealed a full goose breast, half a baked ham, a loaf of brown bread, a jar of cranberry conserve, two bottles of porter and a half bottle of whiskey.

'My God,' whispered Rosie.

'Happy Christmas,' said O'Sullivan and took the opportunity to plant a kiss on her cheek.

'I've another present,' he said. 'One of your damnable scandal-rags.'

He rooted under the food and came out with a slim book, covered in red leather, with the picture of a cowboy etched into the front. The title read, *The Pinkerton's: Tales of Derring-Do to Thrill and Amaze*. He dusted some crumbs from the cover and handed the book to George.

George turned the book over and over in his hands before saying, 'Oliver, I can't accept this. I've gotten you nothing in return.'

'Nonsense,' said O'Sullivan. 'Your constant impositions on my time and your awkward bloody peeler's sensibilities are more diverting than a million presents.'

'You heard about the second one, then?' said George.

O'Sullivan's face clouded and in the drab light of the room he suddenly looked grey and old. He shook his head, 'I'm sobering up, George,' he said. 'And these are not things we should be discussing in front of a lady.'

'Don't worry, Oliver,' said George. 'You'll not have to deal with any more of this horror. I've gotten the G-men in on it. I got a bit of a dressing-down for impertinence, but the Superintendent in Charge could see the merit in it. Medals, Oliver. Medals and newsprint and a pat on the head from the Lord Lieutenant.'

O'Sullivan was busy emptying the basket of its contents and Rosie was busying herself with plates and cutlery. No one was paying much attention to what George was saying. He shook his head and looked on as the good doctor unstoppered the whiskey bottle with his teeth, spat out the cork, took a long pull from it and offered it to George. When George refused, O'Sullivan merely shrugged, cradled the bottle in his lap and watched Rosie as she set the table.

'Punching above your weight, there, Georgie boy,' he commented.

George ignored this and asked, 'Why are you are here, Oliver? It's Christmas Day.'

O'Sullivan took another pull from the whiskey bottle and smiled wryly. His lips were loose and blubbery like strips of fatty meat stitched to his face.

'I am here,' he said, 'because it is Christmas and because one should do one's utmost to spread the joy of the Season of Good Will to those less fortunate than ourselves.'

Rosie harrumphed, clattered a plate down in front of O'Sullivan and began carving the meat.

O'Sullivan glanced at her, laughed and went on. 'I am here because my lovely wife can't seem to leave her theatre days behind her. Ha. Theatre. Dance hall, more like.'

He took another drag from the whiskey bottle. George frowned and looked at Rosie, who shrugged.

O'Sullivan continued talking, his voice a marly sludge.

'There's this chap, you see. A young friend of hers. She invites him to all our parties. She uses my money to fund his wagers. I know she does. I see the way she looks at him. So there he sits. In my house. On Christmas morning. I'll be damned if I am to be bearded in my own den.'

George sighed. He couldn't meet the doctor's eyes. This had been coming a long time. In the dismal surrounds of George's rooms, Dr O. P. O'Sullivan was baring his soul.

'I took a little drink. Then I took another little drink. Says me to meself, "Oliver, that George Frohmell is decent man. Upstanding, doncherknow. He could do with a bite to eat and a bit of company on Christmas Day." So here I am, George. Here to keep you company and to cheer you up. I didn't know you were otherwise engaged.'

He snickered as he said this last word. Snorting like a child who had heard something bold.

'Oh, we're not engaged,' snapped Rosie. 'No fear of that.'

She doled out the food, flinging slices of meat on to George's plate with unwarranted violence.

What was wrong with her? he thought. This wasn't his bloody fault. It wasn't as if he had invited the man.

Attempting to lighten the mood, he said, 'Well you're here

now and you can relax amongst friends.'

But O'Sullivan was speaking as if in a daze.

'I can't stop thinking about that poor girl you had me look at. What was done to her. You wouldn't do it to an animal. How could anyone be capable of such a thing?'

Rosie had sat down and was about to start eating, but the doctor's words had bleached her face of all colour. She was looking at him with wide eyes. Fearful and appalled.

George tried to stem the doctor's words, saying, 'Well you needn't worry about that anymore. G Division will take care of it.'

'Oh, yes,' said O'Sullivan. 'I heard you the first time. The vaunted G-men. They'll have nothing to do with it. Not now. Bigger fish to fry after what happened this morning. I'm afraid these murders will rebound on us, George.'

'What happened this morning?' asked George, delighted that the conversation seemed to be shifting away from anything likely to offend Rosie and prompt her to take it out on him.

O'Sullivan suddenly seemed to notice the food laid out before him, smiled to himself and took up his knife and fork. 'You should try the cranberry conserve,' he said to Rosie. 'Cook makes exceedingly fine cranberry conserve.'

'I've never eaten anything like it,' said Rosie.

Her face was still pale but, to George's relief, she was attacking her food with real gusto. He watched her and noticed, really for the first time, how thin she was. How scrawny her arms and neck were. How sunken her cheeks. She was beautiful, but in the way that a winter tree was beautiful. There was something stark about her, something raw.

Around a mouthful of half-chewed goose O'Sullivan said, 'Cook made everything here. A treasure of a woman. Bread, scones, cakes, the woman can conjure up anything.'

Then his expression soured.

'Except tarts,' he said. 'My wife takes care of those.'

'What happened this morning?' George pressed. A dark feeling was starting to creep over him. A foreboding of something ill-defined but tangible.

'I'm surprised you haven't heard. I presume if you had been at your usual post, slumming it in the barracks rather than actually living your life, you would have heard. Even here, I'm surprised you didn't hear a rumour of the bang.'

George put down his knife and fork and leaned forward. 'Rumour of what bang?'

O'Sullivan washed down his goose with a glug of whiskey and said, 'The Fenians dynamited G Division this morning. Their headquarters, I think. The one in the Castle. Exchange Court.'

'Jesus Christ,' hissed George. 'Was anyone hurt? Why? On Christmas bloody morning. The bastards.'

O'Sullivan slathered a sliver of ham with sauce and said, 'One constable was killed. The sergeant I was talking to said it all seemed rather deliberate. A man named Patrick Sinnott, God rest his soul. The Fenians let it be known he was spreading lies for G Division. Said the Republican movement wouldn't be blamed for the murder of innocent women. Said the murders up in Monto were the work of perfidious Albion and nobody was to be listening to any lies coming out of the Castle.'

George blinked. *Patrick Sinnott.* Jesus Christ, had he killed a man? Had his big mouth, his arrogance, gotten a fellow constable blown up? Jesus Christ.

On Christmas Day?

'See?' said O'Sullivan. 'That is why it will rebound again on us. G Division won't be doing anything except chasing Fenians for the next while. We can't have the Castle dynamited willy-nilly, now can we? It'll be like the Phoenix Park Murders all over again. No one will be even able to sing a ballad or mention the word *Rising* without a detective turning up. They're like Banquo's bloody ghost when they get going.'

George was only half listening. *Patrick Sinnott.* The poor man. What had he done?

'I have to go,' he said at last.

Rosie leaned back in her chair, folded her arms and said, 'I knew it. I knew as soon as the doctor mentioned the DM-bleedin'-P, you'd be off like a shot.'

O'Sullivan paused with his fork halfway to his lips, startled at such language issuing from the lips of a lady.

'I have to go,' George repeated. 'I knew the constable who was killed.'

I set him on this course. I told him to drag G Division into this. Lies about Fenians. A dangling carrot. A baited hook. An unknowing death sentence.

Rosie glared at him as he put on his greatcoat, checked his revolver and tucked it into an inside pocket. She glared at him as he kissed her on the forehead. She glared at him as he said, 'Don't go out. Dr O'Sullivan will take care of you.'

He rested his hand on the latch of the door before leaving. He stilled, as though considering whether this was the right course of action. Then, without another word, he opened the door and was gone.

Rosie stared at the closed door for long moments and muttered, 'I wouldn't marry you even if you asked, you contrary bloody pig of a man.'

'Don't be so hard on him,' said O'Sullivan. 'He's a good man. One of the best.'

'Eat your bleedin' grub,' said Rosie.

George hurried down Sackville Street. The place was emptied. Christmas Day and the old street was a wasteland of grey cobbles and grey buildings under a grey sky. Shops and pubs and even the pagan henge of the GPO were closed and shuttered. The owners and workers at home with their families. At home with their loved ones. And here he was, slogging along in the drear light and the air so cold and damp that it felt like wet oilcloth against the skin. Rosie left sitting with Dr O'Sullivan, him drunkenly prating and her fuming quietly. He should not have left. It was Christmas Day, a time for loved ones. And he loved her dearly.

Here, only the hotels were open. The hotels with their vagrant populations of the well-off and dispossessed, the rich and the wayward. The hotels cast light from their curtained windows and their open doors into the sooty twilight. The laughter from within drowned out the sound of church bells chiming under the wet slate of the heavens. Their merriment mocked George as he walked.

The hotels were open, sure enough. The hotels and the flophouses of the Monto. The flesh-pits of Talbot Street, of the Gloucester Diamond, of Amiens Street and of all the laneways and dead-ends and rancid alleys in between. All of them thriving and teeming and steaming on this day of days, this holy of holies.

A day to spend in the embrace of a loved one.

A time of Peace and Good Will to all men.

Not for an agent of the Crown. Not in this land of shadows and half-truths and knives under the table. Not for the DMP. Not for Constable Patrick Sinnott. And not for Station Sergeant George Frohmell, either.

He noticed the first one as he approached Carlisle Bridge.

Tied to a lamp-post was a poster depicting the same cloaked and devilish figure that had appeared in *The Free-*

man's Journal. Under it was printed the slogan, *Don't let John Bull Murder Your Wives*.

John Bull.

To name a monster. To name a demon. An exorcism or a summoning?

George's upbringing made him recoil from such Popish notions, such ghost stories, and yet his very Irishness made him gravitate toward them. The supernatural. A devil at work in the shabby gullies between Dublin's tenements. The Pooka. The Banshee. The fairy fort and the Morrígan.

John Bull.

They were everywhere. Across the bridge. Down Westmoreland Street. Posters and slogans daubed the walls of once-grand edifices. The old Parliament Building with its colonnades and its weeping granite, its carvings and its coats-of-arms, was splashed here and there with the words *Brit Monsters* and *Up the Fenians* and *Down with the DMP*. The weeping granite of this place of Irish independence, this place that was now a bank.

The posters and the graffiti disturbed George more than he thought they should. He was on edge, just as the whole city seemed on edge. Christmas Day and Dublin was a bonfire ready to be lit.

Up the Fenians.

Down with the DMP.

The killings had to stop before the entire place slipped into pandemonium.

I AM IN BLOOD

Dublin Castle was in chaos. The guard at the gate had been trebled and two soldiers now stood to arms beside the DMP constable on duty. George identified himself and entered Exchange Court. Soldiers were everywhere. Rifles and bayonets and orders bawled out to echo and re-echo from the ancient walls and reverberate again and again until the din was incredible. A field gun had been dragged up and positioned facing the street and two Maxim machine-guns were emplaced behind sandbags to either side. The place had gone mad.

Up a narrow lane, a sort of apse to the main yard, and around to the side of G Division's Headquarters was the scene of Patrick Sinnott's murder. George could see the scorching of the brickwork, the window frames blown away and their glass scattered like chips of ice across the cobbles. Two soldiers were washing the floor of the laneway. Washing it free of the last remnants of Constable Patrick Sinnott. As George watched, one of them said something and the other laughed. How quickly people moved on with things. How quickly people could laugh while water slopped the blood and viscera of another human being about their boots.

George's lip curled and he made straight for the door of G Division's Headquarters. Inside the smell of the explosion was dense in the air. Fireworks and char and burnt pork.

A detective constable was on duty at reception. He was scribbling on a sheaf of paper and his head was lowered, his bald patch gleaming and slick with hair oil. George knew the man.

'Yes?' the detective constable said, without looking up.

'Jesus, Tom,' said George. 'The Fenians are after lobbing a bomb at this building and you don't even look up when somebody comes in.'

'Howya, George,' replied the detective, smiling without any sort of humour. 'I know, I know. But there's a lot of paperwork to get through. I shouldn't even be bloody well here. I should be at home with the missus.'

'So should Patrick Sinnott,' said George.

The detective nodded. 'He would have made a fine G-man. Good eyes. Very good eyes. We were going to draft him out of C Division immediately. Detective Constable Patrick Sinnott.'

He shook his head. 'Poor blighter.'

George leaned forward. 'Look, Tom. I need to speak to whatever Superintendent is in charge of G Division at the moment. It's urgent.'

Tom looked sceptical. 'At the minute you want to see Superintendent Ryan, but I doubt he wants to see you. The army are causing bedlam and the Lord Lieutenant is hounding us to arrest every suspected Republican in the city. There'll be war if we don't keep a lid on things.'

George sighed but persisted. 'I know. I know. But this is important.'

Tom's eyes narrowed. 'Is this about those dead growlers you found up the Monto?'

George tried to hide his distaste at the man's words, failed and went on nevertheless. 'Yes, it is. You lot have to investigate them. I don't think they'll stop. You need to contact Scotland Yard. I think they might be connected to the Whitechapel murders.'

Tom's expression darkened and he said, 'What makes you think that?'

George swallowed and told the frowning detective about the wounds inflicted, the savagery and precision of them, the ability of the murderer to vanish into thin air. He produced a bundle of paper from his pocket. Old photographs of the Whitechapel murders along with those photographs taken of Mary Shortt. He quickly shuffled through them for Tom's benefit.

'Jesus Christ, George,' he said. 'Nobody should be looking at the likes of that. Jesus Christ. Do you want me to show these to the Super as well?'

George nodded and Tom wrote a series of sentences into his notepad and said, 'I'll take this information up to Superintendent Ryan now. Take a seat. I'll be back in a tick.'

George sat in a chair and waited for the detective constable to return. He breathed in the brutalised air and pursed his lips and tried not to read the paperwork that Tom had left open on the desk in front of him. He tried not to think of Rosie sitting in his room on a Christmas evening with only O'Sullivan for company. O'Sullivan who had probably drank himself into a stupor by now. The good doctor had played his hand very close to his chest for years now. But the cards had started to tip lately. The very mention of his wife made him bark like a narky mongrel. Poor bollix. Humiliated in his own home.

A soldier stuck his head in the door leading to the court-yard and said in a cockney accent, 'Ere, where's baldy sloped off to?'

George stared at him. Loyal citizen of the Empire, though he was, George resented these soldiers with their swagger and bluster. Tommies with their foreign accents and alien ways and fumble-footed approach to the city. Tommies who seemed genuinely surprised when they were shot at or knifed in a brawl that sprang from nothing but a comment on the weather. Tommies who knew nothing about Ireland and the history of the place, the old roots that went deep and bitter.

'Well?' said the soldier.

George just stared at him quietly until he grew uncom-fortable and went away.

Eventually, Tom came back. He sat down behind the reception desk and regarded George with genuine sympathy. He didn't say a thing, but every line of his carriage spoke a language flat and unambiguous. A language that spoke to George and told him to go home.

'Fair enough,' said George. 'Let me have it.'

'Look it,' said Tom. 'The boss is after listening to me and to tell you the truth, he thinks we have more important things to deal with at present. We've no time to be wasting on a bogeyman and if there's any connection between the dead whores and the Fenians, we'll find it by catching Sinnott's killer. The Lord Lieutenant is in command here, George. He's directing things as he sees fit. If we don't solve this sharpish and keep it in the realm of the civil authorities, we're looking at martial law in the city. That'd be a disaster. You have to see that, George. We'll come back to the dead whores. I promise.'

George was nodding, but his eyes were directed on Tom's notepad. He had left it open in front of him. The last sentence written in Tom's own hand was underlined and read, *Fob him off*.

Tom noted the direction of George's gaze and hastily snapped the pad closed.

'I'm sorry, George,' he said.

'Not as sorry as some other poor woman is going to be.'

With that, he said goodbye to G Division and went home through the gas-lit streets, past the slogans and the posters, over Carlisle Bridge and past the colossal monument to The Liberator himself. Unveiled in 1882 in front of a cheering mass of the unwashed. It was a balm to their anger, always simmering, as much as a memorial to their dead emancipator. George always felt perfectly insignificant when he passed under that granite plinth with its bronze figures. O'Connell's haughty pose proclaimed George to be a small thing. It clabbered the Protestant blood in him. The arrogance of the empowered underclass. The Catholic as King.

He went home past the bare plane trees and the empty hackney ranks and the shining hotels. The squeals and the roars from the Monto lofted into the quiet night like the clamour from an abattoir. Through the cold night air he moved with the slimy black scraps of last summer's leaves slithering under his boots. His guiding light the woman waiting for him in his rooms. It wasn't a bad star to be following, when all was said and done.

He went home to his Rosie.

★ ★ ★

When he pushed open his door, he saw that O'Sullivan was gone. Dark had entered the room and lurked in every corner and under every piece of furniture. Rosie was asleep in the single armchair, her hair falling across her face and an empty porter bottle on the floor beside her. She was pale and beautiful in the dark like a figure from a fairy story and to George, he supposed, she was.

She woke a little as he lifted her and she moaned in her drowsiness and circled his neck with her thin arms. He kissed her on the cheek and bore her to his bed.

On Stephen's Day morning he woke to a hammering on his door. A voice was shouting, 'Sergeant Frohmell! Sergeant Frohmell!'

'No. No. Noooooo,' groaned Rosie and held him to her under the grey blankets in his grey bedroom in the grey light of the coming day.

'For God's sake,' he said. 'Can they give me no peace?'

He sat up in bed and raked his fingers through his hair and listened to the hammering and the cries from the other room. Rosie placed her hand on his back and said, 'Go, Georgie. You have to go. They need you.'

'I'm so tired,' he said. 'I'm so tired.'

He coughed and sat on the edge of the bed. Then he dragged on his trousers and shirt, tucked his revolver into his waistband and went to open the rattling door.

On the grotty little landing outside a young DMP man was practically hopping from foot to foot.

'Yes?' asked George, already knowing the answer.

'We've found another one, Sergeant. Same as before.'

Same as before, thought George. Same as before and before and before that again, back to the last syllable of recorded time. Murder was in man's nature. No job in the world confirmed that as readily as policing.

'Give me a minute,' he said.

CHAPTER 12:

SUSSEX, SEPTEMBER 1847– DECEMBER 1853

The Work. The Pattern. The second step. The second cut. The first deepest. The first anxious. Every time. Every time no matter. All hidden in the wet and the cold. The catching fog. Ash taste of it in our mouth. The savour of it and the copper tang thereafter. Loathsome in its own deliciousness. Rolling in the mouth. Salt rubber and chewy. All uncooked but warm. And who's this? That noise? Are we seen? Are we scuppered? No. Not here. Never here. The first deepest and finest and the long sigh of it. The second measured. Measured and slow and tender. The tender edge of bright steel. Clean steel. Jars in the darkness. Wet and cold. Filthy woman parts floating in the red dark. Lambs to the slaughter. Filthy lambs. Wolf and sheep and clothing all wet with the cutting with the Work. Quick work and slick work and slop of it after. Quick work and slick work and spick and span work. The red dark and the heavy jars and the fleshy things floating. No blood. Not here. Never here. Hat and gloves and bag. Black and black and black again. The reeking black. The hot black and the cold knife and the practised hand …

See the boy as he grows. Not that he grows far. He would always be a slight boy. Physical hardship always seemed beyond him. Beyond or beneath. It was as though his precise bones were built for something other than the vagaries of rough-and-tumble. His entire being was sharp and clean and dainty, like a scalpel.

When the tutor walked from the cold house, the father was left with no choice but to send the boy away to school. It was either that or watch the boy as he moved silently about the house like some sort of fastidious poltergeist, squaring things away as he went, adjusting the hang of mirrors and prints. The father, uproarious at his daughter's wedding and glorying in the robust ignorance of his eldest son, found it hard to gaze on his youngest. The boy's every movement conjured memories of his dead wife. A wife about whom he thought less and less with every party he attended, every dowager he took to bed and every whore he found pleasure in. Money and advancement was his life now. Money and advancement and the slow clamber of redbrick ever upward and outward and the perpetual churn of steam-driven pistons.

The boy was a nuisance.

In school he was immediately branded a fag and was made to play in goal during football. The older boys took great pleasure in barrelling into him and giving him what for. The school masters were all of the considered opinion that moral fibre was built through physical exertion and so they watched on approvingly as he was buffeted and jostled and trampled on. Day after day after day.

The boy watched them through caged eyes as they stood in their robes like a silent rookery amidst their grey surrounds.

He watched and attained the highest marks in his class in all subjects barring literature. Poetry always let him down.

He returned home at the end of term and gradually became aware of things that made a great skein of anger unbundle within him. His father was become more and more bloated and purple-faced, like his entire being was a blood blister. Dripping roasts and fine wines had spilled his gut over his waistband and he sat in his armchair and scoffed at his son's returnings through loose and blubbery lips. The parties thrown at the manor were become famous throughout the district and the servants spoke in quiet tones about the debauchery they had witnessed.

On his holidays the boy wafted unnoticed through the

corridors and listened to talk of drunkenness and orgies and how his mother would be turning in her grave if she thought this was what her family was reduced to.

The thoughts of other women carousing with his father, other women bedraggled and drunken and wanton, made him sick. The thoughts of whores and women little better than whores twining themselves in his mother's sheets tortured him night and day. He spent his time in the library, arranging and rearranging the books, bitter and angry in that enormous silence.

It was here that he found books that his father and siblings never knew existed. To them the library was simply a room that rich people had. An empty space walled with paper. His father had not read a book in all the years the boy had been on the earth. Nobody in the house had. His father had purchased the library in bulk to flesh out his echoing manor. The books had come from a great estate in the Thames Valley that had been gutted by flame. Some of the books still smelled faintly of burning.

Avoiding the works of the great poets, the boy would pluck books in order, third book from the right, two down, and begin reading, replacing the book if he found nothing of interest. He would vary his pattern from week to week. Creating geometrical shapes from which he would extract knowledge. In doing this at the back of the library, coated in a thin skin of dust, the boy found the novels of Walpole and Shelley, the writings of the Marquis de Sade. In them he found fascination and escape in equal measure. It was here, immersed in sex and death and reanimated corpses, that he found a world that mirrored his own thoughts. He found the old stories of The Black Goat of the Woods. The Rutting Goat of a Thousand Young. The lovely symmetry of the pentagram and all it symbolised. All this he read voraciously. He came to trawl the newspaper columns for reports on murders and executions. The more lurid the better. He was become obsessed and when he went back to school, his bags would bulge with gothic novels and penny dreadfuls.

Christmas of his fourteenth year he arrived home to be greeted on the doorstep by a woman he had never met before. She was slim and clung to his father's side like she was sutured to him. There was a look of trepidation on her face that betrayed her unease at meeting the boy. Somebody had been telling tales about him, it seemed. The peculiar son, come home from school to frighten the servants with his malignant presence.

'This is your new mother,' said his father. His voice even sounded fat, his northern accent blunting the vowels and making *mother* sound like *murder*.

'No she is not,' said the boy and walked past them and into the house.

As he passed, the woman gave a slight yelp and drew away from him and his father's face grew clouded.

'Come back here, boy!' he thundered. 'I'll not have you speak to me or your mother like that!'

But the boy could see thunder was all that was left in the old man. He was grown soft as potter's clay. The boy ignored his blustering and carried his own bags to the library.

His eldest sister, the Duchess, was visiting with her husband. She went to him and found him sitting at a table in the library. Flat and dusty before him was a book, splayed open like a great broken-winged moth. On one page was a drawing of a five-pointed star framing a goat's head.

Without looking up, the boy said, 'What do you want?'

His sister, the Duchess, looked down on her little brother and had he glanced at her he would have seen a copy of his mother's face filled with pity.

'I want you to come sit with us,' she said.

'She's not our mother.'

'I know.'

'I don't like sitting with people.'

'I know.'

'I shan't like her.'

'You don't like anyone.'

She took him by the hand, her odd little brother, and he allowed himself to be led from the library and into the dining room. For the first time in what felt like years he had dinner with his father and three of his eight siblings. But he did not feel happy. He knew he should, but he did not. And looking at the woman who pecked, jerky and sparrowlike, at her food, the woman his father had called his mother, he realised he didn't feel angry either. In fact, he felt very little at all. He was unfeeling as steel. But his thoughts raced and blurred and there was something frenetic in his brain that almost verged on anger, yet was not. Anger, real human anger, was distilled from passion, not the cold of calculus.

That night his father slipped on the stairs and broke his neck. *Fallen in drink* was what everyone said. Nobody asked where the boy was when this happened or how he had gained the head of the stairs so quickly. His new mother wept and tore at her nightdress and wailed. He looked at her and his thoughts followed fast on each other's heels.

Crying and wetfaced and tears all in a flood. Wet on her neck wet on her nightdress. Plastered to her breasts. White breasts in the lamplight all wet and slippery. Slippery steps. Nothing at all to it. Nothing at all.

Below him at the foot of the stairs and standing over the body where it was covered by a sheet and awaiting a doctor, the Duke looked at the boy through narrowed eyes. It would not do to be married into a family of parricides. He would become a laughing stock and pariah overnight. It would not do, at all.

'Such a shame,' the Duke said. 'Drunk, and on such a steep staircase.'

The boy said nothing, but he looked at the Duke and the

I AM IN BLOOD

Duke held his stare for long, long moments.

The next day, as funeral arrangements were being made, the Duchess came into the boy's room.

'Yes?' he said.

She stood for a moment and ran her tongue across her lips. Pink tongue across the furrows of dried lips. She had been crying.

'Alfred, my husband, the Duke. Well, he says we cannot allow you to be placed at a disadvantage because of father's, you know, passing. It would be un–Christian of us. Uncharitable.'

The boy said nothing and looked at her as though she were a curiosity, a foreign animal in a zoo.

'Alfred wishes you to avail of his means to study abroad. To better yourself at some renowned university or college. He says he will provide letters of reference for you.'

'He *wishes*?'

'Indeed he does. It is very gallant of him, little brother. It is an opportunity not one in a thousand English gentlemen have any chance of seizing.'

'And what do you wish, sister?'

Her lips tightened and again her features became a fac-simile of their mother's. This time the boy saw it and his eyes widened slightly. His expression became somehow avid.

His sister sighed and said, 'I feel it for the best, also. You should take this chance.'

'As you wish,' said the boy.

… here and here again. Blood on the street. Blood on the walls. The delicious stink of it. The pork sweet of it tongued around our mouth. Blood on the walls and in the air and then the whistles after. Mindless in the dark and under the gaslights. Mindless as animals. All wedged into pens. All panting in the night. Sweating in the dark. Whistles. More and more. Squealing out in the long night. Hiss of artery. Squeal of breath cut off. Pigs. Trotters. Bog. Irish. No one sees and no one cares. A beaten people. City full of blank walls. Eyeless and uncaring. Faces brick blank and hard. Rough and toothless. And none of their business. Mine. Behind glass. Locked. Filthy woman parts all pale and suspended. Jellyfish hanging in the deep. The taste and smell and the thrust of it. The razor thrust and the averted eyes and the blinkered eyes and the downcast eyes. Servile. The tugged forelock and the tipped cap. Bred to be slaughtered. Slaughterhouse born. Animals bleating. Sheep. Lambs. No one wants to see. The quick work and the short drag. Round the corner and the dark fills the spaces and the rain and the white skin.

The Pattern is all.

CHAPTER 13:

DUBLIN, DECEMBER 2015

Nathan waited for Esther. He'd gladly spend his life waiting for her if only she'd come. Come and stay. Her clothes flung together so that she looked like what Hollywood and shit novels told people vampires looked like. Her face pale and full of emotion and humour. Full of all the stuff that made her the opposite of what she constructed herself to be. Full of hippy-dippy sappy PETA bollocks. Threaded beads and friendship bracelets and every glance sparked something hot and urgent in Nathan's abdomen. He'd do anything for her. Waiting for her in his room at half-four on Christmas Eve afternoon was a piece of cake.

On his bed he had spread a print-out from Google Maps.

On it he had marked the location where each one of the Monto murders had occurred. Or at least where the bodies had been found. Some of the street names had changed over the years. Dead British Prime Ministers and Lords Lieutenant and Under Secretaries and war heroes and philanthropists replaced by dead Irish rebels and freedom-fighters and war heroes and philanthropists. A last kick in the retreating Imperialist arse.

The British had left quite a city. They left it in quite a hurry. And then the Corpo had wrecked the place.

Nathan had looked up what happened to the Monto. It turned out that in the 1920s the Legion of Mary had worked as only the righteous can work and brought the whole show to a grinding halt. No more brothels. No more safe houses. No more IRA Flying Columns. Nothing. Only heroin and petty crime and thievery and shoplifting and casual racism. What an improvement.

Nathan opened the little notepad he had been scribbling in until four o'clock in the morning. In it, he had sketched out characters and events, plot twists and dramatic scenes. In it he had shackled together the skeleton of a story. And the hero, the beating heart of this story? Why, none other than George Frohmell.

Frohmell the outsider.

Frohmell the lovelorn.

Frohmell himself.

Nathan would deny it. If Esther asked he would, hand on heart, say that George Frohmell was taken exactly as he was portrayed in the history. That *The Monto Murders* had outlined a person that Nathan was only bringing to life. He would explain all this to Esther and it would all be a lie. Nathan saw George Frohmell as he saw himself. His name was only the first link.

His name.

He must be related to him. To this policeman from a different century. He must be. Nowhere had he come across that name before. His mother, his real–life–honest–to–God mother, had left him that and only that. Before his Da had rescued him and brought him to live with Samantha. Before his life had really begun, he was a Frohmell. His mother. His mother whom he had never known. His mother whom he had first heard of when a guard called to the door.

This guard with his great heavy face, his great heavy hands, his great heavy accent flat as midlands bog, this guard came into the kitchen and the whole family sat down. Nathan was young but James was younger and Nathan could remember the fear and fascination on James' little face as he took in the guard's stab-vest, his hat, the black block of his radio.

Nathan remembered the guard saying, 'Are you sure?'

It was Samantha who answered, 'Yes. He should hear. He deserves to hear.'

And then the guard said, 'Patricia Frohmell has died.

Heroin overdose. She said to forward her belongings to you. She gave your name as next-of-kin. She knew this address. I think maybe you should explain things. Just to clear them up.'

Who the guard was talking to, Nathan didn't know and he was confused and frightened. Nathan was too young to understand, but he remembered his Da's hands going to his face.

Then the explanations came.

He was adopted. Samantha wasn't his Ma. His Ma was dead.

Every day since that day he had looked at the world differently. He had tried to find his place in it. Tried to find out who and what he was. And now, he thought, he might actually have succeeded. He was a Frohmell. A Frohmell formerly of the DMP. The knowledge of it was like a dove in his chest.

He took a pen out of his pocket and started to jot some ideas into his notepad. He had to go chapter by chapter. Stephen King said that the best advice he could give to anyone trying to write a book was just to get the damn thing finished. Word after word after word. It didn't matter if they were good words. It was the momentum that counted. So he wrote and in his head cycled every crime scene photo he had ever seen. The blood like black paint. The limbs like marble statues. The shadows thrown by the flash all hard and brittle and depthless. Unfathomable as the act of murder itself. The doilies made from flayed skin. The head bubbling in the pot. All these crept into his writing and he just kept going.

Kept going.

Kept going and waiting.

Kept filling each empty minute with descriptions and drama and blood like black paint.

Esther didn't ring the doorbell. Instead, she texted from the doorstep. *I'm outside.*

Nathan planted a fullstop at the end of the passage he was writing and went downstairs. Samantha and James were in the kitchen, having something to eat and talking. About him, probably. As Nathan padded across the too-thick carpet he thought to himself, what to get Nathan for Christmas? Nathan Jacob, the boy who has everything. What could he possibly want?

A Da. A life that wasn't lived alone in his room.

He eased open the door and Esther smiled at him and gave him a little hyperactive wave. Before she could say anything, Nathan put his finger to his lips and motioned her inside. She followed him up the stairs and into his room. Both of them soundless as shadows in the muffling beige of the house.

He closed the door behind them and watched Esther's back as she looked at the map spread on his bed, Sellotape like snail trails holding the different sections together. Her hair fell from beneath her woolly hat and lay against her shoulder blades.

Night falling.

'Wow,' she said. 'This is a lot of work.'

He came around to sit on the bed and patted it so that she sat beside him. They both looked at the map. Esther with polite, academic curiosity, Nathan with something avid in his face.

'This is where they happened,' he said. 'I've marked where the murders happened.'

'The Monto murders?'

'Yep. I'm writing the story of them. I can't believe people don't know about them.'

Esther frowned at him and then looked at the map. She used her index finger to trace the curvature and intersections of the streets. The red dots where Nathan had labelled the victims. The geometry of slaughter under her black-painted nail.

'This was the Monto?' she asked.

Nathan nodded and with his hand traced the streets as he mentioned them.

'It was the biggest redlight district in Europe. It lay between Talbot Street, Amiens Street, Gardiner Street and Seán McDermott Street. Seán McDermott Street used to be called Gloucester Street. You want to hear some of the nicknames the people gave to the alleys? The Furry Glen. Goat Lane.'

His hand brushed against hers. A vinegar tingle.

'What do you think?'

Esther was looking at the map now with real interest.

'This is class, Nato,' she said.

'I think it's deadly. Nobody's ever written a story about this at all. It was all hushed up and forgotten.'

'Why?'

'Nobody knows.'

'Cool.'

Esther licked her lips and let her finger hover over each little red dot in turn. Nathan saw her fingertip tremble. It was as though the fact that each of those red flecks was a life extinguished made her reluctant to touch them. Reluctant or thrilled, Nathan couldn't guess.

'He killed five,' she said. 'Five.'

Nathan nodded.

'But there's only four in the Monto,' she said.

'Yeah. There was a body found in Earl Place. It was connected to the Monto murders. Same MO, I think.'

'*MO?*' she said, smiling that not-quite-a-smile smile.

'Don't take the piss. This is serious.'

Esther laughed. 'Of course it's serious. Five dead women is pretty fucking serious.'

Nathan looked at her then and he saw how beautiful she was in the cold light. He saw her sitting on his bed with her every breath lifting her breasts and his bedclothes rumpled beneath her.

'What?' she said.

Nathan felt his hands twitch with a strange anticipation.

Something alien coursed through him. Something burrowed into his brain and made a nest for itself there.

'What?' she said again.

'Do you—,' he began.

He stopped and she smiled and he began again on a different heading.

'Have you heard from Andrew Callahan, since?'

'Oh, yeah. He rang me a couple of times. He said the writing group couldn't work without me.'

'I believe him,' said Nathan.

She quietened then and muttered, 'The girls have been pretty nasty on Facebook, though. They're saying Andrew and I are an item. That we used to shag each other in his room when everyone else was downstairs.'

'Lies,' said Nathan, flat and hard as slate.

Was it? Was it lies? It had to be. Christ, it had to be.

Esther was staring at her hands now, curled in her lap.

'Thanks,' she said.

'For what?'

'For being a friend.'

A friend. So much more. So, so much more.

Feeling suddenly awkward, he said, 'What I was going to ask you is if you wanted to come into town with me. I could do with some company.'

'What?' she said.

Again and again and again.

Nathan stuttered, 'After Christmas, I mean. I'm going to take a walk around and see where these things happened. It'll be like those books I read but for real this time. Real life. Real life. So I can write about it.'

'Are you serious? You want us to walk around that part of Dublin? Two little rich kids from D4 with a notepad and pen?'

'And a camera,' he said. 'We'll need to take some pictures.'

She was quiet and then her fingernail darted to each red dot in turn. Dates and times and names. Each murder, one after the other.

'Defo,' she said. 'This is deadly.'

When she left, Nathan carefully folded up his map and stowed it away in his schoolbag. Along with it he put a packet of assorted pens, some Sellotape and *The Monto Murders*. He looked down at it. The bag lay open before him like something whose belly had been opened up. He zipped it closed. The locked teeth of the zipper grinned at him. Stitched. Sutured.

Nathan lay on his bed for a few minutes with his notepad and pen and tried to think of a title for his story. Something evocative, he thought. Maybe a quote from one of the poets he did in English. He lay for a few minutes.

Like a patient etherized upon a table.

Then he got up and went in to the bathroom.

It was when washing his hands that he began to think about Esther. About how she sat smiling at him. About her breasts lifting and falling and the brush of his hand against hers. The lack of resistance. The tremble of her lips. Maybe? The slight movement maybe toward him. The smile. The maybe promise in it.

The main bathroom was at the top of the stairs. It was floored in a kind of variegated tile. A red turning to orange colour. Like blood running into pus. It covered the floor in a smouldering flood.

Nathan needed to masturbate. If he didn't, he was going to explode.

Esther's face, her breasts, her pink segment of tongue pushed him on. He'd never before wanted to take his dick in his hand so much. Not even with Kelly Brook smiling at him from his wall. Kelly Brook with just the right amount of cleavage showing. He'd never before wanted to spend himself so pointlessly. It ached.

The burning tiles flowed underneath him like a lick of magma and his abdomen churned like a ball of something else hot and liquid. Nathan slammed the pine lid of the toilet down and panted into the pine fresh air and fumbled with his button fly. His hard-on was putting pressure on the buttons and even his lust-drunk fingers hadn't a problem getting it out. Then he hesitated. Then he licked his lips like she licked her lips and then he began with his hand.

And God, you could grow to love it. I am loving this loving her loving this. Oblivious.

The fake pine in the air rasped through the rough sieve of his teeth and he was deliriously, unbearably oblivious.

Suddenly his fist was gloriously wet and he was shuddering. His breath was a staccato, syncopated arrhythmia. His whole body was a heart murmur.

The main bathroom was at the head of the stairs and the toilet door was all anyone could see as they went up, step by downy step. It was one of those solid 1950s ones. No veneer, no hollow space at its centre. Just a block of wood on hinges covered in a layer of paint that looked inches thick. Nathan felt himself spill across his knuckles and stared at this door, dull-eyed as an addict. And then, in the middle of this, there came a light knock on the bathroom door. The runnels of paint glistened in the light and Nathan doubled over the wilting stalk of his erection as if the knocker could actually see him or something.

The knock came again and Nathan said, 'Just a minute.'

All the while he was thinking how stupid he was. How stupid he was to be sitting there, the seat of his jeans clammy with sweat and his fist sopping with spunk. He just knew that when he got up, condensation would leave the outline of his ass on the pine of the toilet lid.

He thought all this but what he said was, 'Just a minute.'

He turned around and around, looking for the toilet tissue. It wasn't where it should be. The toilet roll doohickey was sleeved in a grey tube of cardboard. Two tatters of white clung to it uselessly. The rest of it was bare. Nathan tried to stand up, to get his now sponge-soft dick back into his jeans and to not get spunk all over himself or the bathroom. He was also trying to find the toilet tissue.

The knock came again and James' voice came with it, 'Whatcha doin' in there?' The words came in a mass. Like he was taking the piss. Like he knew exactly what Nathan was doing. Nathan, however, couldn't say anything. His throat was closing up.

Panic tends to do that to you.

He coughed and said, 'I'm not doing anything. Just a minute.'

And there was the toilet tissue. A full roll of it sitting plumply on the rim of the bath, half hidden by the plastic shower curtain. The shower curtain had small yellow ducks and sailboats on it.

Nathan's hand was starting to drip stuff onto the tiled floor and he began unwinding reams of plush toilet paper to soak up the rest of the mess. God, this was embarrassing.

And then James asked, 'What *are* you doing?'

Then he laughed, joking around like when they were little. As though the intervening years had not happened. And laughing he said, 'Are you wanking or something?'

Nathan almost shouted, 'Jesus no! I don't do that!'

Then he thought, why did I say that? Why didn't I just laugh or something? Now he thinks I'm wanking. I was wanking, but that's not the point.

Nathan opened the door and James stood there swaying a bit like a mast in a high wind. His eyes were half-lidded. If his soul had windows, the shades were heavy with suspicion. If he had a soul. Had anyone? Nathan's hands were wiped and his erection was stowed away. But it wasn't an erection anymore. It was something soft and yielding. Something pathetically boneless and hidden behind the button fly of his best jeans. His best jeans. The jeans he wore to impress Esther.

One cuff of his hoodie was suspiciously damp and he was horribly aware of it.

Behind James, Samantha was coming to the top of the stairs. Her eyes had that vague thousand-yard stare quality that only the pretty drunk or pretty medicated get. At half-five in the afternoon. She disgusted him. Nathan felt that he should take a step backwards because her vision seemed to want to laser its way out the back of his skull. Samantha reached the top of the stairs and stood there stupidly, her hand on James' shoulder.

Nathan looked at them both.

'I couldn't find the toilet roll,' was all he could say.

Then he went back to his room.

CHAPTER 14:

DUBLIN, JANUARY 1893

January 6 1893. Little Christmas. The day when the Three Wise Men arrived at the cowshed wherein the little God child rested. We Three Kings from Orient Are. Bearing gifts and pledges and obeisance. George wondered what the little lad must have made of it. What Mary must have made of it. Her, with the baby gumming at her peasant breast while these great and powerful folk dropped to their knees before her and before the little scrap of humanity that broke from her wet and mewling, like a million other babies from a million other mothers. What made her boy so special? What had he done to deserve those lavish gifts that sat amongst the straw and were snuffled at by cattle? The gold. The frankincense. The myrrh.

What had she done?

And what, George thought, had he done to deserve his Christmas gifts?

The blood. The corpses. The fear.

What had any of them done?

Two days before, the fourth day of January, was the nadir of things so far. The events of that day had made him a figure of fun, of derision. A Guy to be sneered at and a man on fire.

With Rosie taking to domestic bliss much more readily than she had let on, George had found it easier to think, easier to see straight. Three dead bodies and no suspects. But for the last three weeks George had read and re-read the files on every single violent criminal in the city. He had even taken to bringing them home until Rosie, rightfully so, put her foot down. So he stayed behind after his shift ended instead.

He stared at the photographs of the victims. Both here in Dublin and across in London.

He stared at their faces. He tried to read their wounds as a shaman reads entrails.

He knew them like he knew his own serial number.

And on the dawn of the New Year he found his man.

A man returned from England, it seemed. At least *The Freeman's Journal* was right about that. A labourer named Mulvey. He had served time for battery in Manchester and had been locked away in Brixton for the rape and assault of two women. He suffered from syphilis contracted, by his own admission, from frequenting brothels and places of low regard. Tellingly, he had worked as a surgeon's mate aboard the HMS *Dauntless* before being discharged.

He had found Mulvey completely by accident.

George was walking the Monto one evening, talking to any prostitute who did not run from his uniform. As he had done now for a month, day after day after day. The place was busy after Christmas, its grotty recesses filled by men forced to spend more time than was palatable with their families during the Season of Good Will. The place was an ecstasy of pent-up frustration released.

George walked its streets with a perpetual scowl.

How could Rosie exist in such a place?

He had turned the south-east corner of the Gloucester Diamond when two ragged-looking whores accosted him.

'Here, mister!' one of them cried. 'Look what's been done to Maureen!'

The other stood in front of him. Her lips were split and her eye was swelling, a cobalt bruise darkening the socket. She tugged at the bodice of her dress and revealed a long, shallow cut rising from her breast bone and ending under her left ear.

'Look!' screeched Maureen, her voice splintered as a gull's. 'The bastard took a knife to me!'

George listened to the pair, striving to jot down their story without his hands shaking too much. A man named Patrick

Mulvey, well known to the first whore in her youth, had recently returned from jail in England. He was a dangerous man, half-crazed at the best of times, a rabid animal at the worst. He tried to force himself on Maureen without paying and when she resisted, threatened to cut her belly open and do whatever he wanted then.

After her ordeal Maureen had gone to her friend, who identified the man immediately.

'He has a twisted lip and a scar,' said Maureen. 'Bridey here says he got hit by one of your lot when he was a young fella. She says he's done this before but he fecked off to Manchester before you useless shower of bollixes could send him down.'

George nodded and scribbled and tried not to let his excitement cloud his better judgement.

When he had enough information he hurried back to Kevin Street and hauled out as much information as he could about Patrick Mulvey. What he found made his heart jig.

The man had been arrested a dozen times for violence, particularly toward women. When he was sixteen he had served a six-month stretch for battering a barmaid half to death. He had been charged with rape at knife-point, but had absconded before he could be brought before a judge.

And now he was back.

George had used the Castle telegram to send a message to the police at Manchester. The next day he received a telegram headed *Extremely Dangerous*, detailing all the activities of the heinous business Mr Mulvey had conducted across the Irish Sea.

George's excitement built with every word he read and he took the telegram and the whores' testimony and went to seek a warrant for the arrest of Patrick Mulvey.

Dublin was a small city and when they found him it was in a tenement just off Smithfield. George had the place surrounded as best he could with ten DMP constables and he and four others burst through the open door and into the building. The door bounced on its hinges and flung open with a sound like tearing stitches. Immediately, George was through it and blinked. Before him, huddled in the hallway was a family, the father holding a Bible before him like a shield.

Someone must have tipped Mulvey off for when George hammered into the ground-floor hall and stood blinking at the frightened family, Mulvey was already on the stairs. Policeman and criminal stared at each other for a moment and then Mulvey fled back up to the first landing. George and the other constables raced after him.

The stairs gave on to a short stretch of wooden hallway leading to a flaking doorway, once red, now a dull and scabrous madder. Glancing at the other constables, George gestured for quiet and sidled up to the door.

George reached for the handle, gentle as falling snow.

The splintering crash of a pistol ball as it punched through the wood not four inches from his head made George yelp and fling himself in abject shock against the wall behind him.

One of George's constables moved quickly and raised his boot, smashing it into the door's panelling just beside the handle. The door whipped away from him with such force that it rebounded and almost flattened him as the DMP men stormed through.

The room was once a grand nursery, the wallpaper peeling from the streaming walls was once soothing, the colours cream and white, now dappled with fungus. Against the room's only window Mulvey stood in silhouette. He held an old-fashioned muzzle-loading pistol and he froze with the ramrod motionless in one hand, the other petrified even as he clawed in his pocket. The entire room stank of gunsmoke.

The DMP men were on him before he could move.

Under questioning and through lips mangled and swollen, Mulvey informed George and another officer of the date he had arrived back in Ireland. The ticket stub of his voyage was found crumpled and soiled in his coat pocket.

He had come back the day after Mary Shortt was killed. A day too late.

George felt his whole being ready to unspool and drift loose.

'Don't be melancholy, Sergeant,' said his Inspector. 'You

have removed from the streets a dangerous recidivist. He'll do a stretch in Mountjoy for taking a knife to that whore at any rate.'

George looked at him and said, 'What jury will convict on the testimony of a whore?'

He had walked away then, but the story of Station Sergeant George Frohmell's crusade on behalf of the whores of Ireland was starting to become a barrack-room joke. The tale of the shock he received when the pistol ball came through that door seemed to have entered every ear in Dublin in the space of twenty-four hours and with every ear it entered it grew in hilarity.

He was exhausted. Utterly exhausted. Walking the streets was tiring. Grasping at straws was a killing thing.

Now, two days later, it was afternoon and he sat in the lamplight in Dr O'Sullivan's library and stared at a decanter of brandy resting on a side-table. O'Sullivan was talking, but George wasn't really paying any heed to his words. His entire focus was on that hollow lump of engraved crystal and the hot caramel of its contents. The tic in his hands had spread to his face and he could feel the lid of his right eye twitch. Like the flutter of a moth.

It had been nearly three weeks now since he had taken a drink.

'Oh, just take a drop,' said O'Sullivan.

George roused himself and said, 'No. No, I won't.'

The doctor leaned forward out of his own armchair and tossed a newspaper to George.

'You're in the news, again,' he said. 'The darling of the press.'

The headline read, *No Progress in Monto Monster Hunt.* Under it, in the usual cramped type, the article excoriated the DMP and one Station Sergeant George Frohmell, A Division, in particular for making no arrests and having no apparent suspects in the cases of the three murdered women. Mary Shortt. Alice O'Keefe. Betty Quinn. The last of these had been pregnant when she was killed. She had only told a few close acquaintances and George had made sure this detail wasn't released to the press. The killer had taken her womb, baby and all. George was sickened by it. Physically sickened. His hands had started to twitch after that. Like his very nerves were squirming.

The investigation, what little of it there was, had hit a brick wall and the blame was being squarely levelled at him.

'It says you're the Chief Investigating Officer. Did you read that part? You're being hung out to dry, old boy.'

George folded the newspaper and placed it on the table in front of him beside a cup of tepid tea that was growing colder by the minute.

'I'm not even an officer,' he grunted. 'I'm a poxy Sergeant. No wonder G Division wouldn't touch this with a ten-foot barge pole.'

O'Sullivan was nodding sagely and swirling his dram of brandy about in its heavy glass. Its expense could be seen in the way it clung to the inside of the glass like a film of oil.

'He's been quiet now for nigh on two weeks,' he said.

George's jaw clenched and he shook his head. 'He hasn't gone away. I've read enough to know that. He hasn't gone away and he won't ever stop until he's at the end of a rope.'

'The killings in London stopped.'

'They stopped in London. They started here. God alone knows where he went in between. Or where he was before London. Nobody, not Lucifer himself, begins killing as this animal did in Whitechapel. He learned his trade somewhere else and he's perfecting it as he goes.'

O'Sullivan sipped his brandy and said, 'Perhaps this affair with the Fenians has stymied him somewhat. Every safe house and den of iniquity is being raided and raided again. The Lord Lieutenant's blood is up. If They Who Must be Obeyed up in the Phoenix Park think it appropriate to their needs, they'll have the whole city flattened at the drop of a hat. They'd burn the Monto to the ground and have gunboats on the Liffey if they thought it might preserve their positions.'

'He may have gone to ground. He may very well have gone to ground. But he will come out. After Betty Quinn, I can't see him resting on his laurels.'

'I'd really rather not contemplate that, at all, George. Really.'

George remembered how the doctor's voice had stuttered and failed as he had described how Betty Quinn had died. How she had been defiled as she was cut. How the killer had had his way with her even as his blade opened her throat. Had his way with her and left his putrid seed to rot inside her. How her entire womb had been excised and taken.

He remembered the doughy colour of O'Sullivan's face, the disgust and disbelief in his eyes.

'I understand,' said George.

'How's Rosie?' asked the doctor.

'How's your wife?' came the retort.

'Oh, don't be so defensive.'

'She's grand. She has decided that living in sin with a bleedin' peeler is no worse a sin than living in such disgusting digs as she lived in before.'

'Capital!' said O'Sullivan and raised his glass.

'She's a pain in the arse, though, Oliver. She never stops moving things around the place and she's forever getting on to me about the hours I'm putting in. I had some old photographs of the Whitechapel murders on the table that I was looking over. She threw them on the bleedin' floor.'

'She's perfectly correct, George. Those photographs are ghoulish things. Besides, you've been burning the candle at both ends and in the middle for too long now. And what, may I ask, about *her* … how can I phrase this delicately … hours?'

'She's stopped,' George said with the first broad smile that had cracked across his features in what seemed like days. 'She says it's only temporary until we catch this inhuman monster, but I'm sure she'll see sense.'

'She'll have you married, yet. You'll have to turn Papist, you do realise? The lower sort make a point of not taking the soup.'

'I'd wrestle the devil himself for Rosie Lawlor, Oliver. Really and truly and not a word of a lie.'

Dr O'Sullivan refilled his glass and lifted it, declaring, 'To the charming Rosie Lawlor and to traitors to their religion!'

George laughed and took a quick sip of his cold tea. He would never get used to this.

O'Sullivan stilled then and an embarrassment came over him. He swirled the brandy in its glass and said, 'I should really apologise for my behaviour on Christmas Day. Calling over uninvited. Barging in. Disrupting things with my drunken prattling. You know.'

George nodded. 'There's no need to apologise.'

'Oh there, is. I made a fool of myself and discommoded you and your lady friend most abominably. I also said things, alas, that should best remain private.'

'If you did, I didn't hear them,' said George.

'You're a decent man, Sergeant.'

George tried to keep the note of sympathy from his voice. He felt the doctor neither wanted nor needed it.

'You told me before that the heart was a benign tyrant. We can't help who we love.'

'I'm a fool,' said O'Sullivan. 'Don't be listening to me.'

There was a polite knock on the library door.

'Come!' called O'Sullivan.

The door opened and O'Sullivan's butler stood on the threshold, looking like a pallbearer in his black suit and with his solemn expression. He cleared his throat and intoned, 'There's a policeman at the door, Sir. He's looking for Station Sergeant Frohmell. He says his business is urgent and he craves admittance. Shall I let him in, Sir?'

George and O'Sullivan exchanged glances.

'Send him up,' said George.

This was pointedly ignored by the butler, who continued to look straight ahead as though George didn't even exist.

'For God's sake, let him in, man,' said O'Sullivan.

'I shall have him use the tradesman's entrance,' said the butler and was gone.

'Well, well, well,' said O'Sullivan. 'What new surprises have we here?'

George said nothing but got to his feet and began pacing the library's floorboards.

A few moments later a DMP constable was admitted into the library, helmet under one arm and a sour expression on his face. He threw the butler a withering look as the man closed the door behind him.

He saluted and said, 'Sergeant Frohmell. I've been trying to find you all day. Your … your lady friend said that you might be here. I'm sorry if I'm interrupting anything.'

From his armchair O'Sullivan proclaimed, 'Not at all. Not at all, my good man. Have a seat.'

'No, thank you,' said the constable. 'I'd rather stand. If I sit down, I'll never get up.'

George stood with his right forearm braced against a book-shelf, a volume of anatomy at his elbow. When the butler said the word *urgent* a nasty hectic feeling had capered through him. He felt dizzy. Tiredness and adrenaline and the events of the last few days, all at war within him. He stood leaning on the bookshelves hoping there wasn't a fourth body, hoping that the constable and the doctor would not think less of him if he collapsed where he stood.

He licked his lips and pronounced carefully, 'The doctor's man said your business was urgent, Constable. What is it?'

'A letter arrived this morning at the station house, Sergeant. It was addressed to you.'

George frowned. 'Why should that be a matter for urgency?'

The constable looked uncomfortable and his hand went up and smoothed his moustache. He coughed and said, 'It's the envelope, Sir. It caused some alarm.'

'Out with it, man,' said George.

'It seems to be sealed with blood, Sir. I have it here.'

'Holy Saint Patrick,' muttered O'Sullivan. He drained his glass of brandy and got to his feet.

The constable had reached into his jacket pocket and was now standing with a rectangular envelope in his hand. He proffered it to George. George took it and turned it over in his hands, his eyes scanning the paper, the address, the postage stamp. It was still sealed. He lifted it to his face and scrutinised the envelope's flap. It was undeniably gummed down with a liquid that had dried into a sort of sepia crust. He sniffed it and then picked at it with one thumbnail. The stuff flaked away in a filthy little scree.

To George, it looked very definitely like dried blood.

So, whose blood was it?

O'Sullivan came to his shoulder and said, 'May I?'

George handed him the envelope, which he brought over to the window, and in the colourless January light he began to examine the crusted seal avidly.

George turned to the constable.

'What's your name, man?' he asked.

'Constable Albert Doyle, Sir. DMP 2765.'

'Well, Doyle. Have you or anyone else tampered or interfered with this letter in any way before bringing it here?'

'No, Sergeant.'

'Was it delivered to you?'

'Yes, Sergeant. I was on desk duty in the station house when it arrived.'

'It was delivered by post, not in person?'

'Yes, Sergeant. The usual postman. Known him for six months now, Sir. I was sorting through the mail when I noticed how the envelope was sealed, Sir.'

'What did you do then?'

'I showed it to the Superintendent, Sergeant.'

'What did he say?'

'He said not to open it and to bring it directly to you, Sergeant.'

Hung out to dry. Twisting in the wind.

'Thank you, Doyle,' said George. 'You can go now.'

The constable saluted, spun on his heel in a perfect about-turn and left George and Doctor O'Sullivan alone in the library.

George felt the giddiness in him swell up and his stomach crawled. He had never experienced this before but he was abruptly aware, fully aware, of his guts, his bowels, their palpitations and their workings. He felt like he was going to be sick. He had heard old soldiers describe the trembling and the illness that attended those who had been shelled unmercifully. The twitching nausea of those subjected to shock after shock. He felt he could now understand what they meant.

He approached Dr O'Sullivan, who was engrossed in his study of the envelope.

'Well?' asked George.

'It's definitely dried blood,' said O'Sullivan. 'Dried blood or some other bodily excreta. If I were to put money on it, though, I'd say blood.'

George looked at his thumb, where a burgundy grit had gathered beneath the nail. His lip curled in distaste.

'Indeed,' said O'Sullivan. 'There's a very good chance you have someone's blood beneath your thumbnail. And who else would seal a letter with blood if not your murderous monster? His or one of his victim's blood is what he used. The absolute fiend.'

On the envelope's front, a jagged hand had written simply, *Sergeant George Frohmell, Kevin Street Barracks*. The address was not even fully formed, merely details thrown down in the sure knowledge that it would end up in his hands. But it was his name leaping up at him from that plain paper that frightened George in a manner that he was wholly unprepared for. His name in that alien, killing hand.

'He's tried to disguise his writing,' said O'Sullivan. 'He's clever enough.'

George's mouth had dried out and felt for all the world as though it had been coated with ash. He coughed, tried to speak and coughed again.

'Are you feeling well?' asked O'Sullivan.

'Grand,' croaked George. 'Grand.'

'What do you wish to do with this?'

'What else can we do?' said George. 'Let's open the damned thing.'

O'Sullivan dragged a small reading table over to the window and took a silver letter-opener from a drawer. Outside, The Green was lifeless behind its railings. Its trees were bare and twiggy in the cold and the grey sky cast all in washed-out shades, drained and pastel save for the gnarly black of branch and briar, twig and trunk. On the street, cab horses steamed and stamped and champed under the whips of their masters. The rain, at least, had stopped.

George and O'Sullivan looked down at the envelope on the tabletop, George with his hands on his hips and his tongue running along his lower lip. O'Sullivan with the letter-opener poised like a scalpel. Both men looking like surgeons about to perform a delicate and taxing procedure.

'Are you sure?' said O'Sullivan.

'Work away, Doctor,' said George.

'Then, lay on I shall.'

He deftly ran the letter-opener's blade along the crusted seal. It splintered and shattered into hard little crumbs as the blade did its work. Then the doctor set down the letter-opener and reached into the envelope and extracted a letter held between index and middle fingers.

'This, I believe, is for you,' he said, handing it to George.

George took it with shivering hands and splayed it open on the table in the bleak light. In the same jagged hand someone had written:

I AM IN BLOOD

Dear Sergeant Frohmell,

I have sealed this letter with my owne blud so that you know I am to be taken at my word. I am here and youe are here. Youe are looking for me. But youe will not find me. Youe are like the English bobees. The bobees with their blind groping in the dark. They cudn't find me and neither will you. Scotland Yard cudn't find me. Nobodee can ever find me and none ever will. I am not of this earth. I am above it all. The Work and The Pattern is what I live for. Youe have no pattern. Youe or the other bobees. Youe live by rules you do not understand and youe allow filthy whores to live by noe rules at all at all. Why do you care? I won't stop. I won't ever stop until I show youe The Pattern. The Great Goat with a Thousand Young. The rutting goat. When I showe youe youe will understand. I am watching youe Sergeant Georgie. Youe and yours. As youe watch me. But youe will not see me. And youe will not catch me in my work. I ate of their flesh. They are part of me now. Part of The Work and The Pattern.

Cheerio,
John Bull

'John Bull,' George hissed. 'The bastard has taken a name for himself. *We've* given him a blasted name for himself.'

But there was something else. Something in that letter lanced a spike of ice into George's abdomen. Something he couldn't put his finger on. Some phrase.

Before he could really set a shape on his fears, O'Sullivan

picked up the page and was now looking at it curiously. Reading and re-reading it, his finger tracing the lines as he went.

'You know,' he said eventually. 'This fellow is not as uneducated as he is trying to appear.'

George nodded and said, 'Happens all the bloody time. Especially with ransom notes or threatening letters and the like. Most of the time they cut up newspapers and paste the letters onto a page. Sometimes if they like to play games, if they think they're smarter than you are, they do this. Arrogant bastard.'

O'Sullivan was pointing to the page. 'See how the grammar is garbled but it is punctuated so that the sense communicates itself perfectly? There are deliberate spelling errors but none that makes the words illegible. And that phrase, *blind groping in the dark.* That's too artful to spring from an uncultured pen.'

'Arrogant bastard,' said George again. 'He's monkeying around with us. I'll see him swing, I swear it. He admits to eating them, for God's sake. He gloats about it and throws it in our faces. If it's the last thing I do, Oliver, I'll see him dead and buried. Put down like a dog.'

O'Sullivan was a study in academic detachment. He wasn't even listening to George and the sergeant's anger seemed to him a far distant thing, like the glimmer of a star.

'This phrase here seems cryptic, but is of some obvious import to him,' he said. '*The Work and The Pattern.* And also, *Goat with a Thousand Young.* I am at a loss to explain it, George.'

George was frowning now. In his head, half-forgotten stories were coalescing into something almost coherent, something almost substantial that slipped away whenever he tried to grip it.

'What is it?' asked O'Sullivan. 'What are your dratted peeler's eyes seeing?'

'Goats,' said George, his finger jabbing the page in front of him. 'Cloven hooves and horns.'

O'Sullivan was looking at him as though he were speaking in tongues.

'The old stories,' George continued. 'The ones about the stranger sitting down to play cards. Someone drops a card, looks under the table and the stranger has goat's hooves instead of feet. The goat, Oliver. The bleedin' goat.'

O'Sullivan was staring at him, confused and shaking his head slightly.

'What are you talking about, George? What goat?'

George was almost frantic now. Blocks were shifting in his skull and images linked to tales and half-heard stories and all the old traditions came blazing into full consciousness. His Irishness to the fore. This Popish country with its supernatural follies and its history deep as bog holes. Its keening history full of sadness and ghosts. This place that was a contradiction in terms sang now in his blood and in his brain.

He snatched up the letter and brandished it like a warrant.

'The Hellfire Club,' he said. 'Devils and Satanic hocus-pocus and all that. Guff, but dangerous guff if you believe in it. The Pattern, Oliver. That's why he keeps repeating it. The Sign of the Beast. The Sign of the Beast.'

'You're smiling, George,' said O'Sullivan. 'You have that blasted wolf's smile on your face again. Why?'

'He's slipped up, Oliver. The arrogant little bollix has slipped up.'

'How?'

George's smile widened and there were fangs in it.

'Get me a map,' he said. 'Get me a map and I'll show you.'

And still something pulsed unease through him. He was missing something. He was sure of it.

CHAPTER 15:

WURZBURG, MICHAELMAS TERM 1855

The Work. The Pattern. In all the dark and all the rain. Member stiff and standing. To attention. No bobbies. No soldiers. No attention. The parts in the jar. Quick as a wink. Need washing. Blood from the hands. Out out damn spot. Fool. Relish it and hold it and hands slicked with sinning. Oh the power. The Godhand of it all. Altars of sacrifice. Butchers' slabs of fleshflecks and redwet and womanoffal. Filth. The hard crotch and the quick knife. The short drag. Everything just so. The Work. The Pattern. Brand this place. The Mark of Cain. The Work. The Pattern. Harmony from chaos. The Goat with a Thousand Young. Its horned head and its long muzzle and the brand of it on this place. This place as the other places. Goat stink of rutting and grunting in the red dark. Over and over again. Crotch thrust of knife work and fly undone and member stabbing and stabbing and stabbing again and again and again. The hot joy of it. The anger of it and then the release. Make an altar of this place. Make it sacred. Profane and stinking. Edify and baptise. Impose our order. Again and again. The power of Cain in us …

In the upshot it was his astounding intellectualism, as much as the Duke's money, that landed him Wurzburg. Money and influence stretched only so far and the boy's correspondence with the faculty at the college was his own work entirely. He liked the German language. And so at sixteen years of age he packed up his gothic novels and his libertine tracts and crossed the channel aboard the steamer *Alfred the Great*. He smiled at that, though it was a smile of academic whimsy and did nothing to light the dead embers of his eyes.

Wurzburg straddled the River Main in a picturesque whorl of medieval streets and red-slated houses, the Marienburg Fortress scowling down over all from its high tor. He immediately felt at home in the place. The symmetry of the Marienburg, the neat spires of the Palace in the main square, the set pattern of things, all appealed to him. England was a bedlam of a place in comparison. Even at sixteen he could appreciate efficiency. The gothic arches and leering gargoyles, the baroque fluting also set something to chime within him.

I AM IN BLOOD

Without much imagining he could be walking the shadowed terrain of *Frankenstein* or *The Castle of Otranto*.

He found the university readily enough and indeed he found it very much to his liking. He also found something else in Wurzburg. He found Therese Silgnan.

He had attended Wurzburg University for three months when he met her. In all that time he had not had any communication with his family nor had he experienced any impulse to communicate with them. His brother-in-law, the Duke, had provided him with means enough to see out the first year of his medical studies in comparative luxury. He was the youngest student in his class by eighteen months. As such, the Duke had issued instructions to the Provost to place the boy in his special care, to house him privately and to afford him any and all assistance.

The boy therefore found himself sequestered in a small room overlooking the faculty quadrangle and removed from the company of his fellow students. He did not mind this in the slightest. He had spent his entire life alone, even when in the midst of others. At night, when the others would enter beer halls and restaurants and slop and sing and puke and fight, he would wander the streets. Caped in darkness, he watched the bats scud through the air and the shadows dribble down from the arches and flying buttresses like ink spilled from the hidden wells of the Earth itself.

Like all university towns, like all places where rich young

men drank and strutted the nights away, Wurzburg had its fair share of whores. And it was the whores that fascinated him most of all. There was something brazen about them that made the boy stare. They flaunted themselves with the arrogance of aristocracy, sneering at those who came to use them, mocking the drunken fumbling of the desperate and the depraved. Once, he watched as a whore took a tin of Turkish Delight from the bosom of her dress and fed it to a drooling drunkard who sat gaping in the gutter, tugging at a member flopping flaccid and unresponsive in his lap.

Mama.

The nights were growing warm and the café owners had placed tables and chairs on the cobbles outside. He was sitting at one such table the night he met Therese. Across the road, in the dark throat of an alleyway, a prostitute was haggling with a prospective customer, her hand massaging his crotch as she did so.

He was sitting quietly and had become so still that people passed him without even noticing he was there. A cup of cold coffee sat at his elbow and he watched the whore's hand squeeze and release, squeeze and release.

Whores. In my home in mother's bed. Whores filling the world with the stink of them and the wet of them and father taking one. Whores. All of them. Nasty sweat of twining sheets. The laughter of them.

And then a voice said, 'Hello?'

I AM IN BLOOD

He jumped and looked up. Very rarely in his life had he been startled. He hated being surprised.

Beside him stood a girl no older than he himself was. She wore the plain black dress of a serving girl and the white oval of her face was framed by a fall of black hair. On her hands she wore a pair of fingerless black lace gloves. Black and white and beautiful and her eyes blinked at him and in that moment he was stunned. Like something mesmerised, he simply stared.

Across the road, the whore and her customer disappeared down the alleyway.

'Hello?' she said again. 'Would you like more coffee?'

'No,' he said at last. 'I am just leaving.'

She pouted a little, her lower lip jutting forward and he could see the glisten of it in the dark.

'I am sorry, *monsieur*, but you were sitting here and I completely forgot you. It was like you disappeared. Please, allow me to get you a fresh cup. That one has gone cold.'

'You're French,' he said.

He had never felt anything like this before and he was aware of how awkward he sounded.

She frowned a little. His tone and the bluntness of his expression made something in her trill in distant alarm. His eyes were like bullet-holes.

'*Oui*,' she said. 'And you are English.'

'Yes.'

She stood silently and he watched her silently.

'You are a student?' she asked eventually.

'Yes. Medicine.'

'Ah,' she said. '*Bon.*'

'What are you called?' he asked.

'Therese,' she said. 'Therese Silgnan.'

Therese Silgnan.

Then she looked around and said, 'I must get back to work. *Au revoir, monsieur.*'

He watched her leave. He watched her bend to wipe tables. She turned to look at him once before she went back into the café. She looked back at him and smiled.

Was there a promise in that smile? Was there something there to hook him and draw him out of himself? The tremble of her lips. Was this what it was like to feel something? Was there a maybe in that look?

To the darkness he said, 'See you soon.'

When he went back to his room that night, he lay for a long while in the dark and listened to the dogs of Wurzburg howl at nothing in the night. Below his open window someone in the quadrangle coughed and spat and cursed. He lay there and the serving girl's face, *Therese's* face, occupied his entire mind. The delicate petal-moist swell of her lip. The tremble of it. The tremble of her lips. Maybe? The slight movement maybe toward him. The smile. The maybe promise in it.

I AM IN BLOOD

He reached down into his trousers and began to squeeze and release, to stroke and to pant. Just like the whore had done. Thinking of Therese. Thinking of the whore.

… And God, you could grow to love it. I am loving this loving her loving this. Oblivious.

The smell of woodsmoke in the air rasped through the rough sieve of his teeth and he was deliriously, unbearably oblivious.

Suddenly his fist was gloriously wet and he was shuddering. His breath was a staccato, syncopated arhythmia. His whole body was a heart murmur.

The next day he attended a demonstration in anatomy. The class was gathered on the gallery overlooking the table with its cadaver. A woman, naked and the colour of tallow. Doctor Menscher stood beside it with a scalpel and was beginning to draw the blade down along the bone between the only two bare breasts the boy had ever seen. He thought they were beautiful.

The scalpel left a thin red line behind, but no blood. There was nothing vital about it at all. Nothing wet and running.

The evening after the anatomy demonstration the boy went back to the café where he had met Therese. There she was, stepping between the tables and laughing with the customers. He watched her quietly. Watched her move. Watched how her hair fell about her shoulders and how her face made its transition from emotion to emotion. He watched her smile form and crumble away and form again. He listened to her voice, the exotic inflections. He stood there on the fringes of things for a long time.

When she passed close to him he said, 'Hello.'

She almost dropped the tray of empty glasses she was carrying.

'*Mon dieu, monsieur!*' she exclaimed. 'You frightened me!'

'I am sorry,' he said. He said this because he knew that this was what people said in such situations. He felt sorry not at all.

She looked at him and frowned. 'Ah,' she said. 'I remember you. You were here last night. I let your coffee go cold.'

'Yes,' he said.

'Well, would you like a table? Inside or out?'

'Wherever you are most.'

She laughed at this and sat him at a small table beside the door. On her break she sat beside him and looked at his ordinary face and his ordinary clothes, his slight frame.

'How old are you?' she asked.

'Sixteen and a half,' he replied. 'How old are you?'

'Seventeen. You are very young to be a collegian.'

'I am a very quick learner.'

'Yes,' she said. 'Or very rich.'

He smiled and laughed and in that laugh was a terrible self-loathing.

'I have wealthy relatives,' he said. 'Extremely wealthy. I am afraid I do not sit well in their company.'

Therese shrugged her shoulders at this and gestured to the café and the surrounding tables. 'My father and mother moved here when I was ten. I have been employed as their waitress and scullery maid ever since. My brother has gone off to join the Prussian army. Imagine that, a Frenchman in an army constantly at war with Frenchmen. One cannot choose one's relatives, *monsieur*. Even if that means your life is spent as a ragged crow in a nest of peacocks.'

'I hate poetry,' said the boy, 'but that does ring true. A ragged crow in a nest of peacocks.'

Therese rose and tied her apron around her waist and said, 'I shall see you again, *monsieur*. We shall talk further of families and poetry.'

And they did see each other again. The boy began to spend most evenings at Therese's café. Often, when she was busy, he did not exchange more than a few words with her. Often she did not even take her breaks with him. Yet her proximity was the marrow of things for him. A closeness and intimacy that was as much his imagining as it was a physical thing. Sometimes she would brush against him, and those moments would sustain him as he took himself in his hands in the warm dark.

... the Hand of Cain. Reviled for it. Down the generations. Why? The work of God. A pattern right back to the start of time. The birth pangs of the universe. Spew of excised womb. The kernel of things. Omphalus. Here. In this place of dropped eyes. An Altar of Cain. In the filthy streets all wet and running in the night. Streaming. The steam of it rising. The Hand of God and the emptying of us into the filthy woman parts. The steam of them in the moist dark. Our ballsack clenching and the stab of emptying and the quick work and the red gush and the white flesh opened and streaming in the wet dark. Our seed in them and the smiling throat and the yawning belly. The birth chamber clogged with sinning. Rip it out. Carve it out. The emptied womb and the gleaming edge the bitter edge and the brimming jar. The bitter edge and the stiff member. The work and the drag and the just so. No bobbies. None but one. Only one. In the papers. Name in the papers. Same as before. Pen to paper. Same as before. Everything just so. The Pattern. The Pattern. The Pattern.

Over and over again.

CHAPTER 16:

DUBLIN, CHRISTMAS DAY 2015

Nathan woke up on Christmas morning with his phone vibrating under his pillow. God rest ye merry gentlemen. Silent night. Good people all.

Yeah, right, thought Nathan.

He lay for a moment, untacking his tongue from the dry roof of his mouth. Then he slid the sheets of paper that he had fallen asleep scribbling on from his chest and reached for the phone. The screen was black now and it had stopped buzzing, but the little indicator light was flashing to tell him that he had received a message.

He knew who it was from before he even looked at it.

Esther said: *Hey there, how are you? Merry Christmas. Ding Dong Merrily on High 'n' stuff.*

He smiled and went to text her back. Then he paused and really thought about what he was going to say.

He had bought a present for her and it sat on his writing desk, all neatly wrapped with a bow on top. It had taken him three goes to get the corners right. It was a cherrywood box with brass fixings. Inside, cradled in a lap of blue velvet, was a stick of red wax and a silver seal. A moon and stars and all his hopes and all his dreams. Tread softly and all that jazz. A red moon and red stars and his heart bleeding its ache for her.

He thought about her reaction when he finally gave it to her. Would she throw her arms around him? Would she kiss him?

Her text still waited for him.

Lying on his back, he held his phone in front of his face and texted: *Hey there. Merry Christmas to you, too. I hope Santy was good to you. Waking up to your message is the best present I could hope for.*

He read it over several times, his tongue between his teeth and his forehead all crumpled up. Then he pressed Send.

He placed the phone back beneath his pillow and thought about Esther and the shudder in the abdomen and his want for her. Lying on his back, his bed drifted over with scrawled sheets of paper, he took the growing shaft of his penis in his hand. He imagined Esther reading his message. He saw, actually *saw*, her smile. The slight separation of her lips.

When the phone buzzed beneath his head, he almost let himself go. Almost. But he held on. Savouring. He imagined what the text might say. A little flirting sequence of digital letters. Blocky font provoking a giddy little thrill. No emoticons. Nothing so vulgar. Words and rhythm and her face behind it all. Her body behind it all. Her fingers pushing his buttons. A hint that she wanted him as much as he wanted her. A Christmas present to beat all Christmas presents.

When he finished, he cleaned himself with a tissue, took his phone out and looked at the screen. It was dark as cinders now. Lifeless in his hands.

He opened the message and read it. It said: *That's so nice Nato. I sent that same message to all my other friends and you're the only one who texted back. You're such a sweetheart.*

And now it was like a bowling ball was sitting in his guts. He read the message again and what he felt was humiliation. Those words had been pulsing under his head as his head had pulsed with the need for her. His dick had pulsed with the heartbeat of her beauty. Her words, robbing him of his fantasies. Her words, exposing his dreams as things of spun sugar and wafer. Sticky things. Frail things. Things bad for you. Things that rotted your insides.

He sat on the edge of his bed and felt hurt. Scalded on the inside.

He almost threw his phone against the wall. Almost. Instead, he slammed it down onto his duvet, went in to the bathroom and had a shower.

Afterwards he dressed himself in his room and wondered at how quiet the house was. His father's absence chimed like a bell. Everything was subdued. Normally the house was loud with cheesy carols or Italian singers belting out *Silent Night* in Latin. Now, nothing. Silence and the constant pain beneath the ribcage. Everything muted and somehow colourless.

When he went downstairs, Samantha and James were sitting in the kitchen, having breakfast. Back from mass, already. No decorations. No cards on the mantelpiece. He ignored them and poured himself a bowl of cereal and started to go back to his bedroom. On the way out to the hall, Samantha's voice stopped him.

'Happy Christmas, Nathan,' she said.

Without looking at her, he said, 'Happy Christmas.'

Silent house. Joyless and cold.

Ho, ho, ho.

In his room, he sat at his study desk and began to write. Well, not write exactly. He began to plan. He began to sketch out where he and Esther were going to go. What photographs needed to be taken. Stuff like that. Then he went online and began to look up publishers and agents. He filled the vacant lot of his morning with ideas and big plans and ignored the little homunculus that sat in his head, dragging a saw across his nerves and laughing at him.

The knock on the door, when it came, was so quiet that he almost didn't hear it.

'Come in,' he said.

Samantha came into the room. Her slippers made sibilant little noises on the carpet as she moved. She sat on Nathan's bed and looked at him for a long time without saying anything.

'What are you writing?' she asked.

'Just some stuff. You wouldn't like it. It's about a serial killer.'

She looked sad, but she kept talking anyway.

'It's not really my thing,' she said. 'Your Dad would have liked it, I'm sure.'

Nathan didn't say anything but in his mind he was going, Don't mention him, you supercilious witch. Don't even think about him.

She said, 'I know we haven't seen eye-to-eye of late. It's been hard on us all. But your Dad's death has really taken it out of you. Everyone has been saying. Your teachers have rung asking for you. I realise James and I, maybe, haven't been the kindest to you.'

'There's no maybe about it.'

'I know. I know. We were so wrapped up in ourselves. James is so young and so immature. And I thought you were coping.'

'Man enough?'

'No. Nothing like that. It has nothing to do with manliness. You're just so closed off.'

'So it's all my fault?'

'No, I'm not saying that.'

She stopped and sighed and looked at her hands where they were laced in her lap, upturned like denuded crabs.

'Oh, Nato,' she said. 'My poor Nato. We're friends, Nato. I want to stay friends.'

Nathan said nothing for a while and he and Samantha sat alone in the heavy silence and listened to each other breathe and watched each other think thoughts deep and knotted.

Then Nathan said, 'I need to go out later. I'm going to see Esther and then I'm going to visit Da's grave. On my own.'

Samantha nodded and said, 'We haven't opened our presents yet. Would you like to come down?'

'Yeah,' said Nathan. 'Okay.'

For Christmas they had gotten him *The Writers' and Artists' Yearbook* and a voucher for a shopping centre. Samantha gave them to him and said, 'We didn't know what else to get you.'

Nathan was embarrassed because he had gotten them nothing.

He felt strange. He felt dislocated. He didn't belong here and even though Samantha and James were being nice to him and he was being nice to them, there was a subtle dynamic at work here that he didn't like. In their too-big house filled with pristine furnishings and smelling of herbs and the juices of roasting turkey, in this place of money and bland taste, they were like people defusing a bomb. All delicate and precise and careful. No jokes were cracked. Nothing that could be construed as offensive. Everything was anodyne as the beige of the carpet, the *Summer Oat* of the walls. The entire house was suddenly a page from a lifestyle supplement.

Nathan lasted until one o'clock before deciding to go see Esther.

On the way out Samantha said, 'Dinner's at four. Don't be late, darling.'

Darling?

Where on earth had that come from?

To get to Esther's house you went out Nathan's front door, swung left and headed down the Lower Kilmacud Road and then turned left again onto Sweet Briar Lane. Sweet Briar. Blackberries and autumn fruit and black tumours of sunblooded sweetness. Nathan couldn't think of anywhere more appropriate for her to live.

Hardly anything moved on the Lower Kilmacud Road. Christmas afternoon had everyone indoors with their families. Their loved ones. Pulling crackers and playing games. Everyone happy in a whirligig of toys and flashing lights and video games and talking teddies and *The Muppet Christmas Carol* on TV. Michael Caine enjoying himself as Scrooge and working Kermit to the bone. Christmas Day, a time for loved ones and embraces and good company.

When he knocked on Esther's door, her Dad opened it.

'Merry Christmas, Mr Gilsenan,' said Nathan.

Esther's Dad looked over his shoulder and called, 'Esther! That Jacob lad is here for you.'

Then he went back inside, leaving the door ajar. The smell of cooking drifted out into the bitter brightness of the day and Nathan felt his stomach buck with hunger.

When Esther came to the door she was wearing a knee-length black jumper, a black beret and was in her stocking feet. She struck a pose on the threshold and said, 'These are new. Do you like them?'

He smiled at her. 'You could wear a bin bag and look great, Esther.'

For *look great* read *I love you*.

'Thanks,' she said. 'What's up?'

Nathan stood there for a moment. He didn't know how to answer that. What *was* up? Why was he here? What was he supposed to tell her? That Samantha had gotten him a present? That James was being civil to him? That he had been called *darling*? That for all this, the house of his father felt empty as all the million tonnes of wrapping paper rustling across all the million homes of Ireland? That their politeness, his and Samantha's and James' all, felt like hollow plastic? That he could hear it crackling like cheap polyester? That he couldn't bear it anymore?

I AM IN BLOOD

That he had gotten her a present and that he wanted to be embraced? He wanted to be loved? That he needed to see her more and more each day? That she was become the only real thing in his shitty little world?

Was this what he was supposed to tell her?

On Christmas fucking Day?

He said, 'Ehm, nothing really. I got you this.'

He handed her the little cube with its crisp, OCD wrapping job. She smiled at him and said, 'Oh wòw, Nathan. You really shouldn't have. My God, I'm so embarrassed. I haven't got you anything.'

He shrugged and said, 'That's okay. You've been the best thing in my life for a while now.'

Every minute I spend with you is a gift, is what he wanted to say. But instead he said, 'If you want to make it up to me, you can come with me for a walk.'

She threw a look over her shoulder and stepped out onto the path, easing the door almost closed behind her. Almost. Nathan could see sudden gooseflesh dimple her bare legs and she folded her arms across her breasts.

'It's cold,' she said.

'It's December,' said Nathan.

'I'd like to hang out, Nato. I really would. But Christmas in our house is a real family thing. Nobody goes anywhere. Dad would go mental if he thought I was even thinking about leaving the house.'

'That's cool,' he said.

And again, 'That's cool.'

'We're still on for heading into town next week, though, aren't we?' she said. Nathan couldn't tell if the eagerness in her voice was false or not. Whether she had sensed his disappointment and was throwing him a bone.

She went on. 'I'm really looking forward to it. I think it's fantastic.'

'Defo. Just make sure you have your camera and a spare memory card.'

'I won't bring the good one,' she said with a grin. 'We *are* going to the Northside, after all.'

Nathan smiled back at her. But it was a bloodless smile. A smile without any heart.

'Yeah,' he said.

And again, 'Yeah.'

A small furrow appeared between Esther's brows and she looked at him without saying anything.

'I'm okay,' said Nathan. 'I'm grand. I'll chat to you, maybe not this evening, but definitely tomorrow.'

'It's a date.'

Her smile was as weak as his. Troubled and unsure.

He turned and walked down her path and into the street. He heard the sound of her front door closing in the quiet afternoon. She hadn't even opened his gift.

A date.

His life really was a joke.

He wandered then, without putting any real thought into where he was going. His legs working mechanically. Dragging him along the footpath until he found himself at the graveyard that held the remains of his father. The leftovers. What was left when the good stuff had been stripped and consumed. The stuff to be thrown away.

Nathan was surprised for a moment at how crowded the place was. By real-life-honest-to-God living people, not by the buried thousands. People moved between the gravestones and markers with bunches of flowers and a hundred emotions in flux across their faces. The entire gamut of human experience was painted in those strangers' faces. Regret. Joy. Anger. Loneliness. Guilt. The whole shebang.

Nathan sat on the grass beside his Da's grave and watched people of all ages stand over their dead loved ones and think for long moments about their lives and how many Christmases they had spent now in the cold ground. Flowers were left and tears were shed and fond hands were placed on lifeless tombstones. And words accompanied those brief gestures. *See you soons* and *Miss yous* and *Love yous* and a hundred other private things besides. As though they were patting the shoulder and whispering in the ear of someone going on a journey but whom they expected to see again before long. A don't-be-long sort of gesture. A gesture of farewell and longing and affection all at once. And the thousands of graves with their fresh flowers and their silent occupants all gave no hint that anyone at all was listening under the blue Christmas sky and under the still, thronged clay.

Nathan sat for a long while and then, like all the others, he touched his father's gravestone and went home.

Dinner was served promptly at four.

Samantha had been drinking since half-two and was in fine fettle. Her bottle of wine sat in the centre of the table and blocked the line of sight of anyone trying to have a conversation. Not that this bothered Nathan. He didn't really feel like talking. He ate his dinner in silence. He hated to admit it, but Samantha was a pretty good cook.

James, however, was not feeling like Nathan felt and little wiry fissures were starting to web across his veneer of civility.

'What are you doing up there in your room all the time, Nato?' he asked. 'Mam says you're writing. That's pretty gay.'

Nathan ignored him.

'Seriously,' said James. 'What are you writing? C'mon. Tell me.'

Samantha seemed to be lagging some minutes behind events but she looked up from her dinner, frowned and said, 'Don't, James. We must be polite.'

'Why? Why do we have to walk on egg-shells around him? He's giving everyone the creeps.'

Nathan looked at him and frowned. Was that true? *The creeps*?

Samantha raised an admonishing finger.

'Don't,' she said again. 'It's Christmas.'

But James just kept on talking.

'If Dad was here, there's no way he'd let you sulk up in your room all day long with your freaky books and your poxy writing.'

That was all Nathan could take. He jabbed his fork across the dinner table and James jumped a little in his seat. Under his blonde fringe his eyes, his father's eyes, were so wide it was like they were trying to take in the world.

'Don't mention Da to me again,' he said. 'Don't fucking dare.'

'Or what?'

'Or I'll beat the tar out of you, you little shit.'

Samantha was on her feet now. On her feet and shouting, 'Stop it! Stop it! Stop it!'

Then she was dredging her fingers through her hair, her nails harrowing her scalp and saying, 'It's Christmas, for fuck's sake! Christmas. Jesus, can you two not be at each other's fucking throats all the fucking time.'

She looked at James. He looked back at her as though she had transmogrified into some sort of gorgon.

'Say sorry,' she said.

'Why should I —?' he began.

Samantha's voice cut him off. Her voice and the anger in her eyes and the tendons in her neck standing out like cables.

'Because I told you to!' she screamed.

She's cracking up, thought Nathan. She's almost gone. Whatever glue she was holding herself together with was coming unstuck in a big way.

James ducked his perfect chin into his perfect chest and mumbled, 'Sorry, Nato.'

Nathan's swell of satisfaction, his taste of victory soured as Samantha turned on him.

'And you,' she said. 'Don't ever curse at your brother again and don't ever threaten him under my roof. Not ever!'

My roof.

'It's not your roof,' he said. 'It's my Da's roof. He worked for it. And if he was here, he wouldn't be letting you make a show of yourself. Shouting and roaring like you should be on Moore Street. And if you think I'm saying sorry to that little cunt, you've another think coming.'

All the anger and all the frustration of the day, from the moment he received Esther's texts all the way through to now, bubbled in his words. There was a venom to what he said that surprised even him. An anger that came from some region of himself he was afraid to acknowledge, let alone look into. A black place of cruel edges and things that gnashed and tore at each other.

He was as shocked as she was.

'What did you say?' she whispered.

Nathan blinked and blinked again. What had he done?

'Your Da?' she said. 'Your fucking Da. That's all it ever is with you. Da this and Da fucking that. Not a thought for me or what I had to put up with for all those years. Let me tell you about your fucking Da.'

She leaned in on him and Nathan could feel in that moment the entire foundations of his being liquefy and slide away from under him. In her face he could see the ending of his world.

'Your Da was the greatest lying bastard ever to walk the planet. For years he fucked off on business trips and rode anything that fucking moved.'

No, thought Nathan. This isn't happening. This isn't true.

'Your Da. Your charming fucking Da. Every weekend, off he went into town with his chums and came home smelling of perfume and sex. All the fucking time. Every single fucking weekend.'

James stared straight ahead. He wasn't looking at Nathan and he wasn't looking at Samantha. His eyes were dull as limestone. He had heard this before. How long had he known?

Samantha was still talking, her voice a blunt instrument. 'You're not mine, Nathan. God, I wished you were so, so often. You're not mine, but you *are* your rotten father's son.'

The next words she spat at him. 'Your mother, that girl Patricia Frohmell. She landed you on our doorstep. Your mother, the filthy, drug-addicted prostitute. Your mother, Patricia Frohmell. Your father's dirty little secret. His rotten pet whore.'

CHAPTER 17:

DUBLIN, JANUARY 1893

George left Dr O'Sullivan's house with a smile on his face like a gash in a tree bark. The evening had come down with all the weight of the season in it and the lamplighters were out in force. They shimmied up and down their ladders like circus monkeys, all bundled up in hats and coats. And above their heads as they scurried away from the cast-iron lamp-posts, pollen balls of light were left behind to exorcise the dark. Like hanging will-o'-the-wisps.

George was suddenly a man at hunt.

He was no longer on the back foot and like policemen the world over, from Scotland Yard to the Pinkerton's of the barbarous West, he felt the thrill of scented prey in his belly.

He would get his man. As God was his witness, he would have him. The arrogant bastard had gone too far. He had underestimated the abilities of those whom he baited. In this beaten city, in this beaten land, there was so much to be overlooked. So much to be taken for granted. The British had done it for hundreds of years and had reeled away bloodied and confused, time and time again. His own great-grandfather had watched peasants and farmhands butcher his uniformed comrades for the green-painted fantasies of the United Irishmen. The croppies would never lie down. Never. And behind their defeated faces their brains bubbled like witches' cauldrons and plotted and schemed. Their damned language didn't even have a word for a straight *yes* or *no*.

It was easy to see the Irish as buffoons and bog-trotters. Easy to see nothing behind the doffed cap and the tugged forelock. Easy to miss the daggers in men's smiles. And George Frohmell, Protestant, Loyal and policeman though he might be, was Irish to his very marrow.

You creeping bollix, he thought. I've got you.

He walked up Sackville Street and even smiled up at the Liberator on his great pedestal. Still smiling he walked all the way home. And all those people whom he passed along the way averted their eyes for there was something baleful in that smile, something unnatural. It was the smile he sometimes wore when the old anger sang through him and in the grip of drink he would lose all hold of himself. His former fianceé knew that grin and hated it. Hated what it presaged. A destroying. A tearing down.

But there was no drink in him now and the anger he felt was a controlled thing. A thing of awful potential. Like a honed blade.

He would go home and he would write down all of what he knew, neatly and to the point. He would date and sign everything. He would fold it crisply. And then he would go to G Division and demand every detective and DMP man that could be spared to wait in the Monto. Wait at certain specific places and attend the arrival of an entity who had slaughtered three women without remorse or compunction. Slaughtered and cut and consumed. He would do all this, for George Frohmell was on to his man. On to this monster that for all his brutality was really more human than monster, after all. A thing that was the very embodiment of humanity's sordid potential. He was the articulate flesh of those dreams that arise in the black dark and in the depths of drink. The cruellest of George's own impulses released without fetter and without rein. A trampling beast of a thing that reflected back man's own degradation upon himself.

And for that reason alone, he deserved to be put down.

The hallway of his building was empty and still in the dark. He went up the stairs, his feet instinctively finding the hollows in the sagging timber.

He pushed open the door to his rooms and said, 'I'm home, Rosie! And right glad I am, too!'

No sound greeted him. His rooms were empty.

George was suddenly afraid. Since Christmas, Rosie had not ventured outside after dark. It had never been mentioned a single time, not by either of them, but her own *work* seemed to have been forgotten. Without confrontation and without argument, Rosie and George had settled down into a sort of domestic orthodoxy. She cooked and cleaned and he went to work and they bedded together and only the absence of rings on their fingers gave the lie to their happy little family. To live and love in sin was a small sin, when all was said and done. Certainly when compared to all the other vast sins of the world.

To live in sin was much better than to die in sin. Like poor Mary Shortt. Like poor Alice O'Keefe. Like poor Betty Quinn.

Like every other soul that this faceless monster had stolen thus far.

And now Rosie was gone.

George went about his rooms, checking for signs that anything was amiss. He found none and sat at his table by the light of a good oil lamp which Rosie had made him buy. He sat and he thought to himself. She was simply gone out. Perhaps to visit a friend or to buy something. He couldn't expect a note for every little thing she ever did. He couldn't expect her to defer to him or to ask his permission. He didn't need to know where she was at every minute of every day.

She had gone out. That was all.

The thought that she was back standing on her corner in the Monto, flaunting her wares to the slumcrawlers on Buckingham Street, sickened him. It appalled him doubly. First, there was a walking abomination at work in the Monto. And he was afraid for Rosie and for any other lady who walked the lanes of that corrupt part of the city. And secondly, and for so long now he had denied this and pushed it so far down that its presence was like a dormant infection in his system, he despised her selling herself. Even before their current arrangement had come about, the thoughts of her on her back under another man made his guts twist and gorge rise. Now, they almost unmanned him. She was his as much as he was hers, both each other's alone. And that was as it should be.

Distracted by these thoughts, he took the map he had carried from Dr O'Sullivan's out of his trousers pocket and spread it under the lamp. In an effort to avoid thinking about Rosie, he examined it closely.

The simplicity of it all had startled O'Sullivan, but George was sure he was right about this. It felt right. He trusted his own instincts in this matter more than he trusted the good doctor's arch intellectualism.

In the doctor's urbane library, with its books and its tracts on the Rights of Man, George had explained the trigonometry of butchery. The doctor had procured for him a map of the centre of Dublin's fair city. On the map George had marked three small black x's. One for each murder. Not where they had happened, but where the bodies had been found. Poor Patrick Sinnott had been spot-on in his assessment of things. Mary Shortt had lain where she fell, but both Alice O'Keefe and Betty Quinn had been moved. Their bodies dragged yards from the murder scenes, around at least one corner and then placed sitting against a wall.

George was disgusted at the thought that someone must have seen this. Someone must have seen a man dragging or carrying a senseless woman and still no one had come forward with information. And yet the people of Dublin would rave and keen that the DMP were impotent. Their bloody newspapers would howl that Sergeant George Frohmell was incompetent. There was no place like it on Earth.

On his little map George had joined the three x's and stepped back. A neat little triangle had been formed.

If George was right, the pattern needed two x's more.

The goat's head.

The Sign of the Beast.

A pentagram stamped over the heart of Dublin.

He stared at the map for a long while, his forehead cradled in his palm. What could he do to stop another x being planted on his city? Another x to mark the spot. Could the killer do his work and wait until the coast was clear to place the corpse, to continue building his infernal web? Or was it all part of some feverish compulsion that must be done there and then? He could stop him. He could flood the most likely spots with DMP men. But could he catch him? And this was a thought so black that George dared not even contemplate it, but still it persisted. Could he allow another woman to die, sure in the knowledge that her body would be dumped in one of two places? Dumped like a sack of rubbish, spilling offal onto the dirty cobbles. Could he?

He was thinking this when Rosie walked in.

'Jaysus,' she said. 'The wanderer returns.'

'I could say the same for you,' he said.

She was carrying a wicker basket, which she hefted onto the table and then she looked down at him and his work.

'I was down with Mrs Darby downstairs,' she said. 'The poor woman has an awful chest and her lovely little fellas are suffering from it terribly, too. I went and did their shopping for them.'

Rosie Lawlor. The woman of hard edges and brittle tongue. And beneath everything, soft as the human heart.

'I'm after getting us a few bits and pieces, too,' she said. 'Everything goes all mildewed in the blink of a bleedin' eye in here. The damp is fierce.'

'Right,' he said.

The relief that he felt at hearing she wasn't in the Monto

made him relax. He wasn't even aware of the tension across his shoulders until it vanished.

'Right,' he said again. 'Of course.'

'Are you in the right of yourself, at all?'

'Yes,' he said. 'I'm grand.'

'Well you won't be when you hear this,' she said and sat opposite him. 'The darling boys of G Division have been making a right nuisance of themselves. I was talking to Maggie Breen and she was saying that G-men are after raiding Larry Byrne's public house and wrecking the place. They've arrested two of Larry's sons on account of them being Fenians and on account of that bomb that went off. The G-men have them locked up in the Castle. The whole of Amiens Street are wanting to march down there and spring them and there's not a peeler in the bleedin' country that will stand up to them. There'll be trouble, you mark my words.'

'Maggie Breen?' said George. 'A liar and a rabble-rouser and a whoremonger. I wouldn't believe the Lord's Prayer out of her.'

'You believe what you want. She's not the only one saying it.'

George frowned suddenly.

'Maggie Breen? Were you in the Monto?'

Rosie grew suddenly reticent.

'Is it any of your business where I do our shopping?'

'Jesus Christ, Rosie. I told you, I told you a hundred times, not to go there again until we catch this murdering bastard. And here you are wandering around after dark, blithe as a new-born babe.'

'Don't you take that tone with me, George Frohmell! It's not my fault your poxy salary won't let me shop anywhere else.'

'We're not short of money,' said George.

'Oh, yes we are. Don't be fooling yourself. I'll need to get a job or something before too long. Either that or …'

'You will not!' snapped George. 'You'll never have to do that again. Not ever.'

Rosie smiled at him. Her face was plumper and there was a shine to her eyes that had not been there before Christmas.

'My hero,' she said. But beyond the mockery there was something warm. Something tender.

George was talking again and his words came forth without conscious thought. The idea that Rosie might return to her … her *work* … terrified and nauseated him in equal measure.

'Never again, Rosie,' he said. 'If I have to rob a bank. You'll never have to do that again. You deserve more than that. I'll not have my wife sacrifice herself for the matter of a few bob.'

'What?' said Rosie.

George was confused.

'What did you say?' said Rosie again.

George suddenly realised what had escaped his mouth and the realisation flummoxed him completely. He stood there like a man concussed.

'Say it again,' said Rosie.

'My … wife,' said George.

And again, more quickly and with more confidence. 'My wife.'

Rosie was smiling now and she stood and came to him. She sat on his lap and wrapped her arms around his neck.

'I suppose that's the best I'm going to get, is it?'

'I suppose it is,' said George.

'No sign of a bleedin' ring either?'

'Not yet,' he said. 'Not on my poxy salary.'

Then he kissed her and carried her to bed.

Behind him, his map lay in the yellow lamplight, a jaundiced abstraction of a jaundiced city. On its flat surface, the three black x's were like sutured puncture wounds.

The knocking was so soft that for a long time George lay there in the dark before dawn listening to it. He lay and listened and felt Rosie warm beside him and didn't allow it drag him from her. He willed himself to sleep. But the knocking grew in volume and in tempo until it stirred Rosie in her slumber and George slipped out from under the covers before she fully awoke.

He was in his small clothes and the cold clamped onto his flesh and the damp caught in his throat. He cared not a whit. Still, he held his revolver in his right hand as he walked across his room, *their* room.

He was tired but he wasn't stupid.

He lit the oil lamp and went over to the door. He opened it a fraction and looked out onto his grotty landing. On it stood two figures. One was taller than George but sought to disguise the fact by hunching forward in his greatcoat, its cape collar flaring out about his shoulders. The other stood straight as a ramrod. Even in the pre-dawn dark his DMP helmet was a blatant black shape.

A constable and a G-man of some sort.

'What now?' asked George.

It was the G-man who answered.

'May I come in, Sergeant?'

'I don't really have a choice, do I?'

'You are holding a revolver, Sergeant,' said the G-man. 'You can do whatever you like.'

George snorted and then he opened the door and the G-man stepped through. The constable, however, did not. He remained on the landing and turned his back as George closed the door slowly and with some confusion. There was something about the G-man's Ulster accent that he recognised.

'Can I at least put some clothes on?' said George.

'By all means,' said the G-man and sat himself at George's table. The lamplight cast one side of his bearded face in brass and swilled shadow in the hollows and creases of the other. George blinked and blinked again. All thoughts of clothes forgotten.

At his table sat Chief Superintendent John Mallon. The rising star of the Irish constabulary. A detective of supernatural instincts and inhuman tenacity. He was the youngest man ever to attain the rank of inspector when he was promoted back in '69. He was barely thirty at the time. The same age as George was now. And his career had gone from strength to strength ever since. As politic as he was efficient, John Mallon was a man to be respected and feared in equal measure. The fact that he was a Northern Catholic made him all the more remarkable.

Mallon smiled at George's discomfiture.

'Put some clothes on, man,' he said.

George hurried off and slung trousers and shirt on and then threw a coat on over them, to stave off the cold. Rosie mumbled in her sleep but did not waken.

George came back out and stood in front of the Chief Superintendent and saluted. In his coat and his ragged trousers and his bare feet, he saluted.

'Don't be stupid, Sergeant,' said Mallon. 'Sit down. We need to have a chat.'

George frowned but did as he was told.

Mallon leaned forward and placed his elbows on the table and looked George full in the eyes. George met the stare and held it. It was as though he were presenting his very soul for validation.

Mallon smiled slightly and said, 'About the Monto murders. I'm led to believe that you have taken the matter fully onto your own shoulders?'

George still held Mallon's eyes and said as bluntly as he dared, 'G Division does not want to become involved. The Fenians have them chasing shadows again and they are to a man caught up in actions against them. I seem to be the one that this has fallen to.'

Mallon nodded slowly.

'Yes. The dynamiting of Dublin Castle. Poor Constable Sinnott blown up. He would have made a fine detective, I am told. The Fenians say it was because he had it abroad that they were responsible for the whores' murders.'

George said nothing and Mallon continued.

'The thing is, Sergeant Frohmell, that Sinnott had indeed professed such notions. But word is he was only mouthing a canard invented by a more senior constable. A canard designed to pique G Division's interest in the murder of people who, quite frankly, nobody cares the price of a pin for.'

'*I* care the price of a pin for them,' snapped George. 'Sir.'

'I am well aware of that. I would also advise you to moderate your tone.'

George bridled but Mallon went on, 'I am not here to judge, Sergeant. Whatever friends a man keeps and whatever compassions he harbours in his own heart are his own business.' He smiled. 'For the most part.'

His voice then dropped in pitch and he said, 'However, this

senior constable, whoever he may be, that got poor bloody Sinnott blown to Kingdom Come, may have done the world some service.'

George was on edge now, he sensed the ground shifting beneath him and he was suddenly unsure of his footing.

'Go on, Sir,' he said.

'A Detective Tom Dalton, on duty at the Castle the day after Patrick Sinnott was murdered, was in receipt of some rather puzzling information. Something about the Whitechapel murders. So this intrepid officer of the law, instead of letting things go by the wayside, took it into his head that this information came from a source unimpeachable in its honesty and integrity.'

George took in the sardonic tone, the arch of the Chief's eyebrow, but he said nothing as Mallon explained. 'Detective Constable Dalton dashed off a telegram to Scotland Yard and a few hours later received a reply. He brought that reply straight to me. It seems that his inquiry caused quite a bit of consternation in the ranks of our London colleagues.'

George was intrigued now and he could feel the adrenal rush of the hound at hunt course through him again.

'The telegram which we got back from that wonderful institution of New Scotland Yard was from a Chief Inspector Donald Swanson. And it spelled out to me and to all men of the DMP, G Division included, that the murders which are occurring in our little metropolis are not the work of the

Ripper and to investigate it as such was a waste of time.

'Naturally, I thought it rather interesting that a Chief Inspector should reply to a mere Constable and the sentiments expressed were so definite that I found myself growing, I think, *suspicious* is the correct word. And so I had Dalton do a little more digging. And lo and behold, another telegram arrives from our colleagues across the water. In it was the instruction, the order, the demand, that we in our bedraggled little city were to cease all investigations into these matters forthwith.

'We were being *ordered*, by our Imperial masters, to suspend any and all inquiries into the murders taking place in the Monto. The Lord Lieutenant was to be informed and the matter was to be dropped by his command.'

George was stunned.

'What?' he said. 'Why? Why would they wish to bury this?'

'The very questions I asked myself, Sergeant. And so, as a loyal and zealous upholder of the law, I did what I thought I should.'

'What's that, Sir?'

'Sergeant,' he said, 'do you know what the four essentials of policing are?'

'No,' said George, frustrated. 'I confess I do not, Sir.'

'They are truthfulness, sobriety, punctuality and a tremendous care as to what you tell your superiors.'

In spite of himself, George smiled at this.

'And so,' Mallon continued, 'I ordered young Dalton to drop his inquiries and to direct his full attention to the Fenian menace. I, on the other hand, in my own time and using my own resources did a little digging of my own. I have been on very good terms with a Superintendent Williamson of Scotland Yard for a number of years. He was closely involved with the Ripper case before he retired. He was rather more forthcoming than his former colleagues.'

'Go on, Sir,' said George. 'Please, go on.'

Mallon grew very serious then. All levity left his voice and the dry affability of his manner was replaced by something grim.

'Our monster is not native to our city. He began in Wurzburg, where he attended the university as a collegian. He then moved to Paris, where he practised medicine and thence to Edinburgh and then on to London. Behind him he left a trail of ever more elaborately brutalised bodies.'

'My God,' said George. 'Why hasn't he been stopped?'

'Connections and bloodlines,' stated Mallon. 'High-up connections and bloodlines tying him to very important people. That is all I can say without risking the gallows myself.'

George was regarding him with a sense of foreboding.

Mallon wasn't looking at him. Now the Chief Superintendent's eyes were directed at the table between his forearms. He became silent before taking a long breath.

'He kills five,' he said. 'Always five. The organs seem to be important to him, as are the positions of the bodies. He lays them out as though attempting to achieve a pattern.'

George merely nodded.

Truthfulness, sobriety, punctuality and a tremendous care as to what you tell your superiors.

'Of course, you have deduced all this. Haven't you, Sergeant?'

'Some,' said George.

Mallon laughed without humour and said, 'Good man. Good man. And that is why I am here, Sergeant. Because you are a good man.'

'Sir?'

'The DMP cannot do any more. I cannot allow G Division or any other constables to be allocated to these murders. The Lord Lieutenant has ordered it. The Crown has willed it.'

Then his lips warped into a sneer beneath his beard and he snarled, 'But I'll be damned if I'll let this animal walk away again to do this to anyone else. He stops here. It isn't right to do anything other. He stops here.'

Mallon was talking to George, but he got the distinct impression that the great detective was speaking as much to himself as anyone.

'I won't have that on my conscience along with all the rest. By Jesus Christ and all the saints, that weight would break a man. You see where my difficulty lies, Sergeant?'

George nodded. 'You want this animal stopped, but none

of us can be seen to do anything that might bring that about.'

'None of us except you,' said Mallon. 'You have taken this on, Sergeant. In spite of discouragement and shortage of manpower, you have become almost obsessed by it.'

'Is that going to be the story you tell the Castle and the Phoenix Park?'

Mallon looked at him and said, 'It is. And there won't be a trial, Sergeant, do you understand me?'

George shook his head. 'There must be, Sir. Justice must be seen to be done.'

'Nonsense,' said Mallon.

George's lips tightened.

'Look it,' said Mallon. 'If we arrest him, he will never get to trial and you know that as well as I do. You are on your own, Sergeant. With three bodies dead in the Dublin streets and another two to come. Another two and then he vanishes and is gone to some other city to do the same again. We haven't much time, but the clock's not ticking just yet.'

An abrupt droning of voices from the door leading to the landing interrupted him. Without any hesitation Mallon doused the lamp and gestured George to the door.

George rose and sidled across the floorboards in the sudden dark, revolver in hand.

Beyond the door he could hear two voices pitched in low argument.

'Who's there?' he called.

'Excuse me, Sergeant,' came the answer. 'I'm sorry to interrupt but there's a Constable Markey, DMP 4639, out here. He says it's urgent.'

From the bedroom, Rosie's voice, bedraggled and bed-drugged, came bumbling. 'Georgie? Georgie? What's wrong?'

George ignored her and opened the door.

On the landing, Mallon's bodyguard was standing beside a scrawny little briar of a constable. The constable's narrow face looked to have been chipped from a block of teak. His chest was heaving with the exertion of running up the stairs. His eyes were black and staring, as though the night itself had crafted two holes in his face.

Before the man opened his mouth, George knew what he was going to say. And from behind him, in the dark, Mallon's voice came soft and sour.

'Tick tock,' it said. And again, 'Tick tock.'

CHAPTER 18

WURZBURG, MAY 1856– DECEMBER 1857

The Work. The Pattern. Round the corner and down the stairs. Closer now. Closer to the order in chaos. The Godhand of us and the branding of them. The Mark of Cain upon them. The Black Goat of the Woods with his horns and his snout and the hanging genitals of him. The rutting goat of a Thousand Young. The ancient sign of him. Now in this place. In this time. Mark it for what it is. Den of filth. Filthy pit of despair. Us sunk in it. Sunk in to the butt. Drop them on the cobbles. The sound of them. The slap of them and the blood running black into the black dark and black rain. Close now. Very close. Lolling tongue of heavy napping down the middle of the throat of this place. Lamps on the walls. Bright light for to see the dark coming. Falling down. Night fall of shaken hair. The smell of it and the feel of it and the mat of it in the spilled red wet of opened throat of opened flesh. God you could grow to love it. Over and over again. The slitherslap of all the stuff coming out. The slip of it down our throat …

Most of the time, as Therese Silgnan worked around him, he would sit with his cooling coffee and read textbooks and watch the whores ply their trade. He watched as the black alleys swallowed them and their customers both.

As the academic year drew to a close, he received a letter from his sister, the Duchess. It read:

Dearest Little Brother,

I must apologise for addressing you as 'Little Brother'! You are now a College Man and if the Provost's communiques are honest and true (which I have no doubt they are), then you are a most excellent College Man at that! Top of your class at sixteen! How remarkable! We are most overjoyed to hear of your success. Can you remember when I used to call you Bobo and dandle you on my knee? I suppose not, but even then you were a most peculiar and precocious child.

John is doing well. He has taken over the running of Father's mills and has invested quite a lot of money in Indian cotton. I believe he is making money hand over fist. So do not worry. The family is doing very well and we are all anxious that you progress in your studies.

And now to the main purpose of this letter. Alfred has decided that, since money is no object, you should remain in Wurzburg over the Summer months and so have a head-start on the others of your class when the college resumes for Michaelmas. We should all be very grateful to him. He has been a rock ever since Father's accident. He has sent word directly to the Provost and the funds will follow shortly.

We are all so proud of you, Bobo.

Your Sister,

Penelope.

P.S. I shall tell you this although I must ask you to keep it secret for a while yet. I am with child! Imagine! You shall be Uncle to a Duke!

Summer in Wurzburg opened out before the boy like a new dawn. He had no wish to return to England. He had no wish to leave Therese. Lately, he had begun to think that he might be in love with Therese. In his cold way he had analysed what she had done to him. He wanted her so much his abdomen ached every time she spoke to him. He found himself thinking about her when alone. Every dark head of hair he saw reminded him of the midnight fall of hers. He went to the library and read the theories on what love might be. He tried to read the great love sonnets of Petrarch and Shakespeare and dismissed them as the confections they were. Nothing described the fever that was in him. He came to the conclusion that love was a chemical imbalance, a pollution of the humours. Something that could be fed. Something that could be cut out.

Oftentimes he wondered whether she felt the same. All during that hot Bavarian summer the thought played on his mind that she saw him in a different way than he saw her. She spoke to other boys as much as she spoke to him, but there was something different in the time they shared, surely? They communicated in a manner he had never experienced before. He *wanted* to be with her. He *wanted* to hear her voice. Oftentimes he had leaned forward, the fatal words on his tongue, the moment forced to its crisis, only for him to sit back and mouth some petty commonplace. What a coward he was. Unwilling to introduce a note of chaos into the neat order of things.

All that summer Therese Silgnan was his eternal equinox. Unmoving in its perfection.

His life became a pattern. He could predict its every turn as easily as he could straighten a picture frame.

And so it continued for a year more. His studies advanced at a startling pace. His professors were of the unanimous opinion that no one of such supernormal ability had ever before walked through the door of Wurzburg University. It was remarked that the boy's dispassion was what placed him apart. He wielded a scalpel like a master sculptor. He carved flesh with the same unflinching exactness that a craftsman might carve wood. It was as though God's sanctified flesh, his very image on this green earth, were as nothing to him. The boy shaped things as he saw fit.

And as his skills grew, so did his confidence. He was invited to banquets where the discussions were intellectual and bohemian. He was asked for his opinion on matters and he gave it willingly and with cutting honesty. Those whose words were more commonly sleeved in diplomacy chortled at the brashness of youth. And none saw the truth of things. None saw anything dark move beneath the smoke.

For the boy was still the boy. Still the same boy who corrected the angles of skewed furniture, the same boy who bit his brother, the same boy who felt glee at the suffering of the weak. The same boy who stood over his dead father and felt nothing more than if he were looking at something lying in an abattoir.

Down the months and down the years the boy had grasped the importance of human conventions, the dance and dumb-show that people perform to preserve the illusion of normality. He now imitated them with the precision he brought to all aspects of his life. And yet imitation was all it was. He acted *like* he was supposed to. His world had become a simile.

All except Therese Silgnan. What he felt for her burned bright and real and hot.

Summer fell into autumn and autumn in turn died and

rotted into winter. November in Wurzburg brought the season howling down like a wolf. The cold bit and clawed and snow crusted where it fell on roofs and cobblestones. The sky was become a grey slab weighing down on the Marienburg and making the sun a mere memory, a dream of a dream.

Therese and the boy, the boy almost the man, sat on the Old Bridge and looked into the River Main. The strange little English boy and the beautiful French girl, like figures from a fairytale. The water sluiced along under their gaze like something solid, black and muscular. Night was falling and the light fled the town quicker than the lamplighters could work. Winter was a hard season in Wurzburg.

He had spent all day at work in the university. So prodigious had his knife skills become that he was employed to instruct first-year students in the muscular structures of the face. He flayed the white and bloodless flesh as though he were clearing snow. The eyes stared out at him, greying and opalescent in decay. He took particular care with the women. His incisions were as perfectly formed as they were. He sometimes saw his mother in their faces. He sometimes saw the woman his father had offered to him as a replacement. The tears on her cheeks and the tears wetting her nightdress could never come from the dead eyes in the dead skulls under his blade.

Afterward, when he raised his hands to his face, he thought

he could catch the scent of the cold meat from them. The earthy smell of the human dismembered.

Sitting on the bridge beside Therese, he breathed into his hands to warm them and then inhaled that scent, long and deep into his lungs.

'I have something to tell you,' she said.

'Yes.'

'I am not sure how you are going to take it.'

The boy looked at her.

'We have become quite close over the last year or so,' she said.

'Yes,' he said.

In his head a voice told him to reach out and touch her. That this was the moment. Here was the knife edge of time.

'I —,' he began but she placed her hand up to his mouth and shook her head once, sharply.

'Let me finish,' she said, keeping her finger tips to his lips. 'I have come to care about you as one of my dearest acquaintances.'

He frowned now. Some dark presentiment was crawling within him.

One of my dearest acquaintances.

'It is because I care about you so much that I feel you should be among the first to know.'

The boy's breathing was coming harder now and the feel of the black lace gloves she wore was like horsehair against his chin.

'I do not mean to hurt you now, and please believe that I will never do you any harm. You know that, don't you?'

The boy said nothing.

Into his nothing she said, 'I am to be married.'

He bit her then.

Just like his brother who had sparked something within him all those years ago, so too had she kindled something savage. Hate sprang from love and his neat world was in chaos around him. His life, his pattern in its entirety, was suddenly tangled and unseamed.

She scrambled away from him across the parapet and clutched her bleeding hand to her chest. He could taste the salt and copper of her blood. His teeth had knapped a fleck of flesh from her third finger and he chewed it between his incisors. His face, his ordinary face, was suddenly terrifying in its blankness.

He stood with her blood on his lips as Therese Silgnan stumbled away into the dark and he followed. The warmth of her hand, the taste of her blood all balled within him and his member stood stiff in his trousers. Blood and death and all that he had ever been was now condensed and distilled so that his hands strained to throttle, to dig into her so far that he would become a part of her and lap at her fluids.

If only he had a knife.

She fled from him, but he was gaining until from out of the gloom a lamplighter came with ladder and lantern and the boy, the man, turned and made himself one with the night.

The municipal police asked him questions the next day and the officer, sympathetic, understanding of the tempests that accompany young passions, put the incident down to a *lovers' tiff* and all was forgotten.

Therese Silgnan vanished from his life forever.

A month later, just as wreaths and holly were being placed on lampposts and door handles, the man walked out into the streets. He stood; black coat, black hat, black bag. He stood; an avatar of the season.

In his hands the instruments of his trade and in his head consuming fury.

He was unwanted. By all and everything. His mother abandoned him. Left him beached on the ragged shores of this world. The only person whom he had ever wanted had rejected him. And yet they gave it away so freely. That sacred intimacy. Gave it away and took in the rank seed of bastard man. Slice it out. Again and again and again. When you were unwanted, all the women of the world were naught but vessels for wickedness. Slice it out. Wanton and chaotic. Without rhyme or reason. Towing you by the nose and then cutting you off. Like a lamb to slaughter. Unloved. Unwanted. Unmade by them. Time and time again.

They were all whores and from them sprang the fruit of man's destruction. The chaos of the world and the warp of the world and the weft of the world. All needs to be put in its place. Filthy whores need to be put in their place. The right place. The Rutting Goat of the Woods and the Sacred Star and their dead eyes staring. Knife work and bitter work. The Work. The Pattern.

... oysters. Red lobes of slime in the dark. The hard crotch and the sharp knife. The standing shaft and the bitter edge. Round the corner and down the stairs. Cavern yawn of golden light. Us in it. Crow against the sun. The lamps. The brass. The wood. All gleaming here. All polished with fistfuls of notes. Sweat of the underclass. The workers. A nation of slaves. Heads down. Eyes down. No one sees and no one wants to see. Black coat black hat black gloves black bag. Against the light of this place. Man at the desk head down. Man at the door. Top hat and tails and eyes are dead stones in his head. He sees nothing. He asks nothing. Steps beyond and maid coming. Night shift. Like us. She has been in our chamber. The eyes. Suspicious? No. Not here. Never here. Seen not and asked not under the gaslights in the dark. In the red dark. Street now. Wide street. Gaping gash of street. Down the middle. Dead trees. Wider than Paris. Wider than Wurzburg. Wide open for us and the gaslights streaming. Black water. Ever present. Ever flowing down to filthy river. Things afloat. Filthy womanoffal floating there.

Cut out and floating.

CHAPTER 19

DUBLIN, JANUARY 2016

Nathan Jacob lay on his bed. Just as he had done yesterday and the day before that. The New Year had come and gone and with it had gone all the bunting and all the Christmas lights and all the Good Will to All Men. He lay on his bed and felt his life smoulder around him. It was a crash site. A debris field. Everything had come loose and was dislocated. He felt outside of himself. As though the wreck of his world's ending had thrown him clear somehow. Like he was having a permanent out-of-body experience. Like every moment he was dying and dying anew.

Dying from Leukaemia. A disease of the blood. The stuff coursing through his veins was his Da's after all. His Da's and

Patricia Frohmell's. Mixed and merged and sent pumping through him by a heart that was now broken. Corruption in him. Frohmell and Jacob. Jacob and Frohmell. Was there something wrong with him? Something genetic? Something in the blood?

Samantha had tried, for days, to apologise. She sat outside his door and wept for what she had said. She sat on the too-soft carpet and said how she didn't mean for him to find out like this. How the wine had taken hold of her. How she had lost her temper. How hard this must be for him.

She had no idea.

The poles of his world had been inverted and everything he thought right was now proved to be wrong.

He was his Da's son, after all. Genetics and blood and everything bound them, each to each. The only thing that remained of the truth was the fact that Samantha's womb had never cradled him. He was the product of a seedy coming together in some stinking flat somewhere in town. Conceived on a bed damp with other people's sweat. Not adopted but dumped. Not a choice but a consequence. A Frohmell by birth and a Jacob by accident.

What was he going to do?

He had spent every day since Christmas Day lost in his writing. Trying to close himself about in the geography of a world long forgotten. A world of fog and smoke and degradation and murder.

A world, he supposed, that he sprang from. A world of pimps and prostitutes and the men who climbed onto them, all flabby and leering and tasting of drink. Their Viagra-stiffened prongs poking and questing and rooting. The harrowing of it. The brutal harrowing of it. And everything dark and hot in the sticky rooms. Wet on the windows. Breath drops streaking and pooling and stains on the sheets and everything stinking with the reek of bodies and the spilled fluids of it all.

He blinked and shook his head. His thoughts were running together lately. Running away wildly like he had lost control over what he saw in the hollow of his own skull. His imaginings grew wilder with every dilation of his mind's eye.

Since Christmas, he hadn't replied to Esther's texts or phone calls. He just wrote word after word, line after line. Setting the scene. Ripping it up. Setting the scene. Ripping it up. The bin in one corner of his room was overflowing with balls of paper. The marks of his pen like tribal tattoos across them. Blue and aggressive and harbouring unknown messages and unknowable intent.

Samantha had given up after a while. He could hear her crying herself to sleep sometimes.

James didn't even try.

So here he lay, with his very self in tatters and his room a chaos of pages and open books and photographs of those brutalised by chance. For the more Nathan read, the more he had come to realise that fate was down to blind luck.

Nothing was written in the stars. Star cross'd lovers was an illusion created to bluff the people into thinking there was something out there beyond themselves. Something that had its eye on the ball and if you don't understand right now, well the tap of the side of the nose lets you know that it's all in safe hands. All those people in all those books slaughtered because of a chance encounter. At the bus stop five minutes early or five minutes late. This car picks them up or that one does. Going to one bar rather than another. Going out or staying at home. This college campus or that college campus. Random choices that lead you to a cut throat or a crushed skull or to strong hands around your neck.

All those thousands of people, whirling atoms in the currents of the world and all of them harbouring thoughts of a pattern at work. A great plan that they were following.

The more Nathan stayed locked in his room, picking at the food left outside his door, the more he lay there reading, the more his thoughts ran to black. The more he read, the more he realised that anyone who sought to find a true path in this world was a fool. There was no structure to anything. All our yesterdays have lighted fools to dusty death. Those like cattle who trod the well-worn paths and kept their dopey, heavy heads down thought they were playing it safe. But they were wrong. Chance could fling them to the wolves as easily as anyone else. They would subside into history with scarcely a cry. A minor figure, a statistic in a book called *Cannibals* or *Maneaters* or *Monsters*. Their Ma might pour her heart out to the tabloids and get a few hundred quid to splash out on a bad hairdo.

The others, though. The bearers of the knife, the lurkers in the dark. It was they who imposed a plan on things. They worked to a system. They constructed the world as they saw fit. They altered the universe and warped it to a thing of their own designing. Fixed and controlled. Murder as pattern.

And because of this, bad things happened to good people.

The next time Esther rang his phone, he answered it.

'Hi,' he said.

'Hi.'

Her voice in his ear. He could hear the uncertainty in her. He could see her biting her lower lip. The little nubs of her teeth tugging at her flesh. That false intimacy.

'What is it?' he said.

'Um,' she paused. 'Look, your Mam called round the other day. She asked me –'

'Stop right there,' said Nathan. Flat on his back, *The Monto Murders* butterflied on his chest. 'I don't want you to mention her. Her or my ... my father. Or anything else, okay?'

'Okay.'

'Is there any other reason you were calling?'

A long silence. He could hear her breathing.

'Well?' he said.

'Look,' she said. Silence again. 'Look,' she said again. 'I

know you're having a tough time of it and I was wondering if you want to go into town. You know, to take your mind off things. I could bring the camera, if you like.'

The thought had formed words and spilled from his lips before he had any consciousness of it.

'I want to see my Daddy,' he said.

A child lonely and lost and wanting something to hold on to.

'What?' said Esther.

'Remember we went up to the graveyard before? You had that little book with you?'

'Yeah. But I thought you thought it was bullshit.'

'I've changed my mind,' he said. 'If you can help me talk to Da, then I want to. I have a shed-load of questions for him. A shed-load.'

It was four o'clock in the evening and the January bleakness was in the air. Street lamps were buzzing into existence and traffic was starting to build.

Esther met him at the cemetery gates. She was wearing black on black on black and a canvas satchel was slung over one shoulder. Its strap made a gully between her breasts.

'Are you sure, Nato?' she said.

'Absolutely,' he said. 'You have no idea the shit that's been going through my head since Christmas Day.'

'That explains the radio silence.'

'Yeah. It explains a lot.'

'Want to talk to me about it?'

'No. I want to talk to my Da.'

The grave was exactly as Nathan had left it on Christmas Day. He knew Samantha went up to it almost every day, but she left no more mark upon it than the frost did. A good job, too. It was a wonder the tombstone wasn't off-white.

The graveyard was empty, all those thousands of dead forgotten until the next time a seat is empty at a family gathering. Until their families realise with a sudden start that they had forgotten them completely and guilt brought them to the graveside with a bunch of flowers in hand.

The streetlights cast everything in Hallowe'en shades of black and orange.

Nathan and Esther stared down at the grave, now lying smooth and covered with quartzite chippings.

'Are you sure this works?' asked Nathan. The thoughts of what had occurred the last time clung like lumps of sour fat to the inside of his skull.

'I honestly don't know,' said Esther. 'According to the accounts I've read, yeah, some connection definitely forms. The Hyayuntha Indians believe –'

'Stop right there,' interrupted Nathan. 'I don't really care about the theory behind it. Let's just get on with it.'

'Okay,' she said. 'Same as last time. Remember something happy.'

But this time, Nathan could not. Every time he thought

of his father, images of soiled mattresses, of tangled sheets crammed his skull. He could smell sweat in his nostrils.

'Okay?' asked Esther, the little fat book in her hands.

'Yeah,' lied Nathan.

And then she began to read, the delicate pentagram she wore around her neck held in one hand. The language was completely alien to Nathan, no more familiar to him than the last time they had stood here. It sounded vaguely like what he thought Latin should sound like, but there was a guttural hack to it that reminded him of German. It sounded an old language. A language for dark deeds on dark nights.

What would he ask his father? What would he say?

Why.

Over and over again.

Whywhywhywhywhywhy.

This was never going to work. A spur-of-the-moment thing to get him out of the house. It was impossible.

He was about to tell Esther to stop reading. That nothing was happening. And then something crawled into his mind from his hindbrain. Some instinctive firing of some ancient synapse. It was like gooseflesh rippled over the inside of his skull.

And then he heard it.

Above Esther's reading a voice was in his head.

Da?

Da, is that you?

From where it came, he had no idea, but the voice seemed to be inside him. Suddenly there, as if always a part of him. He watched Esther as she read, the strap of her satchel lying where he wished his head to be, and the voice rose in volume and yammered.

Da? Da?

Father and son and boy past and man to come. Over and over again and the red spill of it all. The white flesh. Take her and take her again. The red dark. The weeping dark and quick knife gleaming.

'Stop!' screamed Nathan and his scream cut through Esther's voice and the noise of all the suburban 4X4's making their way home.

And again, 'Stop!'

Esther blinked and snapped the book closed. She did not realise that Nathan was shouting at himself. Shouting at the voice that came unwelcome and unbidden from his Da's grave and crawled up and into his brain.

She stared at him.

'What's wrong, Nato?'

Nathan was shaking his head as though ridding himself of a buzzing insect. He walked away a few short paces and leaned against a headstone. Esther came to him.

'Are you okay?' she asked.

Take her and take her again.

'I'm okay,' he lied. Twice now in fifteen minutes he had lied to her.

'I think we should go home,' she said.

'No!' he snapped. 'I'm not going home. No way am I going home.'

She looked at him. The desperation in his face. The confusion.

'Do you want to go into town?' she asked at last, probing for something that might scour the horror from him. 'We could visit some of those places you're writing about?'

'You want to go up to Monto?'

'Sure,' she said. 'Where it used to be. You need out of here, Nato. It's like you're going crazy or something.'

Nathan twisted his head and looked at the black bag he had brought with him. Book and pen and notepad. That was all he needed. Bag and book and pen and notepad and then gone. With Esther.

'Okay,' he said. 'Why not.'

That voice. Anything to rid himself of that voice. That voice that was not his Da. That could not be his Da.

The 46A into town was always packed. But Nathan and Esther managed to get a seat right up front on the top deck. The windows were slicked over with a film of condensation and when Esther used her sleeve to cut a clear sweep through it, the stuff wept down the glass and gathered along the perished rubber around the frame. Dribbles of exhaled moisture. Panes of grey breath, all misted cataracts in the January cold.

I AM IN BLOOD

Esther tried to make conversation and Nathan genuinely tried to chat back, but their attempts at small-talk were still-born. Strangled at birth. The rest of the bus was a yammering monkey-house of noise. Ninety percent of people had a phone clamped to their ear and were turned slightly away from the person beside them. Shaved apes gibbering away in their own little worlds. Lumps of plastic pressed to their skulls. Nathan sat, and around him the world had lost all its warmth and all its goodness.

He was listening to the radio once and they were talking about the results of this survey that had been conducted. People were asked to list the things they couldn't live without. The internet and people's phones topped the list. Above family. Above friends. Above human dignity. Google and Apple. What a joke. Empty vessels of humanity lodging so much of themselves in plastic and silicon that their souls were become pixelated things. Things owned and peddled by multinationals. Their very selves dictated by an LCD display and whether or not they *Like* a cat playing the fucking piano.

Nathan shook his head. Shook his head at everything he saw about him and then jumped as Esther snaked her arm around his. And because of her touch, the hollowness that yawned all around him puckered closed for a bit. Imagine a bullet wound or an incision for a surgical drain. Imagine the way that looks when it heals. Corrugated around the edges, plugged with scar tissue, but a weak point all the same. If you lift a dog's tail and take a good look at the pursed sphincter underneath, that's what Nathan felt his life, at this moment, to be. A dog's ass. Everything had drawn tight about the hole in his life. It was sealed. Sealed but still there.

He looked down at her and she looked up at him.

Out of her not-quite-a-smile smile her words came silken and slow.

'Don't worry, Nato. I've got you.'

You have me. You have me for as long as you want.

He nodded dumbly and thought he must look like one of those horses that performs tricks for sugarlumps. Mr Ed with peanut butter plastered across his gums.

He tried smiling and it seemed to work for her smile widened and she craned her neck and pecked him on the cheek.

The satin touch of her. The tension of the musculature beneath. The glimpse of tongue behind teeth. The flesh of her. The carnality in that one brief kiss. All this made riot inside him. Down below, down where his hair was coarse and curled like excelsior, down there, something spasmed at the slightest touch of her lips. Something jerked and stirred. Jerked and stirred in dumb, spastic reflex.

'You're the best, Nato,' she said. 'Things'll be grand. Don't worry.'

'I hope so,' he said.

For *I hope so* read *I love you*.

I AM IN BLOOD

They got off the bus in town and went down Talbot Street. Esther made a joke about one of the hundred or so *Euro Valu* shops that crowded the retail market around here. Nathan laughed and his world continued to right itself slowly, finding equipoise in Esther's company. Things were better when she was around. Things felt good. Always.

Down Talbot Street, they turned left on to James Joyce Street and stopped outside the Buddhist Centre. The smells of incense and lemongrass coming out of the place were insane and Esther sneezed. Nathan took his bag off his back and took out his improvised map. Each of the little red marks stood out bright as brake lights. Blood on snow. A mark per murder. Like a perverse sort of exam.

'Right,' Nathan said to himself. And again, 'Right.'

Esther had taken her digital camera from out of her pocket and was busy taking random photographs of the buildings, the people, the rubbish in the gutter.

'Do you think they're aware of the irony?' she said.

'Hmm?' said Nathan. He was trying to get his bearings. Trying to find where Mary Shortt was found, pooled in her own dying.

'The Buddhists,' said Esther. 'Do you think they're aware of the irony of setting up a Buddhist Centre in the middle of where the Monto used to be? Where all these murders happened?'

Nathan paused for a moment and looked at her. It was

statements like that that made him fall for her over and over again.

'I don't know,' he said. 'Maybe that's the point.'

'Good thinking,' she said and kept snapping photos.

Nathan eventually found where he was and took Esther by the hand. 'Come on,' he said.

They walked up James Joyce Street and then swung right onto a little lane flanked by redbrick flat complexes. In front of them, at the end of the lane, was a squat little transformer shed and beyond that a postage stamp of a park. In the January black, the place had a dingy feel to it. Damp and cold and empty. It was floored with tarmac now. Gone were the cobbles on which Mary Shortt had sat and bled her life away, her throat cut and her eyes empty.

'Is this where the first one was found?' asked Esther. She was whispering.

'This is it,' said Nathan. And he too was whispering. 'Mary Shortt.'

He began to write in his notepad while Esther began to take photos of the lane and the surrounding buildings. She crouched and moved and even climbed the railings of the left-hand flat complex, all in an effort to get a striking angle.

'These'll look great in black-and-white,' she said.

'I'm really glad you're here,' said Nathan. Not really replying to what she had said. Just telling her the truth.

She smiled at him and continued to press the button on

her camera. The noise it made was like that of an insect. A cicada chirp in the gloom.

After a few minutes she asked, 'Did your buddy, Frohmell, find her here?'

Nathan tried not to think of his family, the snarl of barbed wire that was his roots, and looked up from what he was writing.

'No,' he said. 'George didn't find her, but he got landed with the investigation. C Division was under strength.'

'Ooooh,' she said,. '*George* now, is it? *C Division*? You sound like you've done your homework.'

Homework. For the last two weeks nothing but homework. Alone. In his room.

'Yep,' he said. 'Homework.'

'Where was she?' she asked.

'What?'

'Where was she? You know, when they, like, found her 'n' stuff.'

Nathan looked at her. She stood with her camera in her hand and her face open and curious.

'Seriously?'

'Yeah. Seriously. This is deadly.'

Nathan slowly took out *The Monto Murders* and thumbed through it.

'Fifty paces down,' he said. 'And sitting against the right-hand wall.'

'Cool,' said Esther and walked down the lane.

Nathan hurried after her, suddenly anxious. Feeling as he did when Esther stood over his father's grave with her little grimoire in her gloved hands. He felt there was a line being crossed here. A transgression that rippled gooseflesh up and down his back.

Esther was standing looking down at a featureless patch of tarmac and concrete.

'Here?' she asked.

'Pretty much. Yeah.'

She handed him her camera and sat down with her back to the glossy marble cladding of a vacant shopfront. One of the glossy abortions of the Celtic Tiger. She looked up at him from the murder scene in which she sat.

'Take a picture,' she said.

Nathan stared at her.

'What?'

'Take a picture. I'll pose for you.'

Then she slumped to one side, rolled her eyes up and let her tongue loll from between her teeth.

'Don't take the piss,' said Nathan.

'I'm not,' she said. 'Is this not how she was found? I'm not taking the piss. I want you to get this right. I can be your inspiration. Your Maud Gonne.'

She said this half-mockingly. She knew. She had to know.

'This is sort of creepy, don't you think?'

She looked up from where she sat and said, 'Absolutely. I love it. You're close to death here. You can feel it. Actually feel it.'

'Are you sure you want me to do this?'

'Definitely. Was she like this? You know, when they found her?'

'No,' he said. 'She ... well.'

He knelt down and propped Esther more upright. His hands sank into the soft padding of her black coat, feeling the body inside it, the heat of it. His hand brushed her breast. He lifted her chin, his hands cupped her flesh, his fingers felt the fine ridge of her jawline. Her eyes looked up at him, wide and close and seemed to drink in him. Swallow him whole.

'There,' he said, and took a step back.

She sat as though relaxing. Her legs spread in front of her, jutting out from under the hem of her coat where it was rumpled up and bunched about her thighs. Her face was tilted slightly upward and her eyes were wide open. The only thing she was missing was a crescent of leaking red banding her throat.

'Take the photo,' she said.

With an odd breathlessness, Nathan stood over her. His hands were quivering and he didn't know why. He could feel adrenaline sluice through him. The glands of his groin trembled. The ghost of her lips burned on his cheek and burned in his abdomen and he pressed the button. Pressed and pressed and pressed again.

Chirp chirp chirp.

Snick snick snick.

'What da fook do ya think yor doin'?'

The shout made the laneway give echo like a ravine, thunderous with noise.

Esther scrambled to her feet and Nathan spun around.

A heavy-set bald man in a Kappa tracksuit and a hoodie was standing at the mouth of the laneway. He held a leash balled around his right hand and a bulldog bucked at the end of it. The dog's mouth was a swamp of saliva and festoons of the stuff slobbered onto the footpath.

The man looked first at Nathan and then at Esther. She straightened the front of her coat and tucked a loose curl of hair back under her hat.

'You arigh' luv?'

'Yeah,' said Esther. 'Fine. School project. Urban Geography.'

'I taught he was *at* ya or sumptin. Ya know wad I mean, yeah? Can't be too fookin careful dese days, wha'?'

'Yeah,' said Esther. And again, 'Yeah. Thanks.'

That night, Nathan lay on his bed with his laptop open and cycled through the pictures they had taken. Esther had photoshopped them black-and-white and they looked suddenly like any other collection of crime scene photos. When he got to the ones he had taken of Esther, he stopped. Esther with her legs splayed, staring at the camera. Everything monochrome. Grey and black and stark and her eyes drinking him in like he was sustenance and stimulant, both.

He lay on his bed and looked at her for a long, long time.

When sleep came, so too did that bitter voice. The voice that was not his own but yet he recognised it in himself. And he in it. A rattling voice. A voice of rust and cold. A voice soulless and mocking.

… a turning-point. A fulcrum in the midst of things. Things turn and turn about. It all rebounds and re-echoes. Oh the symmetry of it. The broken edge of things. Sharp and hard and glistening. The cold of it. The pattern of things and us at the centre. Time and time again. Over and over again. Conflation and collapse. Things turn and revolve and we're all the same in the end …

CHAPTER 20:

DUBLIN, JANUARY 2016

The last place in the entire world that Nathan wanted to be was where he now found himself. Mr Geraghty was at the whiteboard and the sum he was doing stretched all the way down one side of it, began again at the top and kept going. Nathan had written essays shorter than that sum. It was an epic of a sum and Nathan was lost in it. Geraghty was talking as he worked, his back to the class. His speech was full of *of courses* and *as we have seen befores* and *obviouslys*. Nothing he was doing was remotely *obvious* to Nathan. But *of course* and *as we have seen before* the rest of the class didn't seem as con-fused as he felt. They beavered away, heads down and pens scribbling hyperactively.

Nathan fucking hated sums.

Really and truly fucking hated them.

He sat there in the marrowfat-painted classroom and looked around him. He had given up on the sum as a lost cause. He sat there and took in the sickly walls with their glistening cladding of too-much paint, he took in the lads and the girls, hard at it with their brains a sparking constellation of numbers and algebra. Their's was a universe in which he could take no part.

He didn't notice Geraghty turning around.

'What do you think you're doing, Jacob?'

Nathan jumped.

'What, me? Nothing.'

Geraghty stood at the top of the class with his epic maths problem behind him like the backdrop for some geeky stage show. He tossed his marker up. Caught it. Tossed it again.

'That's the bloody point, Jacob,' he said. 'You've been doing feck-all now since you got back from the holidays. It's always a case of *what me* and *nothing* with you, isn't it?'

'Sir,' said Nathan.

What else could he say?

A quick knock on the classroom door and it opened and Mr Sheridan's head poked in at the jamb. Mr Sheridan was Nathan's Year Head and was generally considered to be one of the soundest teachers in the school. There are some teachers who have an air about them. They mightn't ever raise their voice. They mightn't ever even frown. They might be universally liked. Nevertheless these teachers carried something dangerous in themselves that communicated itself through subtle signs. A gesture. A slight shifting of their weight. A charisma that placed all the world as background to their concerns. A suggestion that the Earth spun because they hadn't told it to stop. Yet. These teachers were the spine of the school, the bracing column to which all else was attached. Mr Sheridan, though, wasn't one of these. He was as soft as melted toffee and everyone from first years to the caretakers trampled all over him.

'Sorry for interrupting class, Mr Geraghty,' he said in his deferential way, 'but is Nathan Jacob here?'

Geraghty pointed with the marker.

'There's the very man,' he said.

'Ah,' said Sheridan. 'Excellent. Nathan could you pack your bag, please. I'd like a quick word.'

Everyone, the whole class, went *Ooooooooohhhhh* at this.

Outside in the corridor, Sheridan looked up at Nathan and did that sort of half-smile thing that adults do when they're patronising someone younger than them.

He bobbed his head and did that half-smile thing and said, 'You okay?'

Nathan looked at him.

Sheridan kept doing that half-smile thing and said, 'No. Well. Obviously. You're having a hard time of it. I know.'

Then why the stupid question?

Sheridan was sort of mumbling to himself, as though rehearsing what he was about to say.

Eventually he came out with, 'Um, I would really like to meet with you later, if that's okay with you? Next class. The first period after lunch. I believe you have Irish? The ol' Gaeilge, wha'?'

Mr Sheridan. Year Head extraordinaire.

'What for?'

'Well, a student has raised concerns for you. A student and some of the staff. We're worried about you, Nathan.'

For *a student* read *Esther Gilsenan*.

'Well?' said Sheridan. 'Would you like to talk with me, with anyone?'

'Yeah,' said Nathan. 'Sure.'

And then the bell rang for lunch.

Esther was sitting, as usual, alone in the canteen. The canteen was filled with the noise of three hundred teenagers all talking at once. The canteen was what the main hall turned into at lunchtime. This galvanised shutter thing in one wall was clattered open and revealed a tuck shop filled with rolls and fruit juice and apples and oranges and bananas and all sorts of reconstituted chicken gloop covered in breadcrumbs and masquerading as real chicken. The school's Healthy Eating Policy only extended, it seemed, to chocolate and crisps. Processed white bread and deep fried chicken porridge were all A-Okay.

Nathan wasn't sure, but as he walked over to Esther he could have sworn that some people moved to get out of his way. He could have sworn that some of the fifth-year girls tittered behind his back and he knew, he just knew, that Lorraine Doran was whispering something about him to her little coven of ash-blond friends. All about him the canteen filled with the sticky smells of too much deodorant and cheap perfume.

In the middle of all this, he stood over Esther and looked down at her, sitting alone with her fingerless gloves and her black beret tilted on the dark spate of her hair.

'Alright, Nato?' she said.

'Fancy some company?'

'Yeah, of course.'

She shifted over on the bench and Nathan plonked down beside her and tore the hair out of his eyes where it slumped forward.

'What's up?' she asked.

Nathan smiled at her. He wanted to thank her. Not for setting him up with a meeting in the Year Head's office. But to thank her for thinking of him. For having him so much in her mind. It was a pale imposter of what he felt for her. But it was a start.

'Thanks,' he said. He felt awkward and clod-tongued, speaking to her like this.

'Thanks for what?'

'You know. For caring.'

She suddenly had a funny little frown on her face.

'Have you been smoking something, Nato?' she said.

From under his fringe, Nathan looked at her.

'Were you talking to Sheridan about me?' he asked. 'Or to anyone else?'

She shook her head. 'No. Why would I?'

'Well, I thought you might have been worried about me or something.'

Thought you might be looking out for me like I look out for you. Like I spend every minute of every day thinking about you and I hoped you did the same.

Did she feel for anyone like he felt for her? Did she feel for Andrew Callahan like that? With his white-blond hair and his oh-so-shallow take on the world. Was she that easily fooled?

He felt like getting sick.

Still shaking her head she looked at him and still shaking her head she said, 'No.' And again, 'No.'

Then she seemed to realise what she was saying or maybe she saw something change in Nathan's face because very quickly she said, 'I mean, yeah. Of course I'm worried about you. A lot of people are. But why would I talk to Sheridan? You'll be grand. You said so yourself. You just need time.'

Nathan's head dropped between his shoulders like a poor

beast's under the whip. That one phrase wounded him. He thought to himself that he should not feel this bad, that there was nothing in Esther's words that could explain the sudden wrench under his ribcage. Deep down, though, he knew. He knew the want that was in himself. He knew the import he attached to her every word and look. It was like the augury of his life was spelled out in the lines of her anatomy, in her voice.

Esther looked troubled, as though she understood the effect her words had had on him. To the side of his hanging face she said, 'Your brother was asking questions, though. He came up to me to ask what you were writing about and how you were getting on. He said this sounded lame 'n' stuff but that he was worried about you, too.'

'James?' said Nathan. 'Fuck right off.'

'No. Seriously. That's what he said.'

Nathan hissed out a bitter little laugh. James. The little rat. Worried. About him? No fucking way. The little prick was probably trying to get him in trouble or something. Sending him to the Year Head like some sort of troublemaker. This was like Samantha sending him to that useless psychiatrist. Except it wasn't because he had no Da to fight his corner this time. But he didn't want to think of his Da. He didn't want to think of the man behind those memories. The man who spent his cash and shot his load in the threadbare company of prostitutes.

Shot his load and spawned a son.

Was Samantha lying? Was she capable of that?

Esther was looking at him.

'I actually think he was being genuine,' she said. 'Actually.'

Nathan didn't care whether James was being genuine or not. He didn't care whether his adopted, no, his *half*-brother gave two fucks about him. He cared that Esther hadn't. He cared that the someone who had gone to Sheridan wasn't the person he had wanted to go. For no reason under the sun he felt let down. Betrayed somehow. Like a puppy too stupid to know why it had been kicked.

Every single time he felt the join between him and Esther tighten, she said or did something to create a distance again. And every time she did it, Nathan felt like this. Was she blind to him? After all was said and done, did she think no more of him than of any other stray?

He was quiet for a long time. He felt embarrassed and a weird sort of anger was in him.

'Thanks anyway,' he said and walked away.

Esther watched him go as the bell rang, jangling lunch-time to a close.

Nathan went to his locker before going to the Year Head's room. He dumped some of his books in and sorted out the ones he would need for the afternoon. The corridor was full of girls and boys roaring and shouting and throwing sly digs and shoving each other against walls and lockers and the whole place was an echoing throat of teenage exuberance and sugar highs.

Nathan was closing the padlock on his locker when one of the lads from 6C came up behind him and said, 'You're such a depresso freak, Nato.'

'Whatever,' said Nathan and he turned and left all the roars and shouts and insults behind him.

The Year Head's room was on Mr Shore's corridor. The corridor didn't actually belong to Mr Shore, but this was what everybody called it. Mr Shore was one of those teachers who held absolute authority. Everyone scurried down Mr Shore's corridor quickly and quietly because if he heard you talking while he was in class, he'd come out on to the corridor and very gently and very quietly strip your dignity from you, until your self-esteem was a flayed and bloodied thing. This was hilarious if you were watching it happen. Not so funny if it was being done to you.

Nathan knocked on the big glass door of the Year Head's room. It was the only door in the entire school with a sort of gauze curtain over the glass. To protect the confidentiality of what went on inside. To preserve the identity of those seeking help and advice. To stop the rest of the school taking the piss because you were all screwy in the head and needed a shoulder to cry on.

A lot of lads with anger management issues and a lot of girls with low self-esteem went in there to get off Irish or

Maths. No homework? No problem.

Most of the Year Heads were sound, though. Sheridan's heart was in the right place. He treated people kindly.

Nathan knocked again. He could see Sheridan through the gauze curtain. He was a blur behind his desk and he was putting some papers into a file and then he closed the file and placed it on the desk before him. All this Nathan got only the impression of through the fog of fabric masking the door. Everything in the office seemed nebulous and lacking edges. Slurred.

'Come in,' called Sheridan.

Nathan opened the door and stepped into the office and closed the door behind him again. The gauze hung sustained in the air for a moment like the shroud of a cartoon ghost.

'Sit down, Nathan,' said Sheridan and pushed his glasses further up the bridge of his nose. Sheridan was always doing this. When he was speaking to classes about subject options and discipline issues, he was always fiddling with his glasses. The years of fiddling had indented two red grooves on either side of his nose.

'Thanks,' said Nathan and he sat in the cushioned chair opposite Sheridan.

'Right,' said Sheridan and he shoved his glasses into the cartilage of his nose once more. 'You're a very bright lad, Nathan, and I'd say you could hazard a guess as to why you're here.'

Nathan squirmed a little. This was absolutely mortifying.

Sheridan smiled. 'You have a lot of friends, Nathan,' he said. 'You mightn't know it, but a lot of people think very highly of you. Staff and students.'

Yeah, right. Geraghty definitely wasn't one of them, that was for sure.

He looked at Sheridan, who nodded in encouragement.

'I don't know, Sir,' he said. 'Things haven't been great this past while. I really haven't noticed what people think of me. For a good while, really. It hasn't mattered all that much.'

Except one. She mattered more than anything.

'Have you spoken to anyone about this, this detachment you're experiencing?' asked Sheridan.

'Detachment? Yeah, I suppose that's a good word for it.'

'When we experience loss, especially of someone we were close to, it can often have a serious impact on us.'

'You mean my Da?'

'Yes,' said Sheridan. 'I mean your father. And I mean you.'

Nathan's knuckles drummed on the arms of the chair. He stared at them as if they were someone else's.

Eventually, he said, 'I don't really want to talk about my Da. If that's okay, Sir?'

'Do you want to talk about you?'

Nathan laughed. 'There's not much to talk about, Sir.'

'You've taken up writing, I hear?'

James, you little crawling rat.

'Yes, Sir.'

'What about?'

'Um,' said Nathan. And then, 'A serial killer, Sir. He was in Dublin in the 1890s.'

Sheridan smiled, but it was a different sort of smile now and he lifted a Biro and scribbled something into a notepad.

'Fiction?' he asked.

'Well,' said Nathan. The way Sheridan was writing was starting to creep him out. 'Not really. I'm trying to write a modern account of what happened. A sort of True Crime thing.'

'I see,' said Sheridan. Scribble scribble. Scribble scribble.

'I'm really enjoying it,' said Nathan. And then because he had nothing left to say, he said, 'It helps me take my mind off things at home.'

'How are things at home?'

'Okay.'

'You don't want to go into it more?'

'No.'

'Okay.'

Then Sheridan opened up the file on his desk and took out an A4 sheet. Upside-down, Nathan could see it was a sort of questionnaire with a series of boxes down one side. The paper was a nice, pleasing peach colour. A nice, non-threatening colour. Nathan could see Samantha painting the living room with it.

Sheridan was talking again. He was saying, 'I'd like you to just fill in this questionnaire as honestly as you can, Nathan.

Mr Farrelly, the Guidance Counsellor, feels that it is a good idea for you to do this. You're a bright lad and you'll figure out what it's all about within a question or two, but carry on regardless. A lot of teachers are worried about your grades slipping and the standard of your work in general, but more importantly they're worried about you. They're worried that you're sort of lost in your own life, you know?'

Nathan nodded. What else could he do?

Sheridan spun the questionnaire around and passed it to Nathan along with a Biro.

'Do you want me to maybe stand outside?' he asked.

'No, Sir. It's grand.'

Nathan clicked the Biro and read the questions from start to finish. His first day in first year, his very first day, loads of the teachers did this trick to teach you about how to approach questions. They gave you a big list of twenty questions to do. The very last question, number twenty, after you spending half an hour slogging through the other nineteen, number twenty said: *Only do Questions 1 & 2.*

Ever since that day Nathan read any exam that was handed to him from start to finish.

He looked at Sheridan. Sheridan smiled.

The first question read: *Do you have difficulty falling asleep?*

And on they went until you got to ones like: *Are you in a relationship?*

And: *Do you experience delusions or hallucinations?*

And: *Do you try to avoid dealing with other people?*

Nathan looked at Sheridan. Sheridan smiled.

'These questions are supposed to find out if I'm depressed, right?' said Nathan.

Sheridan nodded. 'Yes. It'll just give us an indication. It might put us on a path to resolving the difficulties you're having.'

'I'm not depressed,' said Nathan. He was suddenly defensive. He felt cornered. Framed. James, the miserable little douche, had set this up lovely.

'If you could just answer the questions, Nathan.'

'No, Sir,' said Nathan. 'Not if I don't have to.'

Sheridan sighed. 'You don't have to do anything you don't want to do, Nathan.'

'Good,' said Nathan. He knew he sounded petulant. Like a four-year-old child. But at this stage he didn't care.

'Look it, Nathan, you're a very bright lad, but the trouble with very bright lads is they sometimes are too busy looking at the world to ever look into themselves.'

'What's that supposed to mean?'

'I once taught in a school where a young man, maybe a bit younger than you, felt so down in himself that he did something very tragic.'

Nathan dropped his gaze to the toes of his shoes. He felt uncomfortable again.

He placed the questionnaire on the desk in front of him

and said, 'Can I go now, Sir?'

'Yes,' said Sheridan, his voice resigned, his breath sough-ing out of his face. 'But please, Nathan. Come talk to me, to anyone, if you start feeling, you know, down or anything.'

'Thanks, Sir,' said Nathan. But what he was thinking was, lately I don't feel any other way. He had forgotten what *up* felt like.

'Oh, and Nathan?' said Sheridan as Nathan got up to leave.

'Yes, Sir?'

'Did they ever catch your killer?'

'No, Sir,' said Nathan. 'That's the thing with the good ones. You don't catch them because you don't see them coming.'

Sheridan nodded and wrote something down. Scribble scribble. Scribble scribble.

Nathan stepped out of the Year Head's room just as the bell rang for the end of class. Mr Shore's corridor was sud-denly filled with a hundred teenagers all muttering quietly to themselves. The corridor was filled with the sound of dry leaves on the wind, susurrate and low.

And into this sound an open sore of a voice belled, 'Ha ha! Look at the state of Nato! He's such a fucking freak!'

That evening, Nathan Jacob sat at the desk in his bed-room. His laptop was open before him and the screen lit his face with a fungus glow. The middle finger of his right hand tapped the cursor and dragged the PDF file he had accessed up and down and across his vision.

That strange anger he had felt for Esther was still in him somewhere. He could feel it like he felt that horrible voice speak to him over her reading.

He had been rewriting a section of his book and on impulse had Googled *Depression Questionnaire*. After a minute he had happened upon the exact one that Farrelly had given to Sheridan to give to him. Lazy shower that they were. Six years of college and postgrad courses to cut and paste something from Google. What a joke.

Now, though, with no one around, no one to judge, Nathan found himself reading the questions one after the other after the other. There was a little matrix at the bottom where you could compute whether or not you were depressed and to what extent you needed to hide the knives.

All the while, as he read the questions, Nathan thought of Esther and the train wreck that his life had become. All the while, until the bright screen and the questionnaire itself became merely background to his contemplations.

For how long he sat there, unmoving in front of the computer, he had no idea, but when he came to himself, centred on the screen was Question 14: *Do you experience delusions or hallucinations?*

Nathan x'd out of the entire thing.

CHAPTER 21:

DUBLIN, JANUARY 1893

Lucy Doherty sometimes felt that the Fitzgerald Arms was the best hotel in Dublin. Sometimes she felt it was a bleedin' kip. Either way, it was where she came to work day-in-night-out and so, in the heel of the hunt, her thoughts on the place did not particularly matter. Every day, in the sourceless, dove-grey of the Dublin dawns or in the hissing gaslight of the Dublin evenings, Lucy walked down from her tenement on Mountjoy Square and mounted the marble steps to the grand foyer of the place.

She had lost a child on those steps once. The snivelling wet of a November night had glazed the hard marble, gleaming and treacherous. She felt her heel go out from beneath her, her ankle turn, and then she was lying on the footpath with people stooping to lift her. The cramps came soon after and then the blood and all the other fluids. All washed into a drain and into the reeking dark with a thousand other human excretions. The sad thing about the whole episode was that she hadn't even known she was pregnant.

Still, with three gobs to feed already, gaping and piping like chicks in a nest every time she walked in the feckin' door, that little slip was probably a great mercy.

If Mick would get off his bleedin' arse and get a job, maybe she mightn't have to mount those steps everyday. Mightn't have to relive that fall every single day.

Still, it didn't do to complain. Who'd listen to you anyway? If it wasn't for the Fitzgerald Arms, she'd be scratching in the rubbish heaps for crusts and potato skins like half the people she knew. The world was the world and there was no use trying to make sense of it, at all, at all.

This evening, she hurried down Sackville Street like everyone else seemed to be hurrying. Every single person's head was down against the weather; January dying with a vicious wind that would freeze the eyeballs in your skull. Everyone's head was down, too, because to look into the face of another human being in this place might be to look into the face of the Devil himself. Four dead bodies, all cut up and sliced and nobody having a clue who was behind it.

The Fenians and the DMP being at each other's throats

did nothing to help matters either. Rallies had been held on College Green and a few bricks and cobbles had been lofted half-heartedly at the police. The police, for their part, had half-heartedly cracked a few pates. But all it was going to take was a full heart. A person with enough commitment to drive home the matter or to storm a police station. Mick said if that happened, they were upping sticks and moving to Liverpool. Life wouldn't be worth living here.

There was a panic in Dublin. A sense of falling that could not be arrested. A sense of a place spiralling down and down like blood in a drain.

Still, it didn't do to complain.

Lucy nodded to Nicky on the door. He stood there every night in his stupid hat and tails, like one of them puffins you got on Howth Head. All he needed was a moustache of silver fish hanging from his chops and he'd be the very picture. Lucy smiled to herself as Nicky touched his hat brim and she went into the hotel.

The first thing she had to do was clock-in. She signed the register, put on her white apron and looked at herself in a mirror. Borthwick, the manager, went mad if you looked at all bedraggled when you were at work. It didn't do to let the image of the Fitzgerald Arms slide at all. It didn't do to look like a denizen of a collapsing ruin, with three skinny children, a bad chest and the teeth rotting in your head. It didn't do to look like what you were.

I AM IN BLOOD

She looked at herself in the mirror, rubbed a smudge of soot from her cheek and went to work.

She knocked politely on door after door and then entered through them one after the other after the other. She turned down the bedclothes, she stoked the fires, she warmed the bed-pans, she mopped up the spills. She ignored the rumpled piles of clothes, the kicked-off shoes, the smells of sweat and of sex. She conducted her affairs with the quiet discretion of hotel workers the world over. The million maids in a million rooms, privy to a million dirty little secrets.

And then she came to the room on the third floor. The room that had been occupied since before Christmas. The room of the dapper Englishman with the grand accent. The room that had lately begun to contaminate the corridor with its bizarre smells. The room that had always, until this very moment, had a *Do Not Disturb* sign slung on its door handle.

There was no sign now.

Lucy knocked tentatively. She had no reason to be wary but she was anyway. She had performed this action a hundred times every day of her working life. The knock. The wait. The opened door and the turned-down bedclothes and then on again to the next. And yet, here, in the bright light of the corridor, a darkness had seemingly stolen upon her. It was as real as the high odour leaking from under the Englishman's door.

She knocked again.

There was no answer.

Lucy looked around, seized by the vague compulsion to simply walk away. To leave this room and whatever alchemy it housed behind her. But then she scolded herself for her childishness, turned the master key in the lock and entered the room.

The smell struck her immediately. It was a chemical stink coupled with something organic, something coppery and meaty in the back of the throat. Like a glue factory or a tanner's yard. Or the smell of a butcher's floor as his apprentice took a mop to it and swashed over the blood and sawdust with disinfectant. It was a red smell.

The room, like all of them on this corridor, was really a suite. It was divided into three parts. The living space, with its couches and armchairs and brass and hooded lamps, was separate to the bedchamber, which was in turn separate from the bathroom, with its enamel bath and sink.

She left the door open behind her, but even at this the suite was dark. Dark and cold. No lamps were lit and the hearth was a dead hole in one wall. The air of the place coaxed goosebumps to bubble across Lucy's bare arms, as though she had been stung by a host of nettles. She rubbed her hands together and breathed into them to warm them up and to get the blood flowing again. Then she went into the bedchamber.

The bed was pristine. It looked untouched and if anyone had slept in it, Lucy admired their bed-making for the blankets and sheets were flat as planes and the pillows plump and inviting. On the bed, a black leather doctor's bag sat, closed and pregnant with implication. Its alien presence on that neat bed seemed to draw all lines of perspective toward it, as though it were a weight on reality itself.

Lucy reached out a hand to touch it. Paused, then turned and left the bedchamber.

It was in the living room that the smell was at its worst. Lucy looked around for its source. In the untouched perfection of the rest of the suite, perhaps the only job she had to do was throw out some rotting piece of meat, some dinner scraps forgotten and left behind a couch.

She made her way about the furniture, fruitlessly stooping and prodding and lifting cushions until she stopped in front of a tall press standing between the room's twin windows. Here the smell was intense. She frowned and looked at the press for long moments. Could a gentleman of breeding and wealth be simply storing leftovers and dirty plates in a cabinet? Could his manners be that lacking? Then again, nothing would surprise her. She had witnessed the manners the upper classes were possessed of. The groping hands, the busy fingers, the pinching and the slapping and the pulling down on to laps where the hard, gristly sausage against her gave the lie to their pretence of jollity and horse-play.

She stood looking at the press and at the stubby key jutting from its keyhole.

The lights of Sackville Street swam up through the webs of the lace curtains and along with them came the sounds of night-time in the city. This was a fine hotel in the middle of Dublin. What could happen here? What was it that gave her the chills, so? A press full of food? The eccentricity of the aristocrat? Was this what was making her so milk-livered? Something she had seen times before beyond count?

She turned the key in the keyhole and opened the cabinet. Before her was laid out a scene of perfect horror. In the cabinet was a variety of jars. And in those jars there floated pale things with hanging tendrils. Bloodless, and all the more awful for it, organs floated in formaldehyde. White and fleshy and crazed with blue-black veins. She recognised a kidney. Suspended and rotating slowly on some invisible axis of the fluid. And then she saw something that brought vomit into her gullet. A human foetus, bald and blue and hanging in the static liquid.

★ ★ ★

He came up the stairs and down the corridor. Black hat, black coat, black gloves. Back he came from a ramble through the frightened streets. The air of the place thrilled him and his stomach rumbled. The frightened streets. Frightened because of his Work. His Pattern.

The Work. The Pattern.

And the one element of this place that snagged the Pattern and threatened all with unravelling. One atom amongst

313

a million. A policeman of all things. A Sergeant. A policeman in the papers hunting him. Hands questing in the dark. Blind groping. Impotent. But not letting go. Not giving up. Not arresting Jews nor making scapegoats. Methodical. Working to his own Pattern.

The policeman interested him. And so he watched and followed. In the dark. In the eyeless blank of the nights. He watched the policeman. Watched his woman. Waif thin and pale. Beautiful. Like ice on thorns. He had sat behind them on the tram once. Sat silent and listened to their drab talk. *Rosie. Georgie.*

Ever since, he imagined what her flesh would taste of on his tongue. The policeman and his Pattern ended just as he sought to end the greater Pattern. There would be no womb to harrow for the Sergeant. The world needed no more mothers.

The policeman would know the final power of man. The power to un-make. And the Sergeant would be broken. Before he left this place, the Sergeant's woman would be part of the great work. The apex of things. And the Sergeant would be broken on the altar of Cain.

He had said it all in his letter, but the grunting beasts of this place had not seen it. They could not grasp the weft of things. The webbings and the threads all taut and thrumming.

He had not felt such a personal hate in years. Not since his father.

Now, on this corridor, in this splendid hotel in the middle of this shabby city, he experienced something else he had not felt in years. He felt fear.

The door to his room was open. His room was never open. He would not allow it. The sign? Surely he had placed the sign? *Do Not Disturb.* Like all the other times before? Was he growing soft? Complacent, in this destitute place with its ham-fisted police and its hooded eyes and its lambs to the slaughter?

Had he forgotten it?

He stopped. And he thought about turning and running away. Leaving before the Work was done. Before the Pattern was complete.

Then his lips grew thin and he took first one and then another step toward the open door. His heels bruised the pelt of the carpet, padding like a heavy hound's. His pulse quickened and with it so did the bloodbeat of the world until the whole of existence throbbed to the hammer of his heart. The itch of his hands. The swell of his crotch.

The red spill of it and the cut of it and our hands around the throat and the crushed thrapple and the eyes and the member hard and ploughing in the cold and the dark. The red dark.

★ ★ ★

The door behind Lucy Doherty closed and she turned around, her gorge already risen and the vomit scalding the well of her throat. She could not scream. The figure stood in the room. Black hat, black coat, black gloves. His face a pale mask in the lamplight. She could not scream. Her throat was gummed with bile. Instead, she managed a guttural sort of yelp. Pathetic in the silence.

She backed away. She needed to get out. Her back collided with the cabinet and its awful contents. The jars clinked and glugged. He strode forward. And he smiled. Oh God, thought Lucy. That smile. Like a dead sun rising. Nothing human there.

Her voice came back at his approach and she croaked, 'I won't tell anyone. I swear.'

That smile stayed fixed as his fist came up and drove into her stomach.

She yawped for breath, doubled over the bolus of pain that clenched below her ribs.

He stood watching her.

Then the hands around the neck.

Then came the knife.

CHAPTER 22:

DUBLIN, JANUARY 1893

The woman sat in Earl Place like something flung by a furious God. She was dead as the cobbles and red bricks that surrounded her, of that there was no doubting. Dead as dead could be, with her throat cut and her eyes opalescent in the weak morning light. Yet, as brutal as her ending had been, there was nothing here to suggest it. No gore swamped the floor of the laneway. No red-drying-to-black caked the front of her dress. But for the fact that her neck was neatly gaping in the new day, the assumption might be that she had slumped here in the quiet death common to dozens of Dublin's citizens. If not for the clean edges of that long wound, it might have been possible to think that the cold and the rain and the hunger had carried her off at the last.

But it was not so, and George Frohmell cursed everything under the sun and, indeed, the sun and the moon and the heavens themselves that it was not so.

'No name yet, I suppose?' he asked.

The DMP man who had found the corpse, Constable John Cooney, was writing in his notebook. He shook his head. 'No, Sergeant. Nothing yet.'

George looked down at the dead body. He looked at the flesh, grey as the sky above him, he looked at the eyes sitting in the puddles of their own rotting and he looked at the throat, wide and leering. He had already checked below, beneath the severe black dress she wore.

Nothing had been done down there. There was some bruising on her thighs, enough to suggest that she had been violated before death, but there was no knife work down there. Nothing carved out. Nothing taken away.

'There's no way she was killed here, Sir,' said the constable. 'There's no blood at all.'

'She wasn't dragged either,' said George. 'There's no trail. Not even a splash.'

In his head, the map he had formulated wheeled and wheeled about. The fourth murder, ten days ago now, had conformed exactly to his own notions. The body had been placed behind a rain barrel in The Long Stand, a nickname given to a narrow little alley off Amiens Street where whatever had to be done had to be done standing up. The murder had happened some thirty yards away but the killer, the *Ripper*, had moved her. Moved her with her womb opened and her private parts sliced cleanly away. Moved poor Molly Hoare. By name and by nature. He had placed her so that four of the pentagram's five points were planted. And he had done so with remarkable accuracy. The angles between them were off by a couple of degrees due to the unchangeable geometry of streets and buildings, but the murdering bastard had nevertheless worked with a fastidiousness that genuinely terrified George.

Everything had so far happened precisely as he had determined. He even knew where the final body would turn up. Maybe not where the murder would occur, but to within a score of yards of where the body would be placed. He had asked C Division's overworked Superintendent to allocate as many DMP men as possible to that part of the Monto. A difficult thing to do with the Fenians threatening revenge and the locals railing at the continued internment of Larry Byrne's sons. *That part of the Monto*. Buckingham Street and its surrounds. Buckingham Street where Rosie, his Rosie, used to walk the cobbles and stand on the corners and sell herself to whoever came along.

He tried not to think about it. For ten days now he tried not to imagine the spectre of Rosie lying stiff and emptied under the starless night.

And then this had happened. This fifth murder. A body dumped in a place not at all in keeping with the pattern. This fifth murder like a misweave in the weft of things.

George stared at the body for a long time.

'Do you see something, Sir?' asked Cooney.

'Does she look like a prostitute to you, Constable?'

'Not really, Sir. She's dressed too neatly. Too soberly.'

'Good man,' said George. '*Soberly* is the word.'

The constable was looking at the body now, too. His eyes roving over it as detached as if it were a side of bacon.

'To tell you the truth, Sir,' Cooney said, 'she looks like a maid. Like a hotel maid or waitress.'

'I was thinking that, too,' said George.

No knife work apart from the cut throat. No knife work down below. No trophies taken. An honest worker. Not a whore. Difference upon difference upon difference.

'Do you think it's the same murderer, Sergeant?'

'Oh, yes,' said George. 'It's the same man alright. I recognise the way he cuts their throats like I recognise my own signature. He does it precisely the same way. Left to right. The exact same in every case. See how the cut is deeper under the left ear?'

'Sir.'

'It's the same monster alright. But he's changed things, here. Why? And where did he kill her?'

George knelt down beside the corpse and lifted its right hand. It was calloused across the pads of the fingers and the palm was thick and roughened.

'She was hard-working,' George said and the constable stepped closer, all the while noting things into his writing pad. 'She worked with her hands. A scullery maid or domestic, maybe. But nothing too hard. Nothing that would involve her cutting herself or causing fresh blisters.'

Then he frowned.

'No dirt, either,' he said. 'No blood and no dirt.'

'Sir?'

'He washed her. In a bath, probably. The bastard washed her before dumping her here.'

'Are you sure, Sir?'

'Absolutely, Constable. He killed her, washed her and then dumped her. Now where do you suppose a killer might happen across a maid and have the privacy to kill her and wash her in a bath without anyone asking questions?'

'Not many places round here would have a bath, Sir. Maybe he has his own little house with his own tin bath?'

'In the middle of Dublin? How many little houses or private rooms do you know within a few hundred yards of this spot?'

'None, Sir.'

'Then think, Constable.'

The constable frowned and stowed his notepad away in his uniform pocket. Then his eyes widened and he said, 'A hotel, Sir. The bollix must be quartered in a hotel.'

I AM IN BLOOD

'Good man,' said George. 'Now you take your notes and your description of her and you round up any other constable you can find and you visit every hotel within a half-mile of here and you make inquiries. Then you come see me in Store Street Barracks.'

'What will you do, Sir?'

'I'll sit here until the wagon arrives to take her away. She deserves at least that. And no photographs this time. I don't want anyone to know this is the fifth.'

'Sir.'

'And Constable. Be quick about this. Quick and quiet. He kills five and then vanishes. This is his fifth. I want him found before he can leave the city. Understand?'

'Quick and quiet, Sir. Quick and quiet.'

George waited until two more constables arrived with a covered wagon and a stretcher to bear away the body. There were no newspapermen this time. They were hovering like vultures around the Castle. Hovering and taking their damned photographs of the premises raided by G Division and writing stories about the poor families of the men arrested on suspicion of blowing up Patrick Sinnott. The Monto murders were fast becoming yesterday's news and George Frohmell was fast becoming yesterday's man.

How quickly people moved on. How quickly they forgot. Killing as routine. Human life lost in the fabric of greater events. What was a life when stacked against the pursuit of money and sensation? What were five?

George watched the constables heft the body onto the wagon and said, 'Take her to the Castle.'

The constables clambered onto the wagon's seat and were about to shake the reins and drive its horses on when George caught one of the bridles.

'On second thoughts,' he said. 'Take her to Doctor Oliver O'Sullivan, 53 Stephen's Green West, first, before taking her to the Castle.'

'Sir?'

'Ask him to just take a quick look and I'll pay him a visit later.'

'Sir.'

'Oh, and lads?'

'Sir?'

'Use the tradesman's entrance.'

George spent the rest of the day pestering C Division's Superintendent until the man lost his temper and threw George out of the station house.

'Who the hell do you think you are, Frohmell,' he raged. 'You're nought but a Station Sergeant. Who gave you the authority to march around like you own the place? Let G Division investigate these poxy murders, just like they investigate all the rest, and have done with it. I'm sick of you hanging around my Division like a bad smell. Who the hell is covering your shifts at A Division? That's what I want to know.'

George had looked him in the eye and said, 'I'm sorry, Superintendent. You can report me to Chief Superintendent Mallon if you like.'

The Superintendent had regarded him coldly, then. Shrewdly. His eyes glittered above his beard.

'Get out of my barracks,' he said.

George had gotten out of his barracks. He sat across the road on the steps of a redbrick tenement and watched all the ragged flotsam of Dublin's human wreckage sift past.

When he saw Cooney coming round the corner, he rose and went to meet him. He caught him by the arm and guided him into the nearest pub. The place was a wooden grotto of spilled drink, tobacco smoke and muttered conversation. When the customers saw the two uniformed policemen, all conversation stopped and the place gradually began to empty. Every soul in the place sidling past the two DMP men as though they were infectious, pints left half finished behind them.

The proprietor looked from his empty pub to the two policemen and said, 'And since you're in bleedin' uniform, youse bollixes probably won't even buy a drink.'

George jabbed his thumb toward the back of the pub.

'Get lost,' he said.

'You're not in a bleedin' Wild West saloon, Sergeant,' snapped the man. 'You can't go ordering people around just cos you've a stupid bleedin' hat on your fat bleedin' head.'

'I've a loaded revolver in my bleedin' pocket, too,' said George.

The man gauged George for a moment. Then he spat into a spittoon behind the counter and walked down the bar away from them, grumbling and cursing to himself.

George and Cooney sat at a table and George asked quietly, 'Well?'

'You were right, Sergeant,' said Cooney. 'Her name was Lucy Doherty and she was a maid in the Fitzgerald Arms. She clocked in last night, but never clocked out this morning. One of the lads ran up to where she lived and read out her description to her husband. He was drunk as a monkey but seemed fairly definite it was her. He wants to see her, Sir.'

'That's fine. Have him formally identify her. Take him down to the Castle. If she's not there, she might have been moved down to Kevin Street. The Castle's full to bursting with soldier boys these days.'

'Sir, without being disrespectful, but on whose authority am I doing these things?'

George had been expecting this question.

'Mine, Constable. If your Super' or anyone else questions you, tell them to come and find me.'

'Sir.'

'Now, about the Fitzgerald Arms. Poor Lucy Doherty arrived for work promptly last night and between then and dawn she was murdered, washed and dumped.'

'Yes, Sir. The Fitzgerald Arms is only fifty yards away from where the body was found and it has a back alley that leads onto Earl Place.'

George felt excited now. His stomach was alive with little kicks of adrenaline.

'Come on, Cooney,' he said.

'Where are we going, Sergeant?'

'We're going to arrest a murderer.'

Ten minutes later George and Constable Cooney stood at the reception desk of the Fitzgerald Arms. The hotel's manager, a Mr Borthwick, was almost apoplectic at the very fact of their presence.

'My God, Sergeant,' he wittered. 'This is most discommoding. The Fitzgerald Arms is an establishment of unblemished repute and yet here you stand, in your uniforms, as though you were raiding a den of Fenian subversives!'

George and Cooney stood while around them the suited and feathered worthies of the Fitzgerald Arms bustled and bobbed like some perfumed armada at anchor. Monocles and eyeglasses were raised to inspect the two uncouth representatives of Dublin's civic guard. George revelled in their surprise and discomfort.

Cooney grinned at the crowd of onlookers. A brazen, pumpkin smile.

'The sheer temerity of this is beyond galling, gentlemen,' said Borthwick.

George looked him squarely in the eye and the man stilled. The old wolfishness was in George again. The old baleful promise of coming violence.

Borthwick was silent for a long while before George spoke.

'There's a good man,' he said. 'A bit of respect for the Queen's own law never goes astray. Now, I'd like you to answer me a question or two.'

Borthwick nodded and Cooney turned to the monied throng gathered about and said, 'On you go, now. Make yourselves scarce. Shoo.'

Above the muttered *Well, I nevers* George said, 'I want you to tell me if you have any guests staying with you from an upper-class English background.'

'Well, yes,' said Borthwick. 'Of course we do.'

'Good. Now how many of those guests have been resident with you since before Christmas?'

Borthwick muttered something and took the hotel's registration book from under the desk. He leafed through it until he found the two pages he was looking for and then frowned to himself.

'There has been only the one,' he said.

'What room?' said George. He tried to keep the eagerness from his voice, but he knew it crackled from him like the charge before a lightning strike.

Borthwick shook his head then and spun the book about so that George could read the entries.

'I fear the person you are looking for has gone, Sergeant,' he said. 'He settled his account very early this morning and left. See, here is his signature.'

Borthwick pointed to a line in the ledger. There, in an elegant hand completely at odds with the savagery it had performed, was a mocking signature.

J. Bull

'I'm sorry, Sergeant,' said Borthwick as he closed the register.

George breathed through his nose. All the frustration of the past few weeks, all the anger that had curdled within him as the bodies mounted and the jibes came more frequent, all this came suddenly to the boil. He felt like he was going to erupt. He needed something to hit. Good God, that murdering bastard couldn't be gone. He couldn't be.

Borthwick stepped away from him. The policeman before him looked like he was about to tear the place apart.

'Are you feeling alright, Sergeant?' he ventured.

'What room?' snarled George.

'I told you, he's checked out, Sergeant. The room is due to be cleaned in half an hour. It's not something that can really be put off.'

'What fucking room!'

The entire foyer was silenced.

Into the silence, Borthwick's voice, very quiet, said, 'Two hundred and six. Second floor.'

Constable Cooney was regarding him with a wary sort of curiosity. George poked a finger into his chest and said, 'Nobody is to leave this lobby or to go up or down those stairs 'til I come back. Do you understand?'

'Sir.'

'And use the hotel telephone. Get as many of the lads over here as possible. We need statements. And a photographer, too. This must be recorded.'

Not waiting for Cooney's response, he took the stairs two at a time, moving like a storm front.

Room 206 stood midway down the hallway. A *Do Not Disturb* sign dangled from its door handle. The door was locked.

George felt that the time for niceties was long past. His anger needed some sort of vent. And so he raised his booted right foot and kicked the door as hard as he could. It gave at the first attempt, rattling on its hinges. The second kick tore the lock free and the door hammered back away from him.

Inside, the room was filled with a gloom like char. That and a reek like a tannery. The curtains were drawn and the colourless Dublin light wept through only faintly. It was a suite. An expensive one, on first impressions. George reached to his left and found the ceramic nipple of an electric light. The wonders of the modern age.

And what wonders that wonder itself revealed.

In front of George was a tall cabinet, standing open as

though to welcome the eyes that beheld it. On its shelves were jars of floating objects. George recognised them immediately and his breathing came harder. With each breath he dragged more of the stench of the place into his sinuses.

Vulva and labia and wombs, floating bloodless like swatches of torn blubber. Kidneys. And there, horribly, was the little life torn from Betty Quinn. Flawless and still in its preserving liquid.

George took four quick steps to the cabinet and pushed the doors solidly closed. He rested his head against the cabinet's panelling and inhaled great gulps of the room's foetid air.

He would not be sick. He would not give him that.

His eyes took in the thick carpet. Took in the blood stain to one side of the cabinet. Took in the burgundy splashes that led to the bedroom and the bathroom beyond.

Like an automaton, George followed the trail of blood. Maybe the bastard had left some clue. Anything at all. Anything.

The bed was immaculate. The corners crisply tucked in and everything pristine. Only the gouts of blood across the floor gave the clue to the monster that had lately denned there.

George pushed open the bathroom door and stopped. Stupefied.

The wall above the bath was painted a delicate dove-grey and on it was plastered the clotted viscera of poor Lucy Doherty. Words. Red words. For him.

Sergeant Georgie,

I am gonn. Long gonn. Youe will never catch me. But I wille make a catch of youe. Your Pattern torn asunder.

Cheerio Georgie,

J.B.

For how long he stood reading that message, he did not know. The humiliation of it. The mockery and the despair.

And something else. Beneath the horror, something sluggish moved. Something that provoked a familiar unease. Where had he felt it before? At O'Sullivan's. Something the doctor had said? Something he had read? Something in those dripping words?

He watched the words on the wall. Watched them as they crusted. What was it? What subtlety was he missing?

Why was he so worried?

He stood unmoving in that stinking place of savagery. All he knew was that, eventually, Cooney's hand on his shoulder spun him round. Behind the constable the room was lit as though by sheet lightning. A DMP cameraman had opened the cabinet and was capturing its horror for all time. Black and white for the blackness at the heart of humanity. White things bobbing against the black of the world.

'Are you alright, Sergeant?'

Another flash of sheet lightning and then George's belly emptied itself all over the tiles of the bathroom floor.

CHAPTER 23:

DUBLIN, JANUARY 1893

After all he had seen, the pale things all afloat in their formaldehyde, all the blood and all the gore. Lucy Doherty's life congealing on a bathroom wall and shaped to mock him by a monster's hand. The monster fled. *Gonn. Long Gonn*. After all this, George spent every penny he had in a pub beside the Rotunda hospital. Then he went home. In the dark.

Rosie smiled when he came in, but it was a smile that died quickly on her face, like something hit and mangled by a steam train.

'What's wrong?' she asked.

'Nothing,' he said. 'Nothing at all. The newspapers were right, after all. I'm useless. Bleedin' useless.'

Her face clouded.

'Have you been drinking, Georgie?' she asked.

He sat at the table and breathed out through his mouth. He was picking a fight. He knew and he couldn't stop himself. The sourness that was in him was there again and it felt like burrs under his skin.

'I have indeed been drinking,' he said. 'I'm only home because I ran out of money.'

'Thanks very much,' said Rosie.

'Don't mention it,' he said. And he hated himself for saying it as much as he hated Dublin and he hated the DMP and he hated the world hanging like a broken bauble in the empty void. A cracked and tarnished bauble with an awful nothing at its heart.

Rosie looked at him and in that instant she could not help herself in the same way that he could not help himself. Her own nature nettled through her.

'You're some bleedin' boy,' she snapped. 'Look at ya. With your horse's jaw hangin' open like a poor walkin' eejit. And the head of ya, cross-eyed with drink.'

She stood over him with her hands on her hips and she said, 'Here we are with no bleedin' money and you pissin' it all away. I've no dress for me own poxy wedding. I don't even have a bleedin' ring on me finger!'

The familiar excuse that he needed. The old anger boiling anew.

He was on his feet and his fist came up in a tight arc.

And then it stopped. Its awful trajectory cut off in mid-air.

What was in him to stop it so, he did not know. It had never done so before. Not ever. In the grip of drink, under its cloak, under its alibi, he had stood over more than Catherine with his knuckles sore and his breath a sea in storm.

But not now. Not here.

Rosie was staring at him. She had taken a half-step backward when he first rose to his feet and now she stood with her eyes wide and her face pale. Like Lucy Doherty in the bloodless morning.

'What were you going to do, Georgie?' she said. 'Georgie?'

Ashamed. More ashamed than at any time in his life, he mumbled, 'Nothing. Oh God, Rosie, I'm so sorry. He got away. *He* got away and it's my fault and now it'll happen again and again and again.'

Rosie looked at him, a swaying golem by the light of the lamp that she had bought. Bought for *their* life together. A light to guide the way.

'I'm going out,' she said. 'I'm going out and I'm not sure if I'll be back. Don't try and find me.'

With that she snatched up her coat and was gone.

Behind her, George pitched forward, stumbling over the chairs and the table.

'Don't, Rosie!' he shouted. 'Come back!'

Then he tripped and he fell to the floor and he lay there

clawing at the boards, a drunk and a fool and a slobbering mess.

After some time he got up and sat for a while with the oil lamp warm on his face. What was wrong with him? He had no drink and no money and all his friends were DMP men and not one of them did he want to speak with now. Policemen were never off the clock. They *were* their job and no matter what topic a conversation began with, it would eventually be dragged back to their work. It was like the weight of what they were forced to do and forced to see anchored them so that it was impossible to fully escape it. They were a ragged brotherhood of scarecrows, stitched into their uniforms.

The job was the last thing in the entire world that George wanted to talk about right now.

No drink and no money and no friends.

Except one.

He rose yawingly to his feet and went to see Dr O'Sullivan.

The good doctor opened his front door himself. He cocked an eyebrow as George stood there looking at him blearily. The walk had mostly sobered him up but the thoughts of Rosie out on the streets or in a pub, headless with fury, made him want the drunkenness back again. The fact that it was his own fault made him want to drink even more.

'Are you drunk?' asked O'Sullivan.

'Mostly,' said George and he began to weep. From where

the tears sprang, he had no idea. It was as though years of unwept tears had suddenly found a weak point in him and began to leak through, like a crack in a pipe.

'Rosie's after leaving me,' he croaked.

O'Sullivan's mouth quirked into a barbed little sneer and he said, 'Oh cop yourself on, Georgie boy. Whatever you might think, Rosie Lawlor has not left you in the lurch. And even if she has, it would rather befit you as a gentleman to take it on the chin and get on with things. Grow a pair of balls, my boy.'

George blinked as though slapped.

'Now, come in at once,' said O'Sullivan. 'I have been waiting on your appearance for hours now and I am in no mood to salve your pickled heart.'

George stepped into the doctor's hallway and ran a sleeve across his nose. 'My heart is more broken than *pickled*, Oliver.'

'Ah, the poetry of the drunkard. The human heart has no bones, George. It cannot be broken. It can be bruised through ill-use only. Perhaps your heart has been ill-used. Perhaps Rosie feels the same about hers. However, there are more important matters to deal with at this minute than the melodrama of your romantic affairs.'

George was slowly coming around. Behind the doctor's sardonic wit was an urgency and earnestness that was quite out of character.

'What has you so vexed, Oliver?'

'That woman you landed on my doorstep this morning. That maid, Lucy Doherty, or so your men informed me,' said O'Sullivan. Then he looked around and ushered George along the hall and into the library.

George allowed himself to be shepherded, his jowls slack and his head beginning to drum.

O'Sullivan closed the library door behind them. George looked around for the brandy bottle, but O'Sullivan was faster. He stalked over to the side-table and picked up the bottle and spun to face George once more.

'Hell's bells, man,' he said. 'What has you in such a state? You haven't been drunk in weeks. This surely has more at its root than Rosie's temper.'

George dragged a chair around and slapped backward into it.

'I've lost him, Oliver. That murdering bastard. I let him get away. A matter of hours was all that was in it and he runs off. Never to be seen again.'

O'Sullivan sat in a chair opposite and placed the brandy on the floor beside him. He leaned forward and said, 'What are you saying, George?'

'He kills five. Five is all. He kills them and then vanishes. He builds his pattern and then is gone. Puff. Like a travelling magician. That woman this morning was number five. Lucy Doherty. Abracadabra.'

O'Sullivan was clenching his lips and his breath whistled

from out his nostrils. The frustration in him was obvious.

'You are a fool, George Frohmell,' he said at last.

George snorted. 'I know, I know …'

'Shut up and listen you oafish bloody sot,' said O'Sullivan.

George stopped talking. He could count the times he had ever heard the doctor curse on the fingers of one hand.

'That woman you sent me today is not part of this monster's pattern. This pentagram that you so cleverly cottoned on to.'

George went very quiet.

'That poor woman was murdered by the same fiend clear enough. But his motives for doing so were completely different from the others.'

'Go on,' George said. Sobriety was returning like an unwelcome guest.

'There was nothing removed. Her body was placed outside the Monto. She was ravaged but not mutilated. The cut throat is the tell-all, but it was cut *post-mortem*. She died due to strangulation. If he is spinning a pattern, then poor Lucy is a strand of a different colour. She doesn't belong.'

George coughed. Then coughed again. All at once he was cold. Cold to the bone.

'What are you saying, Doctor?'

'I'm saying, if he needs five murders to complete his pattern, then he's short one. Lucy Doherty was a murder outside of his plan. He's still out there, George. He hasn't vanished. Yet. Not yet.'

'He's still here,' said George to himself and a note of hope rang through his words. 'There's still a chance …'

And then all hope died. The letter. The letter the killer had written him. *Georgie. Sergeant Georgie.* The note on the wall dashed in Lucy Doherty's blood. *Your Pattern torn asunder.* Nobody but Rosie ever called him *Georgie.* His *Pattern.* His life. His life with Rosie. Dear God, he thought. He's been watching me. And now his mind shrieked. He's been watching *us*.

And into George Frohmell's head came the image of Rosie Lawlor. Rosie Lawlor, beautiful and alone. On Buckingham Street.

He was gone before O'Sullivan could even rise to his feet.

★ ★ ★

Rosie walked the length of Buckingham Street, turned and walked back again. The stink of smoke was in the air in a way that she remembered from another lifetime. Everything seemed closer about in the Monto. More intimate. The walls wrapped you round and the sky splayed across the rooftops and capped the world so that your entire universe was confined and measured by the length of that street, the width of that alley.

She hated this place and yet it convulsed about her like a muscle. It held her to itself.

The bleedin' cheek of the man.

Standing up like he meant to hit her a slap. If he did, it

would be the last slap he ever threw. The stupid, drunken bollix.

And at the same time, he was the best man she had ever known. The best man in Dublin. In Ireland. A stubborn, flawed man who was, nevertheless, head and shoulders above the petty things amongst whom he waded.

A stubborn, flawed, penniless bleedin' man.

One night, she thought. One night more and then never again. She would tell him she stayed with Mary or Annie or someone. A few shekels and she could afford a decent dress. The rings could go be damned. But she would not be married in a frock that was falling apart at the seams and blotched with grease and soot and all the ubiquitous grime of squalid living.

One night more. On this corner in the January night. One night more and then happily ever after.

Down the street, through the smoke and through the drifting damp, came a lone figure. Black coat, black hat, black gloves, black bag.

An avatar of the season.

CHAPTER 24

DUBLIN, JANUARY 2016/1893

Anymore, finding the time to do this was getting to be a pain in the arse. Esther had cancelled twice on him over the past few days because the coming juggernaut of the Mocks filled her whole world. Facebook was nothing but a wall of angst and study tips and predictions that were beyond useless. It was also a wall of insults and nasty little digs. *Nato's a freak. Like. Like. Like.* Insults and exams. Pretend exams to scare you into studying. Nathan pretty much always got an A in English. Pretty much always. Apart from his Junior Cert mocks, where he was handed a C. A fucking C. In the actual exam the following June he aced the thing and, hey presto, when the results came back his inevitable A jumped out at him. The Mocks were a membrane-thin illusion. A duplicate of the twenty trick questions the teachers pulled on incoming first years, year after year.

Nathan didn't really give a toss about the Mocks. Or about the actual real honest-to-God Leaving Cert at this stage.

He cared about getting his book finished. The story of Sergeant George Frohmell. The man he had pinned his entire self to, like a moth pinned to a cork board. He was aware, but only on some vague primitive level, that his shattered identity needed rebuilding. And in George Frohmell he had found firm ground on which to place block upon block. The splintered stones of his being, one upon the other, ruled by the tenets of a man a hundred years dead.

The tenets of his great-great-grandfather, he supposed.

That and the blood. The gallons of the stuff spilled by a man that Sergeant Frohmell never quite caught up with. A man who vanished. A man who was like the great-great-grandfather of Dahmer and Bundy. A man who left his victims spreadlegged in their own gore. Ripe for a photograph. Their blood black in it.

Esther posed as they were posed, with her dark eyes staring and glossy and pulling him into her. Down and ever more down.

It was after school and the winter dark had fallen in a sheet of black ice. His geography teacher had explained how an Arctic High shoved away the clouds like rumpled petticoats and high above exposed the meat of eternal space. All the Earth's heat bounced off into that abyss and left all below freezing and glassed over with cold.

Nathan loved nights like this. Glittering and raw. They reminded him of Esther as she stood outside his house on the day his father was buried. The smell of her in the pure cold. The approach of spring.

He left the house without speaking to Samantha or James. She was gradually coming apart like someone on a rack. Hung, drawn and quartered. He was spending more and more time in his room. He said it was because he was studying for his Junior Cert Mocks, but Nathan knew, he just knew, it wasn't. It was because he couldn't bear to be in the same room as Samantha anymore. He couldn't bear to watch her crack up. What a family. Scattered around their too-big house, with its smothering décor. Each to a room. Isolate and small. Dwindling within themselves, day after day.

Esther was waiting for him by the bus-stop in her black coat and black hat. Her black fingerless gloves.

'Hi,' she said.

'Hi.'

'Where are we going tonight?'

'The Long Stand.'

Esther laughed. 'The what?'

'It was an alley off Amiens Street. It's been built over at one end now and changed a bit, but we'll see what we can get.'

'Deadly. Why was it called The Long Stand?'

Nathan looked at her.

'Oh.'

'How's the studying going?'

'Not good.'

'Really?'

'Yeah. The Institute are saying that Donne will definitely come up, but Shore is saying not to trust them. That they made a balls of predicting Plath in 2012 and that taking short-cuts is a recipe for disaster. He said the Institute was a factory farm for rich kids.'

'Jesus.'

'Yeah. Melanie Kennedy-Doyle said she was going to report him to the Principal.'

'Melanie's a tit.'

'Yeah, she's like mayonnaise.'

Nathan frowned. 'Explain.'

'She's rich and thick.'

Nathan laughed. 'And a bit oily.'

There they stood, laughing and talking like a real couple. Nathan felt that intimacy again. That false intimacy that made a fool out of him time and time again. There they stood, themselves alone under the street lamps. Themselves alone in the whole frozen world until the bus came along and shattered the illusion.

They sat again on the top deck and Nathan huffed the heat of his own self into the cold air in front of him. Clouds of it drifted out and disappeared against the glass like smoke on dark water.

They were just going past the great hulking airport of a place that was UCD when Nathan remembered something.

He turned to Esther and said, 'Did you bring the camera?'

'Ehm,' said Esther. Then she went to say something else but stopped.

'What is it?'

'Dad found some of the photos we've been taking. He asked what the craic was with them. He's not happy, Nathan. He thinks it's weird. He took the camera off me and says I'm not getting it back.'

Nathan felt a strange swell of embarrassment. He also felt angry. It was like Esther's father was intruding into something that should have been his and Esther's alone. Like a clingy friend on what should have been a date. It was theirs. His and Esther's alone and nobody had any right to interfere or gainsay it. To have someone denigrate the time they shared set his teeth on edge. It was like the flat realism of the man's assessment somehow trivialised their closeness. It dismissed the connection between them and dashed his high fantasies all at once.

Weird. Freak. Look at the state of him.

Her father had never liked him anyway.

'Do you think it's weird?' he asked.

'Of course I do. It is weird but that's you and me, isn't it? Peas in a pod. Weirdos.'

She formed her thumb and forefinger into a circle and started doing loop-the-loops with it in front of her face.

Nathan looked at her.

'What are you doing?' he asked.

She laughed. 'This is a weird O. Ha!'

Nathan laughed with her.

'You're insane,' he said.

For *You're insane* read *I love you*.

Peas in a pod.

The bus stopped and they walked through the inner city, past the dregs of the January sales. The final reductions, apart from the last final reductions and the really final reductions yet to come. To Let signs and empty properties where people leaned against the plate glass and smoked or talked into phones or dealt drugs. Then down Amiens Street and left up a narrow laneway.

It reeked of piss and vomit. Empty Polish beer cans made a drift against one wall. The floor of the alley was layered with tarmac, but whoever laid the stuff had done a half-arsed job for it was peeled away in chunks, revealing the old cobbles and brickwork underneath. It was like the upper regions of history were flensed from the place and the raw stuff of its very beginnings was aired to the orange sodium arcs.

With every step Nathan Jacob felt he was walking to meet his past.

'I'm not sure about this, Nato,' said Esther.

'It's okay,' said Nathan. 'It's six o'clock in the evening. In the middle of Dublin. What could happen?'

'I'm sure those women you're writing about thought the same thing.'

'It's okay,' said Nathan. 'I'm a Frohmell. The grandson of a crime-fighter extraordinaire.'

Esther raised an eyebrow. 'I thought you said yer man, Frohmell, didn't catch the killer.'

'Now you're nit-picking.'

'Okay,' said Esther. 'But we can't really take any pictures.'

Nathan frowned and thought for a moment. 'We can use your fancy schmancy new phone. It's even got a little light.'

Esther's face crumpled a little and her brows drew down.

'Okay,' she said. 'One or two pictures on my fancy schmancy new phone and then we're gone. I really have to study.'

'Okay.'

She looked down at the floor of the alleyway and curled her lip at the detritus she saw all about.

'And if you think I'm going to sit down and strike a pose in that shit, you've another think coming.'

'Okay.' He said. And again, 'Okay.'

I AM IN BLOOD

★ ★ ★

Rosie watched the figure come out of the pall like a coalescence of night. He was a distillation of the shadows that clotted the Monto and choked every niche and interstice. Rosie watched him come and felt a nasty presentiment steal over her. She was suddenly and acutely aware that she was alone. Alone in the midst of tenements and flop-houses and the vague forms of punters slinking in and out of them. But there was nobody to see. And amidst the shrieks and the squeals of all the pleasure and not a little pain, would anyone notice hers if she gave vent to it in the empty dark?

Only the once, she said to herself. Only the once and no one shall ever know and then it's over and finished and she would go back to her man and her happily ever after.

The dark figure stopped in front of her. It touched the brim of its hat.

'Good evening,' it said.

English accent. All clipped and plummy. Cufflinks gleaming in the night.

Did she recognise him, somehow? No. His type orbited in a different circle.

'Look it,' Rosie said back to him. 'I'm only out here for an hour or two, so whatever ya want doin', we'll do nice and sharpish and let that be it. It'll cost ya as well,' she said. 'I'm good at what I do.'

The man smiled.

'Sharpish,' he said.

'Cash up front, as well,' she said. 'Cash up front and then a quick fumble.'

'Sharpish,' he said again.

Then he smiled, and in that smile was the death of all things.

★ ★ ★

George almost fell down the granite steps leading from O'Sullivan's door to the footpath below. He was no longer drunk. The adrenaline in him had sluiced all the drink from his system. He was instead a hectic amalgamation of fear and anger and self-disgust.

He was an idiot. Absolute and total.

Every atom of his being was directed in a headlong flight toward the Monto. The Monto where he knew he would find Rosie Lawlor with her head thrown back and her eyes brazen against him. And this was what he hoped. He hoped he would find her and she would lash at him and he would take her in his arms and he would confess his idiocy and his weakness and he would never let go of her again. This is what he hoped. What he feared was a spreading red lake beneath spread white legs and petticoats mussed and pawed at and two dead eyes staring at nothing.

He ran to the top of Grafton Street, past hurrying crowds of people going home, and then he heard the cries. Like a storm at sea or coming thunder, a great cloud of noise rolled over the rooftops down from Dame Street and the Castle. And laced through the dull bass of this thunder was the high lightning of whistles. Police whistles blowing frantic and insistent.

A DMP man came running down Nassau Street, his helmet askew. He wove past people who were moving ever more swiftly and in greater numbers away from the sounds and the whistles. The constable stopped when he saw George and saluted, breathing hard.

'What's the matter, Constable?' asked George.

'Sergeant Frohmell, Sir. There's a disturbance up at the Castle. The Fenians have risen a mob. We're to secure the gates and break it up if we can. Every DMP man in Dublin is on the way. Can you not hear the whistles, Sir?'

The Castle and the Fenians and the poxy Working Class with chips on their shoulders that Atlas himself couldn't heft.

'Hang the Castle,' he said.

'Sir?'

'Come with me.'

'Sir?'

'We're going to the Monto, Constable.'

The DMP man looked at him as though he were raving and began to jog backwards away from him, heading toward the shouts and the cheers and the frantic whistles and now the crack of rifles as well.

The constable looked at the bedraggled sergeant and in

that look was all the scorn and derision that George had brought on himself over the past weeks. All the scepticism for this sergeant with his whore for a fiancée and his obsession with the fate of her sordid friends. This sergeant who had taken his eye off the ball. This sergeant who spent more time trawling the Monto than at his barracks.

All this was freighted in the man's face as he went away from George.

'I'm sorry, Sarge,' called the constable. 'But the boys need help. Can you not hear the whistles?'

George watched him go and then set off again toward the Monto and toward his Rosie. He set off toward a place where no whistles and no shouts rang out. A place without law and without conscience and without help. He moved against people gravitating toward the riot outside the Castle and he was jostled by those seeking to escape it. He was one amongst a Brownian soup of a thousand moving bodies.

Time. Time was what he needed and yet here he was, wading through a mire of humanity, unwashed bodies and stinking breaths and frightened faces all getting in his way. How could he have been so stupid? How could it be so easy to tilt a bottle or pint glass and say to hell with the DMP and Dublin and all its whores and recreants? How easy it was to say to hell with himself. To hell with Rosie. If he were late? Oh God, what if he were late?

A man stood in front of him, his neck craning to look up

along Dame Street in the direction of the Castle. He was as unmoving in the flood of people as an obelisk. If George had had his wits fully about him, he would have noticed the man's avid expression, the burning in his eyes heralding a real burning to come. He would have noticed the club in his hands.

Time, George thought. He needed more time.

George pushed through the crowd and barrelled into the man. They both stumbled and clung to each other for support as legs and arms milled about them.

But George's temper was up and this man was blocking his path. Without thinking, he said, 'Get the hell out of the way, man! I'm on police business!'

He said this instinctively and with all the off-hand confidence that those used to being obeyed heft in their voices. For an instant he was certain the man would step aside with the doffed cap and deferential attitude that bystanders usually demonstrate. For an instant only, and then he realised where he was and what he had just said.

For an instant only, and then he saw the club.

The man's face had curdled on its framework of bone. The blind fury of the zealot burned from him.

'A peeler!' he shouted. 'A bleedin' peeler!'

All around George, angry faces were directed toward him and men began wading through the masses to reach him. He watched them come like a man watching the approach of crocodiles through brown water.

The man in front of him lifted the club and those innocents wise enough to realise what was about to happen wailed and shoved to get away from the scene with renewed vigour. The man's club was wound round his wrist by a leather thong and George realised that any thought of disarming him was futile.

He needed this over with quickly, before the others in the crowd managed to reach him.

Nothing, nothing would stop him from reaching the Monto.

Rosie. Oh God, Rosie.

George fumbled for his gun, but the man in front of him was quicker. He swung the club at George's head. A wide, vicious forearm blow designed to stave in skull and brain and all.

George had seen fellows like this before, though. Thugs and bullies who relied on fear and weight of numbers. Every single year of his life in the DMP he had come up against half-a-dozen such ruffians. And every single one of them had swung at him the exact same way.

George lifted his left arm and the club hammered into his tricep. Ignoring the deadened sensation he clamped down with his arm, trapping the man's hand momentarily.

A moment was all he needed. He had not stayed alive this long by fighting cleanly.

The man raised his left hand half to throw a punch, half to ward off the blow that he expected from George.

I AM IN BLOOD

George, however, had other ideas. He brought his right hand down and up in a savage arc and seized the man by the scrotum. Without any compunction he twisted and crushed everything that was down there with all the viciousness that was in him.

The man howled, torqueing to yank himself away from the agony of George's grip. As he did so, George slammed his left fist into his windpipe. The man sat down heavily, the yawp of his breathing loud above even the noise of the riot. For good measure, George drove the heel of his boot into the man's face.

George now found himself at the centre of a quickly expanding circle of empty space. Into this circle the man's companions now stepped and eyed George warily.

When George was a young boy his grandfather, a boxer, once gave him advice on how to fight more than one adversary. 'George,' he said, 'if you're up against more than one, you've no chance. No one has. If they know what they're doing, they'll hammer the tar out of you. The best you can do is pick one. Point at him and let him know that, if you're going to hospital, then he is too. Then you hit him and only him. As hard and as often as you can. Put him in the sick bed beside you. That's the best anyone can do.'

Those words had come back to George time and time again down through every scrape he had ever found himself in. They came back now.

He raised a finger and pointed at the slightest member of the group. A pale teenager who looked as frightened as George felt desperate.

'Come on,' he said. 'Come on and have a go. But if you do, that lad there, yeah you, you're coming with me. I'll go through every one of these other apes just to bite your face off.'

The young lad took a step backward and the rest looked from one to the other and then at the man bleeding and unconscious on the sunken and filthy cobbles of College Green.

Something unspoken passed between them and two of them knelt to pick up their fallen comrade.

'You'll get yours, peeler,' one of them spat as they bore the dead weight into the crowd.

George wasn't even listening. He was already off and running again.

And as he ran, images of Rosie Lawlor flickered in his mind. From death to life and into death again.

★ ★ ★

Nathan and Esther moved up the laneway and away from the lights and the noise and the rush-hour stop-start of Amiens Street. The dark was heavy here and the laneway had been altered over the years.

Nathan took out his map and used his phone to light it.

'Yeah, we're in the right place. She was found by a rain barrel up here somewhere,' he said.

I AM IN BLOOD

The alley, The Long Stand, was truncated by a high black wall of construction hoarding. On it, printed huge in flowing script, were the words *An address has never before generated dreams of better living*. Looking at it, Nathan wondered what that was supposed to mean. The hoarding with its vacuous slogan blocked the alleyway in front of them, but the construction firm had punched a hole in the right-hand redbrick wall and the alley now dog-legged around this corner.

'Come on,' said Nathan. 'Let's go as far as we can.'

'I don't know,' said Esther.

Nathan looked at her. In the dark her face was white white and her eyes were empty holes. In the filth of the alley, in its stink, her beauty and the summer smell of her were like the flecks of brightness in the stone of built concrete.

Beyond everything, he wanted her so, so much.

'Come on,' he said again.

They went down the alley and round the corner and this was as far as they could go. A JCB, yellow and huge on its caterpillars, blocked their way, its windows sheathed in steel sheeting to stop the local scumbags doing what they did best.

Esther began to take photos and Nathan began to scribble in his notepad. He smelled the air, the dank of it. He jotted down some synonyms for *dank*. He breathed in the chill of the place. The dead winter feel of it. Through his jacket and on his skin. The knowledge of what occurred here was hot in his brain. The knife work and the other stuff. The killer's spunk found in the body. The release he must have felt. The pent-up explosion he must have felt.

Beside him, Esther was warm and her breath made clouds that he stepped through. Feeling her against his skin. The feathery essence of her.

'Can I have the phone?' he said.

She gave him the phone. The phone with its little white light. With its megapixel camera. She stepped close to him and the heat that came off her was like a blow. She stepped into him and with a pucker of his lips he could have kissed her first on the forehead and then on the lips and then he would not have stopped kissing her. Again and again and again and again and again.

'I told you, I'm not posing,' she said.

And then she stepped away from him.

That coming close and then that pulling away. The infuriating tidal heave and withdraw of her. In and out. In and out of love. All the time.

'Ah, go on,' he said.

The black-and-white of a crime scene photo. Everything black and white when nothing was black and white. Everything was shades of grey and her face pale amongst them. Her eyes black black black against the grey. Definite and stark and all like in those books he read. Her lips slightly open. The tongue behind the teeth. The questing musculature of it. The throat behind that. Could she drink him in, after all? Was the promise there, after all?

'Ah, go on,' he said again.

There was a throb in his abdomen. An insistent pulse of a thing. Almost painful.

'Not happening,' said Esther. 'Can I have my phone?'

She stepped toward him and Nathan stepped, too.

He was moving on autopilot. His brain had locked into a cold and lifeless slab. But something was stirring way back in some primordial cluster of nerves and synapses. Some unthinking part of him that was old when the world was young. Something primal.

Her face was tilted up towards him. Her brows slightly furrowed. Sort of amused. Or bemused. Her lips quirked into her not-quite-a-smile smile.

And Nathan bent his own lips to them.

For the first time he let go of himself. Let go of all the petty insecurities and narcissism that had prevented him ever doing this before. He surrendered to that ancient part of him. And from out of that mindless pulp of brain matter a voice howled in triumph.

For a moment only was he lost in that kiss. For a moment only, while his groin tightened and his hips strained. His hands lifting to touch, to feel.

Then she was pulling away from him. Her fingers going to her lips as though she had been scalded.

And now her face had on it an expression of pure pity.

'Oh, Nato,' she said. 'My poor Nato. We're friends, Nato. I want to stay friends.'

And there it was. Samantha's words in Esther's mouth. And as though that were some sort of dam bursting, thoughts of his real mother, Patricia Frohmell, flooded through him. A whore. Conceived in the filth of a sty. The rutting stench of it. The sticky putrescence. And his father grunting atop her.

He wanted to scream the walls of the world down around them.

Women seem wicked when you're unwanted.

'Nato,' Esther said. 'What's wrong?' She went to step away from him.

But he was moving now with real purpose. His hand came up and touched her shoulder and when she turned, he let it fall and glanced his fingertips against her breast. Skimming it, but just enough. Just enough.

'Nathan?' she said. There was confusion there but something else, too. Fear, maybe?

He stepped toward her and the beat in his abdomen grew into a ball of soreness and he reached up to where her coat was buttoned and he snapped one button open. Her little pentagram spilled free and dangled silver in the black dark.

She backed away from him until she was against the rough of the wall.

'Nathan,' she said again. 'What are you doing?'

I AM IN BLOOD

Nathan kept coming. In his head, he wasn't really himself anymore.

… The Work. The Pattern. And the words around the alley. Round the dark alley and the quick thrust of it and the hard crotch and the white skin and God you could grow to love it here. In the dark. In the red dark. The button pop and the white skin and the oh God of it in us. The member stiff and standing and the eyes closed and the dark and no one to see and the end coming. The coming and the coming again. Again and again and again and again and again.

★ ★ ★

George stood at the mouth of the lane and gagged like a broken horse. His breath came in great sickening whoops. He stepped into the dark. One step and then another.

The Monto was become half emptied. Whore and pimp and opium dealer all sloughing off to watch the poor of Dublin vent themselves against the Castle gates and the soldiers and the DMP. Those that remained were shacked up in the grotty inward parts of whorehouse and tenement, on their backs or on their fronts and sweating in the January night, their faces disinterested and their minds elsewhere.

George had collared a girl who worked her patch on Buckingham Street. *Worked.* He had collared her and because of his frenzy and into a cloud of his alcohol-stinking breath she had told him where Rosie was.

She wasn't there.

And he couldn't find her.

Oh God, he couldn't find her.

Now he was staring into the lightless depths of a laneway. A foetid ravine between two rows of countless mortared bricks. Was there something down there? Something hunched? Something that slobbered in the dark like a monster from a fairytale. A troll under the bridge?

His eyes lost their blindness. Before him was a figure. Black coat, black hat, black gloves, black bag. And under him was another. Her white legs in the dark. Limp white and outflung. The black figure over her. The animal movement of him in the night. The frantic thrust of him in all that dark and all that filth.

And then something caught what little light there was and it gleamed like a splinter of winter itself. Ice bright and bitter.

'Get off of her!'

George was roaring and he pounded down the disgusting yards that separated him from them.

The black figure stood away from his victim. Her dress collapsed about her like the fall of a stage curtain. In the dark the figure's organ was a suddenly shrivelling thing, drooping and spilling a grey thread from its tip. Like a pale glow-worm against the black blank of the figure himself. And in his hand he held a long knife.

And now George could see his face.

It was an average face. Unremarkable. The face of a million

other men in a million other cities. A face George had seen before and would see again. It was the face of the everyman.

For the first time in his entire career, George's revolver came into his hand without him having to fumble for it. It was as if the heavy little lump of metal was as eager to end this as George was. As eager for revenge.

All thoughts of arrest had vanished. All compassion, all lust for justice, replaced by the brute urge to kill. Blood for blood. The oldest arbitrament the world had ever known.

The black figure was straightening up now. His knife held above his head. The squat prong of his member dripping his seed onto his shoes.

Rosie, oh dear God, Rosie lay prone at his feet.

This figure, this monster, stood straight up and said, 'I will go peacefully.'

I will go peacefully, as though it were human. As though some human value could be applied to it in the cold and in the dark

At an arm's length, George levelled his little revolver and fired.

It made a crack when it fired like a small firework a long way off.

The creature's oh-so-unremarkable face was blotted out for a moment by the muzzle flash and a blue afterimage swam across George's vision. Then it cleared and George saw the face before him opened in awe at what had happened, like it was party to a vision of unspeakable wonder. Behind a mask of powder burn, the eyes blinked once and from a small hole above its left brow a thread of wine-dark liquid wound down.

Then, without a word, the figure keeled over and collapsed into the slops and the leavings and all the dross that lay at its back.

Without even looking at the killer where he lay surrounded by the detritus of the destitute, George bent to Rosie.

He had let her down. Let her down and down again. Until here she lay, on her back, in a festering laneway in a forgotten city.

She was pale and still and her right jaw was swollen where she had been struck. She must have fought. Of course she had fought. George smoothed her skirts where they were fallen over her thighs and his fingers touched her forehead, her closed eyes. Her lips.

Her throat uncut, he noticed. Uncut and unbloodied.

No blood. No blood anywhere.

And then Rosie's eyes opened and she looked at him.

'Georgie,' she said. 'My Georgie.'

The following day, Maguire's Crematorium on Lombard Street played host to Station Sergeant George Frohmell and Chief Superintendent John Mallon. While the rest of Dublin cleaned up after the riots outside the Castle and nursed sore heads and bruised limbs, George and Mallon watched as old Thomas Maguire committed an unnamed corpse to the flames. When they were done, all that was left was a rat-grey powder. A monster's essence reduced to a heap of colourless particles. It was as it should be. Mallon and George collected the cinders in a plain tin can, once used for holding molasses, and took it to the salt sea at Ringsend. There they dumped the ashes into the sea and watched the waves gnash them into nothing.

Then they went home.

CHAPTER 25:

DUBLIN, FEBRUARY 1893

George and Rosie were married on St Valentine's Day. He whose bones were sat in Whitefriar Street Church. His mark on their blessing. The ceremony was attended by none other than Assistant Commissioner John Mallon, newly promoted and proud in his dress uniform. Many passed comment at his presence, but few could fathom it. They were married in a Catholic church and George left his religion behind him and turned his back on all the old Orange bluster. All the old *Croppies lie down* guff and gladly said *Yes* when the padre asked him the all-important question. He didn't feel one bit different because of it. The Host melted on his tongue not like dead meat at all. When you got right down to it, it was all a bleedin' joke.

He kissed Rosie and everyone cheered and she was happy with her man at last. And no one noticed that she touched her belly more than was usual. Not a one, except Rosie herself, knew that under her own bosom was incubating a thing not of her own doing. A little fluttering thing that made her sick in the grey mornings and grew day by day in the secret grotto of her womb. An innocent little thing, sprouting unnoticed by all except her. And with every flutter, her mind returned to what had been done to her. The meaty paling of that monster's shaft. The pain and the terror of it all.

But something good would come of this. She knew. She was determined. She and her man would raise this child and not a sinner would know the squalor of its conception. Not a sinner, save her.

This little person burgeoning inside her would be a Frohmell from the first to the last.

And down the long generations the badness would be thinned and nature become subordinate to the happy tyranny of upbringing and that would be her triumph at the end. She would be the incarnate dam of cold revenge and the bald, blue thing that would eventually slither from her would grow to be upright and decent. A Frohmell. Like his Da.

Beyond blood and beyond provenance. Generation upon generation down the long spans of time, grinding the evil from the world until it was reduced to its smallest part in the slow immensity of the trundling years. Smaller and smaller, thinning and vanishing like a cry on the wind. Like ash on the water.

Never again to return from the pit to which it was consigned.

Therein lay her victory.

Not even a memory left to clamber up and up the eternal blasted slope from Hell.